Mainely Power

By

m Langdon Cost

M. Langdon Cost

ISBN: 0-75966-837-X

This book is printed on acid free paper.

1stBooks - rev. 09/12/01

Prologue

Harold Dumphy crept through the flickering shadows of the records department. There was something he was looking for, something he had to know.

Something was wrong.

But he could not quite put his finger on what...

Or who...

As a matter of fact, Harold had no evidence whatsoever. He had been in the security business for twenty years now and had never run into a problem of any depth. But this time there was the suggestion of a scandal, a potential catastrophe that could rival Three Mile Island.

It wasn't hard to prowl through the empty building now that everyone had gone for the evening. All the doors were locked but that is what the keychain at his waist was for. It wasn't as if he were doing anything illegal. He was after all the head of security for the plant, just trying to do his job. There was no one to go to without some sort of evidence. Who would believe him, a middle aged nobody?

Harold wasn't sure what it was that had given them away. The tightness in the face of the plant's out of state inspector. The locked doors that did not need to be locked. The extra security guards added to his staff without his input. It was not any one thing but a multitude of unknowns that came crashing together into one screaming pile of unanswered questions.

What was he doing here? A smarter man would have turned a blind eye, or resigned.

Harold found the room he was looking for, housing the reports on safety standards prepared by the national inspection team. He hoped to find some clue here. Certain safety standards were no longer being met, he was sure of that. And sure that he couldn't possibly have been the only one to notice this.

Forty-one years old. Balding on top. To compensate for this lack of hair, Harold had grown a mustache, drooping thick and bushy from his upper lip. He had always been fit, but just in the past year the food he ate seemed to be stopping in his midsection, pushing his belly out like some surprise pregnancy and accusing him each morning when he stepped out from the shower. There were dark circles under his eyes, a worried, haunted look lurking somewhere deep in his pupils. Not very long into his ten-year-old marriage, Harold had noticed the bored look in his wife's eyes when they made love; not long after that her social obligations had begun to pile up.

Perhaps if he took a stand his wife would desire him once again.

The file cabinets were locked but Harold did not question the sensibility of forcing the lock with the Swiss Army Knife he carried in his pocket. There was no going back now. He clutched his small flashlight in his teeth as he worked.

Harold had been thirty years old when he had taken the job as assistant head of security here at the Maine plant, a rising star known for his hard work and diligence, if not for his keen mind. He had moved to Maine from New York and almost immediately had begun dating Janice. One year later they were married and he was on top of the world.

Then the descent had begun. Day by day he got older. Night by night he lost his wife. They had not made love now in three years. It must be some failing on his part.

He had been promoted to head of security only because there was no one else left to take over when his boss had moved on to another job.

But it was time now to take a stand.

First he would confront the creeping terror in his workplace.

Then he would confront his wife and her social activities.

It was going to be all right.

Harold wore skin-tight latex gloves for the job. It would be these very same gloves that would kill him, wrapped fiercely around his throat. It would not be the cold shock of the water. It would not be the water seeping down his throat or the blow to the back of his head.

Death would come from the impersonal, sterile, latex gloves he wore to leaf through the papers in the file cabinet in the early morning hours in the records department.

At least he had finally taken a stand.

Chapter one

"Damn!" Goff Langdon cursed under his breath at the harsh sound of his alarm. His ex-wife had compared this very same alarm to a truck backing through the bedroom at 5 a.m. When properly riled, Amanda would draw this metaphor in great detail, the churning wheels, clanging metal and general all around torment that had become the room they shared. It crossed Langdon's mind from time to time that perhaps all his marital difficulties could be traced to this simple clock.

But there was no one around to argue with on this particular morning; there hadn't been anyone in quite some time. There was only the rustling and banging of another creature quite ecstatic to be up. Goff reflexively covered his face as a dark shadow came flying through the air with an eager whine, a clack of nails on the edge of the bed. He groaned. "Get off me, you worthless mutt!" A wasted insult. If nothing else, his dog knew his own fine breeding, knew that his ancestry would make the Prince of Wales blush. His grip on Coffee Dog starting to loosen, Goff twisted his body to the side and felt...nothing. Then the Thwack! of the cold floor. The edge of the bed had come and gone.

This entire early morning ritual from the still-clanging alarm clock to the All-Star canine wrestling, took no more than fifteen seconds, but already the downstairs neighbors were banging on the floor. Goff never knew just how the Beans could get a stick into position so quickly unless of course they waited poised for the opportunity. With a deft movement that bespoke years of experience, Langdon, or maybe it was the dog, unplugged the clock and the infernal noise ceased.

Goff lay without moving, as did Coffee Dog, his puppy teeth clasped around his master's ear lobe. Goff waited a moment before conceding defeat. "Okay, okay. I'll give you the canned food for breakfast." With one final wrench the pup twisted the man's head to prove his superiority, then trotted calmly to the kitchen.

The phone suddenly rang.

Both man and beast froze—for this was truly a strange occurrence. There wasn't much of this sort of thing in Goff's cramped apartment these days, unless of course it was one of those infernal sales machines. It takes a pretty lonely person to wait past the recording for that human voice to come on the line trying to sell weedwhackers or whatever the hell it was. But it was too early even for those talking headaches just doing their jobs. This had to be something real.

On the second ring Goff plucked the receiver from the cradle and croaked a greeting, an early morning rasp.

"Is this Goff Langdon?" A sharp, almost derisive tone.

Langdon found himself angry. "It's not his gay lover." "Is this Goff Langdon?" Patient. Waiting. Flat.

Langdon stirred uneasily in his hardwood chair, wanting suddenly to be free of this moment. "Sure, this is him." There was a pause before the voice continued, "I know where you live."

The phone went dead. "Big deal you jerk-off," Langdon muttered in the silent darkness of the Maine morning. "I'm listed under 'L' in the phone book."

With a strange sense of foreboding Goff Langdon went about feeding the dog and climbing into the shower. He took an ice cold shower every morning—to recirculate his blood, to clear the cobwebs from his mind. He never quite rinsed the shampoo all the way out of his hair. The result was dandruff. Too tired to handle a razor. This did not make him lazy. He was a Private Detective. Bookstore Owner. Environmentalist. Football Fan. Red Meat Eater. He voted Independent, sometimes Democratic, never Republican.

By the time he made it out to his car Langdon had all but forgotten the early morning call. It was hard to spook or impress a man who had become disillusioned with life at the tender age of twenty-eight.

It was late November in Maine, which meant the temperature was somewhere near the freezing point. Maine was a place of pristine beauty, summer, fall or winter, there not really being any such thing there as spring. It was the cold that kept the rest of the United States from moving to the state; if the cold were overlooked then there was no better place in the entire world. Langdon had long been thankful for the climate's providing a barrier against the spread of civilization into his backyard.

Langdon rode with the top of his convertible down. The car was a Chevy Impala or something like that, he could never quite remember. An early 1970's model. It was still dark and his hair, still wet from the shower, froze, but he hardly noticed. Langdon had never been much for the details of life. Coffee Dog rode with his paws balanced on the front windshield, his ears blown straight back.

The two went directly to the diner, as breakfast was the most important meal of their day. The waitress greeted them both by name, not commenting on any number of things—such as the wind-blown redness of Langdon's face, the icy spikes of his hair, and the fact that his companion was a dog. They were regulars.

"Hey Goff, did you catch that game last night?" This from the large woman working the cash register, her face already warmed by the ovens and beaded with sweat.

"Watched it at home with my buddy here. You see Danny T., you tell him he owes me five bucks." Goff slid into a booth that overlooked the street and smiled up at the waitress. "Alison, has the paperboy gone and gotten himself sick?"

"Sorry Goff, the gentleman over there has the paper."

Without turning his head, Langdon chuckled. "What gentleman? You mean Larry? He can't read anyways. Give him the advertisements from the middle, maybe the women's lingerie section to finger through..." Normally this would have caused Alison to blush, but a certain stillness in her face caught Goff's attention. "Not Larry, huh?" A nod. "Probably not even somebody I know would be guess number two."

With deliberate calm Goff Langdon rotated his head ninety degrees to the left and right smack into a face he'd heard very recently. The face that went with the cold derision of the voice on the phone that morning. There could be no doubt of this. It was like knowing that John Wayne's voice would be gravel, or Keanu Reeve's that of a surfer dude; sometimes the senses crossed over, sight and sound mixing and matching and becoming apparent to each other.

The man was slender, dainty, even foppish, but by no means soft. His head was narrow, oddly like a banana, protruding slightly at the forehead and the chin. He had no facial hair to speak of, almost as if it had been waxed away. His eyebrows so sparse and lightly-colored it took careful scrutiny to see them. The man grinned at Langdon, his smile filling his face but not reaching his steel grey eyes.

Langdon smiled back and said, to show he had put the face to the voice, "So, I know where you eat your breakfast now, don't I?" He waited for a reaction, for anything at all.

The man took the bluntness to a whetstone and sliced back his reply. "Good morning Mr. Langdon." Coffee Dog growled deep in his throat, more a vibration felt in the table than a sound. "It would seem that I have taken the paper usually reserved for you. Please accept my apology." Langdon made himself smile slowly. "Just the sports pages and maybe Calvin and Hobbes."

"Of course my dear man, help yourself." The man spoke not with politeness but as if issuing a challenge, the opening move of a game of chess.

Langdon rose to his feet, stretching to his full height of six-feet four-inches, momentarily pausing to consider how Easy Rawlings would handle this situation. More than likely the Walter Mosely hero would have been overcome with rage at what he would have deemed a racial power play and would have escalated the situation to raw violence until the palpable tension was a spent and useless puddle on the ground. "In that case I may just take 'Big Nate' as well." Langdon had his own style, and it wasn't his style to ask questions.

The opening move of a chess game is often the one that determines the outcome. Langdon knew enough to know that when someone is pressed for information before he's prepared to give it, he'll generally lie. When this silly-looking guy with the manners of Oscar the Grouch and the dress of Groucho Marx was ready to come through with what this was all about, well, then, Langdon would be more than willing to listen.

Half an hour later Langdon was in the middle of his weight lifting routine, today being his day to work shoulders and arms. The gym was something Langdon greatly enjoyed, getting his blood flowing, allowing him time to enter the day on his own terms. Life was a great balancing act, a melding of mind and body. It was impossible to reach one's full mental potential without a healthy body, impossible to build a healthy body without focus and iron will.

Nine o'clock.

Freshly showered and in a crisp dry-cleaned shirt, Langdon arrived at his bookstore—actually more a much-loved hobby than a business that was anything close to profitable. Thanks to the death of his crazy Aunt Zelda who had a special affinity for him and a written will to match, Langdon was able to supplement his faltering private eye business with a mystery bookstore that had no loan repayment. The book business was pretty much suicide, the margins just not being there for any independent store to compete against the mega-stores sweeping the nation. But if the store were bought and paid for, as it was, and the payroll were small—well then, it was easier to get by and do something he enjoyed.

The population of a small Maine town like Brunswick could not support a venture of such limited and specific interest as a mystery bookstore—but these same statistics also scoffed at the concept of a private eye in rural Maine. Langdon had always gone his own way in life. He'd always believed in the philosophy that if you liked what you did for work, then you didn't need much else. It seemed to be the trend of members of the present generation to slave forty to sixty hours a week at jobs they didn't like just to make enough money to take a two week vacation in the Virgin Islands, buy a jet ski to ride on Saturday afternoons, drive a brand new car and basically live the American dream of capitalism. Why?

His father had always told him, "Goff, do whatever you want in life, but make sure that you do it correctly. If you're going to be a ditch-digger, well then, be the best damn ditch-digger there is."

The glass door he now pushed open had two inscriptions, the top of the door reading "The Coffee Dog Bookstore" and the bottom "Goff Langdon, Private Detective". The store sat right on Maine Street, the only truly "Maine" Street in the state. Brunswick was a throwback to the way things used to be, the small local stores owned and operated by people who lived in town. Maine Street was the widest center street in the state, two lanes going each way, brick sidewalks stretching luxuriously in front of stores such as the natural food store, the bakery, the coffee house, the video store—the owners of each establishment comfortably greeting customers by name.

The Coffee Dog Bookstore sat right in the center of all this, with long picture windows displaying a sampling of what lay inside—the most extensive collection of mystery books in all of Maine. These books had shaped Goff Langdon's life, starting with Encyclopedia Brown, the Hardy Boys and The Great Brain, and progressing with time into James Lee Burke, Dashiell Hammett, Raymond Chandler, James Crumley, Stephen Greenleaf and John Dunning among others. Goff wasn't always sure that their vast impact on his life had been a good thing.

After all, it was more than likely the reason for his wife's leaving him.

No time to ponder that this morning. Lights. Turn the coffee maker on, flip the power switch for the computer, pick out some good jazz for the morning sound and put money into the cash register.

At 9:30 A.M. on the button two things happened. Flipping the open sign up, Goff also opened the door for Chabal. The mother of three though only thirty-one years old, Chabal had somehow managed to retain the figure of a college co-ed. Wisps of blonde hair poked out from under her navy blue beret, tickling the delicate balance that was her face, swinging in front of the green fire of her eyes and clinging to the freckles so prominent in this morning's chill. Five-feet two-inches tall, about eye level with Langdon's upper rib-cage. Pert is the thought that always came to his mind to describe her, but he knew better than to voice that thought. She was the only woman he knew who called him Langdon. He liked that.

"Yo, Langdon, what up?" She said.

He knew that she'd been up since five to get her kids ready for school. He also knew that she did not drink coffee and that this energy of hers was somehow a natural gift. "Glad you could make it in, sweetheart," he muttered. His wife would have taken offense at this same moniker, even if uttered right from the lips of Dashiell Hammett's Sam Spade, but the woman in front of him merely grinned mischievously back, sending hot flashes all through his spine. "The store is yours," he said, "you all set with everything?" Without waiting for a reply, Langdon floated towards the back of the store where a small door blended in with the bookshelves. "I'll be in the office. When some lady comes in looking for me, just send her back."

"All right Boss," she mocked.

Langdon, or was it Spade, merely waved his hand over his shoulder in dismissive fashion, pretending exasperation with this person who was his friend, his associate, his secretary, his teacher. She was his desire too, but one he'd never act on, for sometimes the wanting is much better than the having-had.

Stooping to fit through the small door he took an appreciative look back at the lithe figure now bent over the books on the coffee table. Chabal knew Langdon would be stealing this glance, and was basking in it. The best streets in the world go two-ways, and so it was.

The office was small, cluttered, without windows—in short, the office a private dick was supposed to have. The clutter had no real purpose, but seemed to fit. Business was slow, for what really happened in small-town America?

There had been the case of the lost dog back in August—but that canine had turned up on his own, having found the hunting life to be a little harder than the domestic life. Violence, from bar fights to personal vendettas, was generally settled in Maine without outside intervention; neither the victim nor the antagonist tended to want attention brought to their plight, usually the result in one way or another of the demon alcohol. It was the cheating hearts of the population that constituted Langdon's real mainstay.

Langdon spent much of his time as a detective with a camera, following people on their lunch hours to some secret rendezvous where they lived out their fantasy that the grass was always greener on the other side of the fence. Small town life made this a very delicate matter, for on more than one occasion Langdon had known at least one of the partners in lust, and faced a real conflict of interest in bringing the evidence he'd gathered back to their spouse.

But even this was not really enough to make a living from, so his aunt's timing in leaving him a parcel of money to open a bookstore with had been perfect. Except, of course, in that this had been the straw that broke the back of his three year marriage. Amanda, who had been a much better girlfriend than wife, had been hoping that Langdon would finally concede defeat and move home to Atlanta with her, where, she'd argued, private dicks were making money hand over fist and were never, ever, short of cases.

But leaving, for him, had never really been a consideration.

At this point in the memory train, a light knock at the door caused him hurriedly to pick up a 'Publishers Weekly' and call for an entrance. The woman who entered the room had not one straight edge; she was full of curves, not overweight but bulging out of her too-tight clothing. Her perfume was perhaps a little strong, but not overpowering; the same could be said for her make-up. She wore gold earrings, some sort of pendants swinging gently against the sides of her well-tanned cheeks. Her high heels didn't seem practical for the time or place.

"Mr. Langdon?"

He didn't rise, just nodded his head, taking everything in—going for the quick first impression that would allow him to judge what he was about to hear. In his work, Langdon had found the first impression to be indeed the most important—for a nervous man was liable to hedge the truth, a confident woman would not give out any more information than she had to, a guilty person would be stuck on claiming his innocence while an innocent person would be lost in fascination over what had actually happened, and so on.

He did not know why she was here, only that she'd called and set up an appointment. His guess would be, based on her appearance, that it was a sexual offender case, the offender being her husband, the sex taking place without her. And she wanted out, with a large paycheck.

"I want you to find who killed my husband," she said in a calm voice.

Langdon jerked visibly. A murder case? "Please have a seat, Mrs. Dumphy."

"Janice, please call me Janice," the woman said, her voice tickling his ears with small insistent caresses. She settled into the chair in front of him, leaning forward ever so slightly, her blouse one button too low.

"Perhaps we could start at the beginning..."

"You don't know who I am, do you?" She said. He shrugged. "Janice Dumphy, my husband was Harold Dumphy, died two months ago yesterday? Do you read the papers or have a television set, Mr. Langdon?"

It began to come back to him in bits and pieces. Her husband had been found in the river near the old railroad bridge, floating face down, blue around the ears and quite dead. It had been a suicide, or so the papers said. Job stress, family stress—whatever the case, the man had gone off the deep end. Literally. "Why do you think your husband was killed Mrs...I mean Janice?"

"He told me things about work, things that were going on that weren't right. He wasn't sleeping nights, wasn't eating well."

"What things?"

"Harold had been working security for plants all over New England for fifteen or sixteen years. He knew there should have been inspections that weren't happening, there should have been maintenance work that didn't happen, things were kept secret that there was no reason to keep secret..."

Langdon stared at the woman for a long moment as she babbled away. She was obviously under a lot of stress. "Whooaa, slow down Mrs. Dumphy." A broad smile creased his weather-beaten face. "Let's take this one step at a time."

"He thought they were sabotaging the plant."

"Who?"

"Don't you understand? They're playing God..."

"You suspect his employers?"

Janice Dumphy stifled a sob, a low guttural intake of breath.

And then it came back to Langdon, where Harold Dumphy had worked. DownEast Power. The nuclear power plant.

Chapter two

Langdon eased out of the small office with a slight whistle to garner the attention of his sleepy dog, who lumbered to his feet and jogged irritably along. Langdon was heading out to meet Sergeant Jeriamiah Bartholowmew, more or less a friend of his, for lunch. The sergeant wasn't technically allowed to discuss ongoing investigations like the Dumphy matter, but Langdon was buying and Bart was always hungry.

Langdon put the top of the convertible up—the temperature had dropped a little since the morning, and twenty degrees was below even his threshold. Hog Heaven, where he'd arranged to meet Bart, was a drive in restaurant with fine, greasy food. The waitresses weren't on roller skates, but then you can't have everything. Also, they didn't serve alcohol. Langdon stopped for a six-pack of Geary's beer along the way. He didn't intend for Hog Heaven's policy to interfere with his putting back a few while he ate, and probably a few more after that.

Langdon understood that he was the worst kind of drunk, the kind who didn't really drink much more than socially when things were going well, but whose gloves came off with a little disturbance. The heavy drinking hadn't started until after Amanda had left him. On his good days Langdon knew he had to stop; on days like today he rationalized his drinking in keeping with his specially-tailored mind-body philosophy. Sobriety leads to discontent, to the need for more than it is possible to obtain, while drunkenness brings each and every one of us back to his basic self—propelled by instinct, by the need to fight at the drop of a hat, to pick up and sleep with any available member of the opposite sex. Jokes are funnier, television sit-coms are bearable, MacDonalds is heaven—life is just so much better with the edge dulled. With an unsettled pleasure, Langdon twisted the cap off the Geary's and tipped the bottle high in the air. The fine taste of the beer equalled and then began to override his self-contempt.

Bart, a large, shambling man, approached in the rear view mirror, having parked a ways down the street. He deeply resented having to skulk around like this whenever he stopped to eat: people in general seemed to get a kick out of timing the food breaks the police took, and Hog Heaven, right off a main through-road, was not the place to pass an inconspicuous afternoon eating. Not unless you wanted people calling the local radio personality to deride the stereotypical police trend of sitting around in coffee places while criminals ran roughshod over the law.

Bart tapped the roof of the car. "About time you put the top up! You know, we have people calling the station to report sighting a crazy man driving around. It's too damn cold!"

Langdon grinned at his friend. "Is that all you have to think about in that job of yours?"

By this time Bart had managed to settle his enormous bulk into the passenger seat. He eyed Langdon, picking up on an unintended edge in his voice. His glance fell on a newspaper Langdon hadn't quite managed to stuff behind his seat, one he'd picked up from the library earlier, with a clear headline from the morning after Dumphy's death. Bart reached for the door handle. "I'll tell you right now, the price of lunch is not worth the hassle that I see coming from you, so I'll just go back to my car and get my own lunch."

"Hold on, hold on just a second would you," Langdon shot out of the corner of his mouth. A sudden rapping at the window interrupted him. He rolled down his window with a bland face. "Hi Bess, what can I do for you today?"

The waitress shook her head. "Goff Langdon, you're sitting here with your lights on. This means that you must want to be served something. I am a waitress here. I would be the one to serve you. And stop drinking that beer, you're going to get me into trouble." The girl was only nineteen, a little too high-strung, but a good girl none-the-less.

Bart snapped across at the bird-like creature, "Girl, stop your yapping and bring us some fried clams and french fries. And a coke."

There was not a chance that Bess would sound off again; she wouldn't have in the first place if she'd known Bart was in the car. Everyone with any intelligence was terrified of the bad-tempered man with the badge. Langdon was one of the few who knew that his bark was much worse than his bite—though Bart's hot temper had actually been the ice breaker leading to their friendship.

As a high school student Langdon had, like everybody else, been terrified of the bear of a man. There were some cops you might sass, even some you might blatantly defy, especially when you were the captain of the state championship football team, darling of the town, cock of the walk—but Sergeant Jeriamiah Bartholomew was not one of them.

Langdon had had his first proper introduction to Bart after his junior year in college when he'd worked one summer as a bouncer for Goldilock's Bar.

Bart had come to the bar one night in jeans and a stained, faded t-shirt. He was quite obviously drunk, the first and only time Langdon would ever see him so. "College boy," he'd snorted, by way of letting Langdon know he had his number.

"Yes sir," Langdon had said. He wasn't supposed to allow any intoxicated person to enter—but Bart was the police, large and angry at that, and Langdon was willing to make an exception.

"I'm here to kick the shit out of some boys who've been dealing to high school students," Bart said. "I think you know who I mean."

Four young men had recently taken up Goldilocks as a hangout, men in their early twenties, handsome, polite, well-dressed. And the biggest suppliers of cocaine in Brunswick. The whole town knew what they were doing.

Langdon left his post to look for the owner—turning around after just a moment to see Bart, without warning, lurch and break a bar stool over one of the dealer's heads. The man—who bore an odd resemblance to Don Johnson—crumpled to the floor with no grace left whatsoever. A melee ensued—tables, chairs, pictures, dartboards, everything being knocked to the floor, the aging owner Goldilocks suddenly appearing to leap over the top of the bar to help Bart. Langdon didn't want to get involved, least of all in a knock down, drag-em-out fight between the cops, a bartender and a gang of drug dealers. But suddenly there was Bart, pinned down—and without his conscious knowledge Langdon's feet took the two forward steps necessary to hit the dealer who was pinning him down.

The next day, the police chief himself had paid a visit to Langdon's house. Someone had made a complaint about Bart's off-duty vigilante work. The Chief was wondering if Langdon would verify it.

Langdon gave the Chief his most winning smile. "I didn't see a thing, sir."

The Chief couldn't make a case against Bart—and seemed to hold Langdon personally responsible for this, treating him with thinly-veiled contempt on all their subsequent encounters. And Bart seemed equally grateful to Langdon—a gratitude he expressed not in so many words, but by watching out for him like a gruff, beer-bellied, ill-tempered fairy godmother. On the one occasion when he'd mentioned that night, Bart had implied without actually saying it that the fact that the men were dealing drugs with everyone's knowledge meant there must be some sort of cover-up in town, possibly involving the Chief. But they hadn't discussed it since.

Bart was busily digging into the food Langdon passed over to him. "What do you want?"

"The Harold Dumphy suicide." Langdon paused for a minute, as he tried to read his friend's face. A brown head suddenly appeared from the back seat—snatching the top six or seven fried clams from Bart's basket and slobbering over all the rest. The Coffee Dog munched the clams noisily down. He was probably one of the only dogs in the world who enjoyed fried clams—but then again, he liked everything that was edible and several things, like sneakers and bottle caps, that weren't. Bart eyed the clams for a minute before digging back in. When eating something fried, what did a little dog slobber matter?

"What do you want to know?"

"Who killed him." Fifteen minutes earlier Langdon would have phrased this as a question. But Bart's edgy tone and earlier nervousness had taken away many of his doubts.

"I don't know."

"It was a murder then?"

Bart sighed and looked away, tapping the passenger window lightly with his fingers. "There were a lot of loose ends to be looked into. And then the case was closed. Suicide. It wasn't my case, but it sure as hell didn't seem so cut and dried to me."

"Details..." Langdon prodded gently, not wanting to cut this flow of information.

"Tommy, it was his case, said there were some strange bruises around the corpse's ankles. There were bruises all over the body, jumping off that bridge and hitting the water and all. But around the ankles?"

"You mean he was dragged there?"

Bart half-heartedly munched at a few more clams before speaking. "I don't know, the case was closed and they buried him."

"What else?" Langdon tried to speak quietly, tried not to betray his excitement. A real live murder case.

"He had none of the classic suicide indicators, no signs of depression. An all-around happy, self-motivated man who was going places. Nothing I can put in so many words. Just how I feel."

Langdon's eyes were narrowed to mere slits, his beer forgotten in his hand. "So how does Brunswick P.D. get away with calling it suicide?"

Bart took a healthy haul off his beer, draining half of it in one huge gulp, burping, pausing, then answering with a lowered voice, "Three days before he bought it, he took out a large life insurance policy."

That was that, then.

But Langdon's mind kept working. If there had been evidence that seemed to suggest murder rather than suicide, why was the case closed so abruptly? "Dumphy doesn't strike me as a stupid man," Langdon said slowly, picking his words with care, "Surely not dumb enough to think the insurance policy would be paid up if he offed himself."

"Rumor around the station is maybe he didn't actually want his wife to collect. Like maybe she forced him into getting such a large policy. Or maybe even he took out the policy knowing he was going to commit suicide and that his wife wouldn't be able to collect."

"Any special reason for this blissful matrimony?"

Bart yanked another bottle out of Langdon's cardboard Geary's box, his third beer in twenty minutes. Langdon hurriedly finished his own beer so he could lay his hands on the last one before the bear next to him got to it. "This is all speculation, you understand, nothing you can quote me on?" Goff gave a level stare to show the question wasn't necessary. "The word on the street is the Dumphy widow was yanking more chains than just her husband's."

"She'd had an affair?"

"Not just one affair. The woman's a goddamn franchise. She's got more men in her life than you had beers in this car, and neither one was enough. Is that all you need to know?"

Goff slowly chewed on a fry, staring at the lithe figure of one of the waitresses attending to the car across the way. "So, the theory goes, the husband either finds out about, or can't take, her little dalliances, takes out a policy on his own life, then nullifies the chance of anybody collecting, such as his wife, by jumping off a bridge? Sounds pretty well thought out for somebody utterly despondent over the fickleness of the woman he married. So depressed in fact, that he kills himself."

"It doesn't smell right at all." Bart polished off the rest of the clams. "Hey, flick your lights back on, I wantta' get an ice cream sundae." He looked at the empty six-pack box. "I sure as heck could use another beer, too."

Langdon slowly smiled. "There's a bottle of Jack Daniels in the trunk that I was saving in case I ever broke down in a blizzard."

After the ice cream sundae arrived, and Bart returned from the trunk with the JD, Goff resumed his questions, "So, they have any kids?"

Bart shook his head no.

"Who was Mrs. Dumphy making it with?"

"Nobody who'd admit it."

"Who?"

"Greg Carr from the appliance store out on Bath Road. Stan Jacobs from the town council. Some clam digger that lives out to the trailer park on Maquoit Road. Pick a name, chances are you'll be right." He took a swig and then glanced at Langdon. "Been awhile for you, hasn't it?"

"What."

"You know what I mean. I haven't seen you with a lady, or any sort of female for that matter, since Amanda left you."

Langdon didn't answer.

"Come out with me this week, we'll see if we can't get that little problem straightened out." Bart washed down the last of the fudge topping stuck in his mouth with a generous haul off the bottle.

Langdon made himself smile—Bart didn't mean any harm. "Not to change the subject." He had one last question. "You said earlier that Dumphy had none of the classic signs of depression—but then you say the official line is he was depressed, so depressed he took some life insurance policy and then screwed his wife by not letting her have it. I don't get it."

"Tommy told me that the guy, Dumphy, was acting strange the last few days, jittery, hyper but with dead eyes, you know, the look like something's tearing you apart."

"Who told him that?"

"Christ, Langdon, what is this, the Spanish Inquisition? You know the procedure, he talked to some of the guys Dumphy worked with at the plant, he talked to the neighbors, he talked to the relatives, the paperboy—who by the way was making it with the widow."

"And they all said he was acting strange?"

"They all said he was acting strange."

Langdon looked out the window for a full minute, working through what he'd heard, trying to pick a thread to follow.

Bart spoke as if following Langdon's train of thought. "There's only one angle, if there is an angle. And that is the guy was murdered and there's some sort of cover up going on. Which, by the way, is only supposed to happen in the city, not in Brunswick, Maine."

"So why aren't you doing something about it?" Langdon was immediately sorry for the question. Bart had his own life to live; he didn't mean to judge him.

In a voice Langdon had to strain to hear, Bart answered, "I hope that's what I'm doing now."

Chapter three

As he drove from Hog Heaven back towards town, Langdon called in on his cell phone to check for messages. He could hear Chabal smiling at him when she said, "You're a popular man today." He'd gotten a response, earlier than he'd thought he would, to a deliberately cryptic message he'd left at DownEast Power. Sometimes it was good to stir the pot and see what happened. Especially when you had no leads.

Langdon ripped most of the top off of one of the cans from his freshly purchased six-pack of Bud and took a huge swig as he dialed the number. Back in college he'd participated in beer chugging races and discovered the simple truth that the larger the hole you made in the can, the quicker you could drink.

The woman who had returned his earlier call to the Public Relations division of DownEast Power was an Abigail Austin-Peters. She spoke now in a voice completely devoid of emotion. In his message he'd mentioned Harold Dumphy. "The Harold Dumphy case is closed," she said. "The police have closed their investigation."

Now was Langdon's chance to be creative, to stir the pot further, threaten and cajole. But what he found himself rather lamely saying was, "His Widow doesn't seem to think it's closed." After a measured pause, Ms. Austin-Peters agreed to meet with him for lunch at the 'Wretched Lobster'.

Langdon chucked his now-empty can into the back seat where Coffee Dog had been sleeping for long enough—getting no more than a groan in reply. Whoever had coined the phrase "a dogs life" had never met the Coffee Dog.

Langdon had half an hour left before he was to meet Ms. Austin-Peters, and absolutely nothing to do in that time. He decided to go to the restaurant early. It occurred to him that he'd already had lunch, no more than forty-five minutes ago, but never in his life had he gotten to the point where he felt he just couldn't eat another bite. For that matter, it wasn't as if he ever got hungry either. Sometimes he forgot to eat for days on end, usually when he was caught up in something important. This was not to say that he didn't enjoy food; on the contrary, he felt that the taste of food was one of the few things that made life worthwhile.

Langdon decided to wait in the downstairs bar. "Richam, get me a beer would you?"

Richam, the bartender, finished polishing the glass in his hand, inspecting it briefly before hanging it on the rack. He eyed Langdon and Langdon could feel him calculating, based on his appearance, how many beers he'd already had. Langdon looked away. They were old friends; Richam knew him too well. "What'da you want today?" Richam was one of the few black men in Brunswick, a rake thin man with a military bearing. As Maine towns go,

Brunswick did have its share of ethnic diversity, between the naval air station and the college—but Richam was more than a migratory figure. He lived here. Worked here. Had a family here. Was happy here. Most of the African-Americans who were here in Brunswick were here because this was where they'd the misfortune of being stationed, or because Bowdoin College was the best school they'd gotten into. Richam had chosen Brunswick.

Langdon cracked, "I'm feeling a little risky today, why don't we go with something new." But he could hear the self-disgust in his own tone, disgust for this small town and for the life he'd made for himself.

Richam pulled a Geary's from the cooler, twisting the top, pouring the beer, handing it over. "You've been drinking too much of late."

"Yah, probably."

"How many does this make for the day so far?"

"It's a phase."

"It's a weakness."

Langdon smiled, enjoying the rhythm of this banter even though its subject was himself. "You probably won't believe this, but I've been striving to reach that moment of crystal clarity that occurs somewhere between sobriety and a drunken stupor."

Langdon had first met Richam about five years earlier, when Richam was just recently arrived, an immigrant from an island off the coast of South America. Richam had gone to college in the U.S. with the owner of the Wretched Lobster; when the politics of his country had become too intense, he'd called in a past debt and moved his son and pregnant wife to Maine.

Langdon had entered the bar one day to find four rough-looking clammers addressing Richam as "Hey nigger" while they ordered drinks—a term they seemed to think was as impersonal a form of address as "Hey you". Although Richam appeared to be a person who could handle his own problems and was planning to, possibly with the aid of the gun Langdon suspected—and later confirmed—that he kept under the counter, Langdon somehow felt responsible for the attitudes of his fellow Mainers and stepped in. His attempts at educating the four men about racism were for naught, but for his part Richam learned something about the difference between hate and ignorance, a lesson that would serve him well during his future years in Maine. And he and Langdon had become fast friends.

"Where's your mutt?" Richam was no longer interested in pursuing a conversation about Langdon's drinking that he had no chance of winning.

"Ah, he's still upstairs running around terrorizing the restaurant. Don't they love that dog upstairs. Can't imagine it does much for business, though."

"So what are you doing here," Richam said. "You're not so far gone that you'd be here at this time of day unless you wanted something."

"As a matter of fact, I'm meeting a lady here for lunch."

"A date, I suppose," Richam teased.

Langdon chose to ignore this and took a slug off his Geary's. "What can you tell me about the Harold Dumphy suicide?"

Richam flicked his eyes briefly over the now-empty room. "His wife spends a fair amount of time here."

"That's my client!" Langdon chortled.

"Use protection."

"Very funny."

"I mean that in more ways than one," Richam said, his powerful features fixed intently on Langdon. "She gets around a lot, but don't let her fool you, that's one tough lady who knows what she wants and means to get it."

Goff played his early-morning meeting with the woman through in his mind. He knew he could trust Richam's judgement. Richam listened. Mulled over all he heard. He knew people and liked very few of them. "What are people saying about the suicide?"

"What does she say?"

"Says it was a murder."

Richam smiled humorlessly. "Tell you who did it?"

"I'm the one trying to gather information here. Why don't you answer some of my questions?"

"The man didn't commit no suicide." Richam had the speech of a well-educated man, but often abbreviated his grammar to fit in with his customers. It had become habit.

"People keep telling me that," Langdon murmured. "Any ideas on who may have wanted to do it?"

"No." This was said a little too quickly, a little too forcefully.

Langdon frowned as Richam turned his back to wipe off some more glasses. He rose, making a note to himself to press the matter at some future point. "I've got to go see what my dog has gotten into, make sure they haven't called animal control on him yet." Langdon carried his barely-touched beer with him. He'd been too embarrassed to drink in front of Richam after the reprimand he'd gotten. But once safely through the swinging doors, he took a long swig.

Coffee Dog—all forty pounds of him—was perched upstairs in the lap of a navy blue skirt, the material as well as the animal hugging a woman's rippling edges.

"You must be Mr. Langdon," the lady attached to the skirt stated.

Langdon raised his eyes slowly up from Ms. Abigail Austin-Peters' feet. She was fit, well-dressed and tan, keen and observant. And quite beautiful. Langdon stumbled his large frame into a seat across from her. He found himself in this instant intensely jealous of his dog.

The restaurant they sat in was a crisp whiteness in comparison with the rough-hewn bar downstairs. Fresh tablecloths adorned the finely-crafted tables, each fitted with designer pottery dishes and a lone and solitary flower in a bottle. Every bottle was different. As was the flower.

Ms. Austin-Peters looked warily across at Langdon. Her dark eyes were hidden behind jagged eyelashes and prominent cheekbones.

The woman seemed to be all points. Elbows that jutted out in front of her and bony knees. There was no width at all to her nose, as if someone had drawn a line on her face and then raised it for the blind. Her shoes were pointed. She wore a necklace that appeared to be a fir tree. Even her breasts poked their way out of her blouse as if pointing to something behind Langdon, making him want to look over his shoulder to see what he was missing.

"You are here on behalf of Mrs. Dumphy?"

"She's my client." Langdon was suddenly not sure why he'd come. Had he been hoping this woman would confess? He wished he didn't have the beer base he did in his blood—but there was no changing that now. He was caught at that embarrassing point in drinking when everything seemed just a little too slow, most of all him. The only thing for it was to push on and enter the stage of not really giving a damn, for here one could talk, go with hunches and think pretty much clearly—that is, in a free-form sort of way.

When he called the waitress over to order a beer, Ms. Austin-Peters ordered a Wild Turkey on the rocks. A slight curl to her lip hinted at how much she relished this form of drink.

"What does the widow of a suicide victim want with a private dick?" There was no hint of a smile on her face. Langdon liked that.

"Do you know the widow Dumphy?" Langdon asked casually. He was fishing, trying to get some kind—any kind—of reaction from her. But there was none.

"Christmas Parties. There was some sort of award ceremony. She caught my attention, but not as much as she caught the attention of my male colleagues." This was said with a slight edge of sarcasm. She tapped her nails against the water glass. "What are we here for?"

"Lunch."

"I don't eat lunch."

"Drinks, then."

"Is there a point to all this?" Langdon thought he caught a glimmer behind her cool edge. Though she was acting as if she wanted to be somewhere, anywhere, else, she was intrigued. With a wave of her hand she had another drink on the way. The first had gone down with only a slight wrinkle around the eyes.

Langdon made himself lean casually back in his chair. Now was the time to use his special talent for exasperating people. "Let me tell you. I wasn't sure why I even called you, just reaching for straws, stirring up anything I could. The fact that you called back so soon and the fact that you agreed to meet me makes me think one of two things." Langdon was surprised to find a Wild Turkey on the rocks now sitting in front of him. "Either you're a very bored lady with not much to do except make luncheon dates with strangers, or maybe, just maybe, there's more to the Harold Dumphy case than meets the eye. And maybe my call scared the dickens out of you."

The lady didn't miss a blink. "Are you saying that you don't think Harold Dumphy committed suicide?"

Langdon just shrugged and folded his arms across his chest.

She tapped her glass again. "I would have to agree that there were some discrepancies in the police report. But what does that have to do with DownEast Power?" With a sort of carelessness that was very becoming, the lady Austin-Peters chewed the ice from her third drink, snapping each cube, rolling the chips over her tongue, never, not once, taking her steady gaze from Langdon's face.

"What I'm thinking," Langdon said, picking each word with great care over a tongue that had become thick with drink, "Is that if Harold Dumphy didn't commit suicide—then either his death was accidental or it was murder."

That last word was heavy in the air between them.

"I still don't understand what that has to do with DownEast Power?" Abigail Austin-Peters tossed the remainder of her drink to the back of her throat, her eyes gleaming with the sudden fire, hot-burning and inquiring.

Langdon plugged on. "Harold Dumphy was in charge of security at DownEast Power?"

"Yes." Licking her lips to get the last of the Wild Turkey as she waited for another drink.

"Do you think it possible that he found something that he shouldn't have, or got involved in something over his head?"

"Like what, Mr. Langdon?"

"We are dealing with nuclear power, Ms. Austin-Peters, we are talking plutonium, uranium, fission, radioactive waste. Any number of things somebody may not have wanted him to know about."

She glanced at her watch. "What are you trying to say?"

"I don't really know," Langdon replied through a black cloud that was slowly descending from the ceiling, making it hard to see clearly. "Aren't you in the least worried that something strange is going on at DownEast Power?"

"No. A man commits suicide who happens to work at the plant. It's unfortunate, but that's all there is to it." Abigail Austin-Peters had taken his measure and understood his weakness. He'd been classified as not a threat.

He tried one last stab. "Why are you here?"

In response, Abigail Austin-Peters looked at her watch again and slid to her feet. She spoke in a polite, slightly annoyed tone, "I really have to be getting back to work now." She jostled Coffee Dog gently off her feet. "Thank you so much for the drinks." She placed a twenty on the table, the final insult. "Here, this should cover it. Goodbye." With a stoop to pat the dog, a step, a flutter, the lady who was all angles shot out of the Wretched Lobster and was gone.

It was 3:45 p.m. It had been a rather full day. The beer and Wild Turkey sat heavily in Langdon's stomach, making everything sort of fuzzy. As if the room had been squeezed, rounding everything, expelling most of the light.

Coffee Dog began pulling on Langdon's pants leg, tugging persistently, urgently. He had more intelligence than a dog needed to have. He looked Langdon over warily for moment with his yellow eyes before trotting to the door downstairs and disappearing. Langdon made it to his feet, staggering towards the door one step at a time.

A shadow suddenly loomed in front of him, blocking the light from the door. An arm draped itself gently across his shoulders. Coffee Dog was right at Richam's heels.

Richam was far too wise to tell a drunk that he was drunk. "My wife has been wanting me to ask you if you've heard from Amanda," he said, a thin pretext of conversation.

Before Langdon could argue, resist, or even reply, he was sitting on a bar-stool back downstairs. Spilling his guts. In the morning he knew he'd hate himself for having unloaded on Richam—but now, in this weakened state, it all came out. Amanda. His daughter. Tears of anger and sadness ran down Langdon's cheeks and he made no effort to wipe them away.

When Chabal arrived at 5:45 p.m. after shutting down the bookstore, two hours of black coffee had brought some clarity back to Langdon. And Richam knew more than he cared to about Langdon's personal life.

With one look at Langdon's red eyes the mother in Chabal kicked in, as if one of her kids had scraped his knees on the playground. She was all business, pulling him from his delicate perch at the now-crowded bar.

"Thanks Richam," Langdon said, too embarrassed to look at his friend. "Sorry to hit you with my problems."

"Why don't you come over this weekend and see my family?" Richam asked gently.

Langdon paused when he was a few steps from the bar, turning back to ask a professional question. "You know many women who can slam four Wild Turkeys down in half an hour and not even blink?"

"Who are we talking about now?" Chabal's voice had an edge to it.

"The lady that you took the message from. The one from DownEast Power."

"She was quite a looker, or so the hostess upstairs claims, a real high flyer," Richam said, interested in seeing what reaction this would get from Chabal.

"Kind of makes you wonder what she's doing living in the middle of Maine. Working for a power plant."

Chabal was irritated. "Let's go, I can't be standing around here all day." She pulled her keys briskly from her purse. "Like I need to be playing nursemaid to a grown man." Langdon flushed and Chabal relented slightly, making it into a joke, "Just because he pays my check. Next thing you know, he'll want me doing his laundry."

Chabal drove a Volkswagon bug, a sort of oddity in Maine but one that fit her personality to a T. She also managed to drive too quickly—not fast, for those heaps can't get any real speed, but quickly, as in accelerating too quickly from a stop, braking too quickly for a stop, not braking at all to go around corners. Always pushing the limits.

"Thanks for bringing me home, Chabal." Langdon said. "Just one of those days I guess."

Chabal looked expectantly at him when she stopped in front of his apartment, willing him to stay, to ask her up, to keep quiet, to get out of her car. It was all very hard but at the same time very sweet. It was nice to be able to enjoy time like this. "Take care of yourself, Langdon."

It came as no real surprise to Langdon that the widow Dumphy was sitting on his stoop. He silently thanked Richam for thrusting coffee at him, sobering him up.

"Hello Mr. Langdon," Janice Dumphy said, "I've been waiting for you." She was dressed all in black. Black jeans. Black sweater. Black boots. Black jacket. She had on one of those fur hats that the Russians have made famous. Also black. But mourning was not what she seemed to have in her mind.

"I've got to feed my dog," Langdon said. "Then maybe we can go out and get ourselves a cup of coffee?" This was meant to be a statement, but came out weak, questioning.

"Do you mind if I come up while you...feed your dog?" Her voice was teasing, slightly mocking. She knew the effect she had on men.

"Please do." Langdon had always had a real weakness for women, though usually only for those who wanted nothing to do with him. He was cursed with this strange affliction, that the females he found to be interesting, enticing and intellectually challenging pretty much thought him a dope. Chabal was an exception, but in a way fit the rule too because she was married and not allowed to have any real interest in him. Not that she could admit.

There was no light on over the stairs, so the widow found it necessary to hold onto his waist, close enough behind him that they both almost tripped. Langdon fumbled with the keys, too many keys on the darn ring.

"Did you find out anything today that you should fill your client in on?" Her voice was slightly husky.

"Did you give your husband any reason to kill himself?" He shot back.

The Widow Dumphy took this in stride, "What would it take for you to kill yourself, Mr. Langdon?"

"We can't keep asking each other questions without any answers." Langdon knelt to pour the dog food into the bowl. "Please tell me if you gave your husband any reason to kill himself." Coffee attacked his food as if he hadn't eaten in weeks.

"My husband was a strong man. It wouldn't be easy to give him reason. He might have killed me. Or one of my lovers if that's what you're working around to. But he wouldn't have committed suicide."

"Fair enough."

"Are you a strong man, Mr. Langdon?"

"I would never commit suicide," he said. Not any time soon at least, he added to himself.

"You seem very strong," she said. Wide-eyed and, as if he were all she'd ever wanted.

It wasn't hard to see how she picked up her men with such ease. "Strong?...I tend to eat poorly, drink too much, not sleep enough, let sales-people walk all over me, give to every charity that asks. Even my dog has my number."

Janice Dumphy's eyes were very dark. She leaned against the counter next to him. Wind whistled around the eaves of the house and a very faint hum could be heard from the downstairs neighbors conversing. Coffee sensed the moment, looking up from his now-empty bowl, ears alert, eyes dancing.

Langdon pulled away and walked to the sink. "I guess I need to ask you the names of the men you've had relationships with over the past couple of years, Mrs. Dumphy." He was trying to move the conversation back to firmer footing. It wasn't every day that a murder case was offered to him. He wasn't going to blow it by giving in to a desire that didn't go any higher than his waist.

"Relationships? You mean, like, the milk man and what not? My brother? Who do you mean?" Oh-so-innocent.

There was still enough Wild Turkey in Langdon's system to allow him to deliver the next low, but necessary, blow. "More like the paper boy who I hear tell was delivering more than the paper, or the clam digger who was raking more than clams..."

"Okay. Okay. I get the point." The Widow Dumphy was proving to have a few hard edges. "Do you want details or do you just want names?"

"A few details wouldn't hurt, none of the bedroom variety, though."

She leaned back again and smiled. "The last man I slept with was Greg Carr, he owns the appliance store on the Bath Road. He lives with his wife and two kids in a house just down the road. But he has a lovely summer place out on Bailey Island. I've gone there with him four or five times over the past six months. Is that the kind of stuff you want?"

"When was the last time?"

"Two weeks ago."

Some grieving widow.

Before Greg Carr there had been a long list of men. Thirteen to be exact, over the past two years, ranging from a solitary fling to extended affairs that sometimes overlapped. The woman kept herself busy. The youngest was sixteen at the time, now seventeen and a junior in high school. Probably he'd told all of his friends about his escapades with a married woman and none of them believed him.

Janice Dumphy had settled onto his tattered and torn sofa. Her sweater proved to be of the button down variety, for it was most certainly buttoned down right now, in the sense that most of the buttons were undone. "Won't you have seat," she said, patting the sofa next to her.

"What do you want, Janice?" Feeling his resolve dwindling, Langdon struck out, meaning to force the issue, to dull the moment, whatever it took to avoid doing what he didn't want to do.

"You're not a very good detective if you can't figure that out."

Langdon made himself stay where he was, leaning against the wall. He kept his voice low. "Mrs. Dumphy, I am very much a man of weakness. I go through cycles. For a while I go through the routine that is life. Then, on a consistent basis, the devil rears its ugly head in me and I want to drink too much, smoke cigars, chew tobacco, gamble, go to strip bars and generally make a mess of my life. Usually, if I have a good drunk, this is all erased and I start with a clean slate. That's the part of the cycle you've caught me at today. I'm not interested. If you want me to do some investigative work for you, fine, but that's it."

It was only after the widow had slammed the door, stomped down the steps and driven away in her Camaro with a squeal of tires that Langdon realized he could really have used a ride back into town. It was cold out.

Langdon had decided to walk. It was only a three mile hike back to town, and besides, Coffee Dog could use the exercise.

It started to snow as they left Langdon's apartment. The wind was already gusting at a high rate, making visibility poor. But neither man nor beast noticed—one caught up in his thoughts, the other happy with the cascading flakes of snow. It took forty-five minutes to traverse the distance between home and the College, during which time the dog became somewhat disillusioned with the novelty of the storm.

It wasn't often that a nearly frozen Neanderthal of a man walked into the library of a small, preppy, liberal arts school with his canine beast at his side and proceeded to the computer terminal. The young college student at the entrance desk was so intrigued by this sight that she decided not to enforce the 'no pets' rule. Besides, what was the man supposed to do with the dog, tie him outside in the storm?

After a few minutes, with information scribbled on an index card, the man and dog disappeared into the stairwell.

It was hours later, midnight to be exact, closing time, when the stocky college sophomore from Texas approached Langdon in the upstairs stacks. "Excuse me, sir, it's closing time." His head jerked up from the books he'd been bent over, as if he'd been caught in some inexcusable act. "We're closing for the night," she repeated, "If you would be so kind as to leave."

Langdon smiled, his whole face creasing. "I'm sorry to hold you up..." He paused momentarily, feeling for a foothold, "But do you think you could help me out?"

The shy-looking student seemed intrigued by the the bedraggled man, or maybe it was the Coffee Dog. "What can I do for you?"

"Well, I'm trying to do some research on nuclear power and I can't seem to find anything on DownEast Power. Does that sound right to you?"

"Did you try periodicals?" the student asked faintly.

"No, no I didn't check them..."

She eyed him quizzically, "What is it exactly that you're looking for?"

Langdon frowned, puzzlement racing across his features, "I'm not really sure..."

The student waited patiently. She was an intense and thoughtful girl.

"Let me level with you," a weary Langdon began, needing to talk, to try to work out the confusion in his muddled mind. To top off a very interesting day of threats, new clients, murder cases, blackout equivalent drinking and attempted seduction, he'd just spent the past several hours wading through text books dealing with the process of breaking apart atoms and creating energy through fission. "I'm a private detective working on a murder investigation, a murder that may involve DownEast Power."

"You mean the nuclear power plant?" The student pondered whether the man standing in front of her was entirely sane. The dog raised his lazy head from its resting place against a heater.

Langdon pressed on. "I'm wondering if there's something the murdered man might have stumbled on there. Some reason he might have been killed."

The girl was thinking, trying to follow him. "We're not talking hydro energy here or some other safe alternative. I mean," she paused again, "we're talking about the same process that's used to make nuclear bombs."

So he continued, hitting her with what was consuming him, "If something weren't right at a nuclear power plant—if something had to be hidden—what would it be about?"

There was no hesitation in the slightest from the student. "Nuclear waste."

Chapter four

The student hesitated, shifting her hefty outline back on her heels, face trapped in a pose of indecision. Langdon had just asked her out for a drink. He wanted some simple sanity in his corner for a few moments. "Maybe," she murmured, as if afraid this was just another cruel joke of the kind the members of the male sex seemed to like to play on girls like her, making them feel important and liked, and then pulling the rug out from under them.

He held out his hand to put her at ease. "My name is Langdon."

"Patti Smith. My friends call me Peppermint Patti."

"What should I call you?"

"We'll see." By this time, Patti had moved to a seat across the table, smiling shyly. Her brown eyes had nothing to hide, young, innocent and very much alive, dancing without movement. Her hair was a deep amber red, pulled back into a tight bun, probably to fit the image of a librarian. Several freckles were scattered across her square rigged nose. She was not actually overweight, just a big boned girl, probably—judging from her drawl—right off the farm from down south somewhere.

After a moment she looked away, embarrassed. "I'm not old enough to get into any bars."

Langdon smiled. "I have friends in high places."

They stopped for the girl to punch out on her time card and grab her jacket. "You mean you want me to walk all the way downtown with you in this weather," Peppermint Patti exclaimed. She gave a casual wave as they headed to the door to the elderly woman who was the sole remaining body in the library.

Now it was Langdon's turn to be be embarrassed. "Do you have a better idea?"

"Well, don't you have a car?"

"I do, but it's down by the bar," Langdon moaned, "At least I can give you a ride home later."

"Why don't we just take my jeep," the girl asked sweetly.

"You have a jeep parked right outside, I take it," Langdon muttered, feeling as if the girl were teasing him—but not totally disliking that feeling. "Why don't we just take your jeep then, if you're afraid of a little snow."

"I could meet you there if you'd rather walk." Peppermint Patti was enjoying herself. Her broad face was flushed with excitement now, a much healthier red than its earlier embarrassed glow.

The jeep proved to be a brand new Jeep Cherokee, fully decked out, black and silent looking in the night. The girl was not hard up for money, Langdon thought, appraising the cool splendor of the vehicle.

"So, where are you from that you're so afraid of a little snow," Langdon bantered, feeling more at ease now that they were actually on their way.

"Texas, Lubbock, Texas," she said.

"What the hell is in Lubbock, Texas?"

"No snow for one," slashed the girl, showing some fire, "but not much else, or I sure as heck wouldn't be up here in some province of Canada, trucking around with some Eskimo with his wolf cub who claims he can get me into a bar that probably closed long ago due to the storm!"

"Hey don't get me wrong, I don't have anything against the south, I just wouldn't want to go there for more than two weeks at a time. I even named my daughter Missouri in honor of the south."

"Missouri...what's the last name." Peppermint Patti stared intently through the frantic windshield wipers.

"Langdon."

"Oh, silly me, I thought that was your first name."

Langdon grinned in the darkness of the jeep, thinking that perhaps he had chewed off more than he had bargained for with Peppermint Patti Smith. "Goff Langdon. Pull into this parking lot right over here."

"You're taking me to Goldilocks?" Peppermint Patti stared skeptically at the sign to the bar.

"Something wrong with that?"

"Bowdoin students don't ever go here and the few that do usually get beaten up."

"You've got the wrong information on the place Pepper, do you mind if I call you Pepper, the rest of the whole nickname thing is too long for ordinary conversation. I'm afraid it won't live up to the myth."

"So I should leave my blackjack in the car?" Peppermint Patti smiled, her nervousness fading, but then there was the sound of a car horn and her face froze with fear. "Oh shit. That cop is staring right at us." It was Bart, sitting in the front of his parked cruiser, peering through the storm at Langdon.

Goff smiled as he opened the Jeep door. "Wait here." He whistled for the Coffee Dog when he got out, but the dog remained rooted to the seat in back, eyes wide, pleading to not make him go out into the violence that Mother Nature had whipped up for the residents of Brunswick this evening. Bart was smiling. "Langdon, is that you?"

"Well, it sure as hell ain't Santa Claus!"

"I thought it was, but I have no idea what you're doing in a Jeep Cherokee with Texas plates with a girl who's young enough to be your daughter. In the middle of a snowstorm no less." Langdon just shrugged. He expected Bart to go on with his slightly irritable teasing—but there was a seriousness in Bart's eyes. "Can I talk to you for a moment." Bart pushed open the passenger door and Langdon walked around the cruiser and got in. In the sudden silence after

Langdon closed the door, Bart flicked on his wipers and tilted his seat back a few inches.

"What's with the girl? Is she as young as she looks?" Bart was curious.

"Pepper? She's old enough to know better than to get caught up with me, she's just helping me do some research."

"Yah, right, I had a girl help me with my homework when I was in high school, boy did she help me out, but she was my age at least."

"What do ya' got for me?" Langdon wanted to move the topic away from himself.

"Bowdoin student?" Bart was happy to see Langdon out with a female, even if she wasn't legally old enough to get into the bar Langdon was about to take her into.

Langdon wasn't interested in chatting. "Bart, for Christ-sake, what do you want to talk to me about?"

The big man withdrew momentarily in reaction to Langdon's sharp tone. He made him wait for a few moments before telling him. "Harold Dumphy." He paused for another moment before continuing. "I talked to Tommy, you know Tommy, I told you he was the one working the case."

Langdon tried to keep his tone cool—though he sensed that Bart was about to tell him something big. "He was the one who decided it was a suicide and not an accident or murder."

"That's just the thing, that ain't how it happened. I got him off in a corner tonight after he had too many beers and he spilt the beans."

Langdon pressed him gently. "Beans?"

"Word came down from up top for him to drop the case and to go with the suicide ruling."

"Up top?"

"The Chief himself. Took no argument, threatened Tommy with dismissal from the force."

"Is that all?" Inside Langdon was like a pinball game in a lightning storm. He was now certain beyond a shadow of a doubt that he was working a murder investigation.

"Is that all?" It took Bart a moment to realize Langdon was kidding. He shook his head, exasperated.

Langdon touched his arm briefly as he opened the door to step back outside. "Thanks Bart, I owe you one." He didn't hear Bart's muffled reply—which was probably only an insult anyway.

When Peppermint Patti didn't get out of the Jeep to join him, Langdon approached the window, waiting several seconds for her to crack it open.

"You coming?"

She stared out at him with contempt. "So you can bust me for underage drinking?"

Langdon smiled at her suspicions. “He’s a friend of mine, just wanted to say hi.”

The window went back up smoothly. The Jeep lurched forward, catching Langdon unaware. When she made it to the back of the lot Peppermint Patti had to turn around, an awkward three point turn that was actually four or five in the bad visibility. She managed to pick up some real speed as she came screaming across the lot through the pelting snow like a bat right from the depths of hell. It was a sign that she must not really have wanted to leave that she stopped the shuddering mass of metal almost a full foot from the erect figure of Langdon blocking the way.

The window went down. Langdon walked on shaky legs around to the opening. It was a good thing the lot had recently been plowed, or there was no way the jeep would have stopped in time. Peppermint Patti now looked smug. “I would have run your sorry ass over but then I remembered I still had your dog and I sure don’t want him as a room-mate.”

“So, let me get this straight, you’re mad at me because you thought we were being arrested for pulling into a parking lot outside of a bar, and for this reason you almost left, no, no, I mean, you almost ran me over?” Langdon, raised the second beer from the pitcher that was on the table in front of them. When the two of them had entered bickering back and forth, the bartender had immediately filled a pitcher of beer and brought it over to the table, setting it between them without comment. Coffee Dog was busy jumping on the man and then quickly sitting down and showing how good he could be (give me a treat! the dog silently screamed at the bartender), his entire body quivering with excitement at the potential for food. Goldilocks, the bartender, quietly produced a dog biscuit from his pocket and walked away from the table and Coffee Dog, whistling a tune. Coffee Dog followed a close step behind, eyes glued to the biscuit going up in the air, up, down, up, down, the dog’s head was like a yo-yo. Suddenly, Coffee Dog struck, like a Python going for the kill he shot through the air and plucked the falling biscuit from midair, having swallowed the biscuit whole before his feet touched the floor. Goldilocks laughed and filled a bowl with water and set it down for the dog.

Pepper did not drink all that much in the natural course of her life. She was on her fourth beer. Her anger was beginning to subside, leaving her feeling a little silly, but hey, what did it matter? “**No, let me get something straight,**” she said, tired of being made fun of, “You named your daughter Missouri Langdon?”

“That’s her name. My wife started calling her Missy as soon as she was born, though. After a few months I started calling her E, just to be the opposite of my wife.”

“Your wife?”

“Ex.”

"Not for long, one would think, if you're still making that slip."

"Just about six months now."

"Separated for six months or divorced for six months?"

The girl didn't miss a trick. "Separated."

"So, you're still married."

"Technically." Langdon was uncomfortable with the conversation.

"What happened?"

"We didn't really like each other." Langdon. Amused at the twenty questions.

"So who does Missouri live with?"

"Not the guy who is out in the wee hours of the morning drinking beer with some college student."

"Where's the ex?"

"Last I knew she had ended up in Daytona Beach, Florida, dating some MTV personality."

"And you call her 'E'?"

"Yes."

"Short for Missouri. Do you have some ties to the South or something, you know, like your mother was born on a riverboat full of gamblers, one of which won her hand and you in a poker game?"

"To tell you the truth," Langdon smiled at the spunky youngster in front of him, not sure why he was about to tell her what he had never told anybody, including his wife, "It was sort of in honor of the South because I admired their spirit in the Civil War. Honor. Chivalry. The South was like some ancient mythology, Arthur and the Round Table or something. These are traits that I would like my daughter to possess..."

Pepper was smirking as she poured them both another beer from the bottomless pitcher, "Isn't Missouri considered a Western State."

(Was Missouri a Southern or a Western State? He wasn't exactly sure, now that he thought about it. Perhaps it was a good thing he had never told anybody else the real reason behind his daughters name.) "I guess I could of named her Virginia, or Carolina, or Georgia but none of those names had the originality I was looking for."

"At least they had the Southern twang'." Peppermint Patti continued to grind the point home.

"Are you sure Missouri isn't a Southern State, because I actually liked Nevada better but I figured that pretty much had nothing to do with the Civil War."

"You weren't a history major by any chance, were you?"

"Listen, when I said I would tell you the whole thing, I didn't mean my life story, just the case I'm working on."

"You take many geography courses in school?"

Langdon was frustrated but not unhappy, "Can we get on with our conversation?"

The alcohol had warmed Peppermint Patti's face to a burnished cherry color. She'd let her hair cascade down from its stern bun. Peppermint Patti eyed Langdon playfully. "So tell me Mr. Private Detective, what is the case you are working on?"

She listened attentively as he told her, drinking steadily from her mug. Langdon omitted the details of what had happened earlier in the evening with the widow Dumphy, saying only that they'd scrapped, but told her everything else in full. When he had finished he summed it all up. "There you have it. This morning I was threatened, offered a real live—no pun intended—murder case, got drunk under the table by a nuclear power woman, and then probably fired from the case by a sexually active grieving widow before the day was done."

"And yet the first thing you did was to go to the library to do research on the case?"

A tall, gaunt man with a thin, greying mustache was watching Langdon from the bar. Langdon knew him from the bookstore—Limington was his name, Ellsworth Limington III. He owned most of the town of Woolington—ski resort, restaurants, hotels, etc...When Langdon met his gaze he made his ways towards the door and left after looking back one last time. Something bout this interaction made Langdon nervous. Was he getting paranoid?

Peppermint Patti was watching him intently. "What did you ask me?" He said.

"You probably have no client, yet you persist in researching the case," Pepper replied.

"I'm sorta interested in the whole thing now. It's like starting a puzzle and then having it taken away from you. What do you do? Maybe you go buy your own puzzle so you can finish it."

"Or maybe you get somebody else to buy the puzzle for you."

Langdon nodded slowly, surprised at the girl's intelligence and ability to read his mind.

She continued. "DownEast Power might be interested in the case, if you can convince them that Harold Dumphy found something suspicious at the Plant."

"DownEast Power would definitely be the place to start," Langdon agreed. "But what if what Harold Dumphy 'found', was something the officials at the plant are trying to cover up?"

"Like what?" Pepper had an intense look of concentration, squinting her eyes, caught up totally in this game of detective.

Langdon replied, "According to what I found tonight in the library, the inspection of these plants is pretty intense. There are actually three inspectors from the Nuclear Regulatory Commision who go to work every day at DownEast Power. There are also entire teams that come in for in-depth analysis, twenty people for a couple of months. This just happened three months ago. So I doubt it's any physical defect in the plant. But it is possible."

Peppermint Patti went back to her earlier musings. "Maybe the utility companies that own the plant would be interested. What's the big one?"

"Casco Bay Power is the majority stockholder."

"At the same time," Pepper thought while she talked or talked while she thought, "CBP wouldn't be too hot on you finding something wrong there either, not if it was serious enough for them to have to shut down the plant."

Langdon stared at the college student and realized that the two of them were right in sync, it was one of those things. "I could always take what I have to the state and see if they would be interested," Langdon said without much enthusiasm. "But they have their own people that do this sort of thing, so if they were really worried they'd drop me like a hot potato and send a special investigation team in."

"How about some sort of environmental group?" Pepper asked excitedly, "I know a couple of students at Bowdoin who were big into some campaign last year, what was it, 'Flower First'. It was a grass roots sort of thing, but I think that may have been the party that won, the Governor's party."

Goff realized that Pepper had hit the stage of drinking that was absolute clarity, a brief period in which the doors of the mind opened, allowing everything to crystalize, to have logical beginnings, middles and ends—that is before it all shut down, leaving the individual a blithering idiot.

Almost on cue, Pepper somehow missed her mouth with her next swig of beer, and dumped the entire contents of the glass down the front of her blouse. It was a lacy, white material. Langdon found himself suddenly staring at the twenty-year old Texan's bosom, not without some enjoyment.

She froze for a moment, her boldness and playfulness disappearing, as she reverted in her mind to an awkward, overlooked, overweight outsider. A tear formed in the corner of one eye, followed by another. She rose to her feet, knocking against the table and spilling the half-empty pitcher onto the floor. She fled, leaving her pocket book and her jacket.

Langdon picked up her things and whistled for the Coffee Dog—the dog was already in hot pursuit, obviously thinking the girl had decided to play a game with him. They caught her as she reached her jeep and realized that it was locked, that she had no key, that she had no jacket, that it couldn't have been much above zero. Coffee Dog, not realizing the delicate nature of the situation, began jumping on the girl, thinking that now that he had caught her she might want to wrestle, roll around in the snow, play chase or just generally be entertaining.

"Coffee, get down," Langdon hissed at his dog.

Pepper stood with her arms crossed, shivering violently.

"Let me give you a ride home," he said.

"Give me my goddamn keys!"

"You have two choices, a ride with me or I call a cab."

She eyed him apprehensively. Coffee Dog looked at both of them forlornly.

"Me or the cab?"

Pepper wrenched her jacket from his fingers, pulling it on with her back turned, "Okay, let's go."

Langdon drove through the white shroud that enveloped the night, starting to feel the exhaustion of the long day. Once again, he was leaving his car behind, which would probably mean another walk through the developing ice storm. Pepper didn't speak the entire way and Langdon respected her silence. But as they approached the snow shrouded college, he thanked her for the idea of contacting an environmental agency. She was staring out her window and didn't turn her head. He wanted to comfort her somehow—but he knew that whatever he said would only make her more embarrassed.

When he got to her dorm and attempted to return the keys, Pepper shook her head in the negative. "You keep the jeep, bring it back whenever it stops snowing. Just park it in this lot and leave the key under the mat."

Coffee Dog pleaded with him to accept.

Langdon drove the jeep the few miles to his apartment, his head stinging from the smoke of the bar, his body aching from the day's stress. Janice Dumphy, Abigail Austin-Peters and Peppermint Patti all in one day. But he smiled at the thought of Pepper, and wished her a silent good night.

Langdon was not surprised to see the slender, sallow faced man sitting at his kitchen table reading the morning paper. It was just after 3 a.m. It was the same man who'd been reading his paper this past morning, an eternity ago.

"Mr. Langdon," the fop sneered, his voice crisp and proper.

Coffee Dog stood in front of Langdon with a low growl or what passed as a growl, his body tense—but at the same time conveying an attitude of 'when do we get to go to bed'. Langdon told him to go sit down. The dog agreed but did keep one eye open from the corner, never leaving the face of the intruder.

"Where have you been?" The man said. "I've had a long wait for you."

"Making snowmen."

"How do you expect us to get along with that sort of attitude?"

Langdon filled a plastic cup with water. "I've had a long day. Could you just deliver your message and be on the way."

"Who says I have a message?"

"Your kind always works for somebody else Mr...?"

"Shakespeare."

"Shakespeare. You're no more than an errand boy, a lackey, a messenger if you will. So what is the message so I can get to bed."

Anger at Langdon's last comment curled Shakespeare's lip. His eyes were hard and unforgiving. "I came to ask that you stay away from the Dumphy case, Mr. Langdon. I have even brought a sum of money to pay you for your troubles."

"What I want to know," Langdon began with exasperation, "Is...what is the Dumphy case? I probably would be passing it off as the greed of a not-so-grieving widow for her insurance money if some faggy, excuse me, sensitive sort of European fellow named Shakespeare didn't keep popping up in my life?"

"I am just trying to nip an embarrassing situation in the bud, Mr. Langdon." Shakespeare had his anger under control for the time being. "There has been no crime, and as a matter of fact, this has nothing to do with DownEast Power. My benefactor is a gentleman here in town who would like to keep the nature of his relationship with the widow Dumphy a secret, for his family's sake. This is how I knew you were going to be offered the case. She told the man who hired me and he was unable to dissuade her. That is all. No espionage. No crime. Just a desire to keep private affairs private."

Langdon didn't believe him. He doubted that conversation would get him anywhere—so he slammed the man in the face without warning.

Shakespeare went over the back of the chair into the wall without uttering a word. He lay without moving. Langdon had thought it was only in movies that people could be knocked unconscious with a single blow. With a sudden fear he reached down and felt for a pulse on the icy wrist. He was alive.

Langdon quickly set about searching his pockets. There was a long, black pistol, worn and dangerous looking. There was a driver's license with the man's picture—Lawrence Shakespeare, from New York City. Langdon copied down the license number and the address. That meant nothing though, for this sort of man could always get fake identification. There were no credit cards. No pictures of friends or family. Nothing but the license and six crisp fifty dollar bills. But in his jacket pocket there was something more—an envelope which held ten thousand dollars. This then, was the amount of the payoff.

Langdon took this money and put it in the oven which as far as he knew had never even been connected much less used. He searched the man for other weapons. Strapped to his leg was a slim, very sharp looking blade. Langdon put this in the drawer with his kitchen knives. He emptied the gun of bullets.

He filled a black pot with cold water and dumped it over the inert figure. Shakespeare stirred, jerked, then reached for the empty holster at his chest. There was a large red welt on his jaw. In degrees his composure returned. His eyes were absolutely flat and without emotion.

"I will kill you."

"Not this morning you won't."

"Where is the money?"

Langdon smiled. "I have it."

"You accept the offer then?"

Langdon opened the door. "I'm thinking it over. In the meantime I'll just hang onto the money."

Chapter five

Darkness.

Man and beast came awake as one.

Jolted out of sleep.

Rolling, reaching, pawing.

A deadly scramble with sleep, with noise, with any sort of rationality that does not exist in that half world between night and day, dreams and thoughts, hot and cold.

For the second morning in a row it was the phone. Langdon retrieved the receiver from the floor, where it had been knocked in the wild melee of man and dog that the ringing had created.

There was no trace of sleep left in Langdon's tone as he barked into the phone. He'd slept for no more than ninety minutes. He yanked the cord back from Coffee Dog, who'd somehow got the notion that it was time for tug of war. Langdon paid no attention to the banging on the floor from the Beans downstairs.

The voice on the other end of the line was laughing, "I'm surprised to catch you awake at this time in the morning."

It was Jimmy 4 by Four, Langdon's lawyer. When Langdon was done with the string of obscenities that he felt such an early morning call merited, he fought back a sense of dread. Why would his lawyer call him this early?

Jimmy seemed to read his thoughts and spoke to reassure him. "It's your daughter Langdon, I got you visitation rights."

Langdon sat very still in the middle of the floor for a few minutes after he'd hung up the phone. The last Langdon had heard, no one had even had a location of his wife and daughter. Amanda had simply disappeared with Missouri into the void of the South. There had been rumors that some MTV personality or professional golfer was the new man in Amanda's life—rumors that grated on the very inner being of Langdon. Even though he would not admit it to anybody, not even himself, Landgon still had feelings for her. There had been good times before the bad. It was a part of his life that he missed, deep down, a part that he hid well underneath his gruff exterior of nonchalance.

In the car on the way to Jimmy's office, Coffee Dog watched him with doleful eyes.

* * *

Jimmy 4 by Four had grown up in New York City, in the Bronx, and had fought his way into Rutgers University, his ambition driving him like a train, never slowing to pick up any passengers or baggage along the way. Graduating seventh in his class, he had been accepted into Yale Law School, working nights and weekends—working at any job he could, to pay off his monumental student loan's. That loan was like a ball tied to his leg and it wasn't any beach ball.

He got a job with one of the most prestigious law firms in New York City, becoming a partner in just four years. He worked fifteen hours a day, seven days a week, and billed for most of them. He was a legal genius, without a doubt the rising star of the firm.

Smoked four packs of cigarettes a day.

Drank somewhere between twelve and fifteen cups of coffee a day.

Lived in a highrise that he never saw awake.

One morning Jim Angstrom, as he was known then, woke up and said 'enough'. By eleven-thirty he was driving north in his BMW. At 2 in the afternoon, somewhere outside of Hartford Connecticut on 84 East, he traded his BMW straight up for a Volkswagon bus that sat in the furthest corner of a used car lot. The car dealer thought he was taking a real chance with what he assumed was a stolen car, but the 'greed of the deal' got the better of him. Within the hour Jim Angstrom was back on the road, maxing out at forty-five miles an hour, half in the slow lane and half in the breakdown lane—and that was how he arrived in Maine. The bus had broken down in Topsham as he was cruising up the highway, intending to reach the back woods before stopping—but sometimes fate intervenes in these matters, for he never left the Brunswick/Topsham area.

He passed the bar in Maine, taking some light contract work to pay the bills, smoked a lot of pot, grew a beard, lived in a house without plumbing, had an outhouse, did some painting and sculpturing. There were a series of live in girl friends, drifting in and out of his life like the clouds that passed overhead when he lay on his back for hours in the fields. He lived in the woods of Bowdoinham, Maine, and was happy.

Fifteen years later he had begun to emerge from his self-imposed isolation. His cocoon opened to reveal a deeply confident, content man who truly enjoyed practicing law and interacting with society. The therapy had not been quick, but he was now a fully recovered workaholic. He could put in a day's work and leave in the middle of a project without taking any of the stress home with him. Somewhere along the line he had become Jimmy 4 by Four, legally changing his name.

Langdon had several times tried to pin him down on the origins of this odd appellation, but had never been given an answer.

* * *

"What do you got for me?" Langdon had taken but twenty-five minutes to get down to his lawyer's office.

Jimmy 4 by Four struck a match, studied the flame, pondered the fate of a thin unlit cigar for a moment, and carefully lit the end, inhaling deliciously.

"Your wife's in Philadelphia right now," he said, "Staying with her sister." Cigars had taken the place of pot in his small collection of luxuries in life.

Langdon leaned back in his chair across the desk, not pressing for details, knowing that there was no hurrying this man, that the information would come in its own good time. Jimmy 4 by Four had come from a world in which there was never enough time to do all, say all, be all that he wanted and needed. Now time passed only when he wanted it too. If he wanted or needed time to stand still, well then, time stood still.

"Me thinks," Jimmy continued, "that she would be happy enough to have a break from being the mother to a three year old child. Maybe even for as long as a month."

"I'm on my way," Goff answered, doing some internal mental calculations. "I'll be there...about seven hours from now."

"The drive can't be done that quickly." It was an easy nine hour trip doing the speed limit, not including stops.

Langdon paused only briefly on his way to the door, "Just tell her I'll be there about two o'clock this afternoon."

It was not until Langdon reached his car that he realized his lawyer was right behind him. "You goin' somewhere?" Langdon snarled.

"Its been awhile since I've been to Philly." 4 by Four said to Langdon with a carefree, vacation-attitude.

Langdon shook his head. "I don't have time for you to pack a bag."

Jimmy smiled. "I'm not bringing a bag."

"But I need you to call Amanda." Langdon muttered.

"I called her right after I talked to you on the phone. Told her we'd be there by two." 4 by Four answered with increasing smugness, much like a cat playing a mouse, a Kung Fu master throwing his pupil. "Besides, you forget to ask me where Amanda and Missouri are. Philadelphia ain't exactly like Brunswick, country boy. You might have a little harder time than stopping the first pedestrian you see and asking them where Amanda Langdon lives. As a matter of fact, if you did that, you'd probably get your dumb ass shot. So why don't you quit the damn complaining and let me in the car."

Langdon did as he was told.

After all, the man did have a point.

* * *

It wasn't until Portsmouth that any conversation passed between them. Langdon was swearing softly under his breath.

Jimmy 4 by Four frowned. "What?"

"I was supposed to return somebody their Jeep Cherokee this morning." Langdon had driven the jeep to where his car was, not having time to return it to Pepper in his hurry.

"A friend?" Jimmy 4 by Four gently pried.

"Somebody I just met."

Jimmy smiled knowingly. "Must be a female."

"Why do you say that?"

"No guy you just met is going to let you take his jeep with the promise to return it in the morning."

At that moment, 4 by Four's beret disappeared into the backseat. Coffee Dog had come awake and snatched the hat away. With a quick move that took the dog totally by surprise, the lawyer went over the seat in a flying tackle and pinned him down. Jimmy held the dog with one hand by the collar and with the other hand deftly flicked the hat out of the dog's mouth with minimal slobber.

Sprawled in the back, his feet sticking over the front seat, his face now being eagerly licked, 4 by Four continued his train of thought, "Not to mention that she probably let you take the jeep so you didn't have an excuse to stay at her place."

"She's twenty years old."

4 by Four's smile deepened. "Bowdoin student?" Langdon's astonished face in the mirror was all the answer needed. Jimmy continued, "Its pretty elemental that only a Bowdoin student could afford a Jeep Cherokee at the ripe age of twenty. Which, by the way, brings me to the question of what were you doing with a minor in the eyes of alcohol?"

"What do you mean 'a minor in the eyes of alcohol'?"

"I mean she may be old enough to fool around with an old geezer like you, but she still can't legally participate in your favorite activity, going to bars..."

Langdon ignored the barb. "We were just talking, she had some insights into the case I'm working on."

"The Widow Dumphy?" Jimmy kept the smile from his face only with great effort.

Langdon swung his head around for a moment in surprise, despite the fact that he was driving. "Now how the hell do you know that?"

"Richam stopped by last night," Jimmy said, "He seemed a little worried about you."

"If this is the point at which you tell me that I need to start going to AA meetings, well then, you can just skip it." Langdon glanced down at his speedometer—which had began to creep above the rock steady ninety miles an hour they'd been traveling at thus far.

"That's not what he was worried about," 4 by Four retorted, "And by the way, if you think that having your lawyer in the car is going to get you off of going to jail for going this fast, then you better think again."

Langdon steadied the rumbling beast back to a dull 90—which in his exasperated state didn't feel nearly fast enough. "What in hell is Richam worried about then?"

Jimmy sat up in the back seat, hugging his knees, speaking more cautiously as he read the annoyance in Langdon's tone. "Well, he was talking to Bart." Langdon rolled his eyes in disgust at this collusion of his friends. Jimmy continued, "And the thought seems to be that this Dumphy guy was killed for something he knew, something you seem to be stirring up. It doesn't take Sherlock Holmes or even Watson to know who the next victim will be."

Langdon answered dismissively, eyes glued to the road, his head pounding. "Oh, come on, this isn't some penny detective novel with guys and gals being shot up left and right. This is real life. There ain't nobody gunning to kill some private dick in small town Brunswick."

"Its not just in New York that people get killed for no reason, not anymore, anyway," 4 by Four said, taking care with each word. "New York has moved to Boston which has in turn has come to the suburbs and believe it or not, Brunswick is the suburbs now."

"What's that supposed to mean?"

"Maine is changing quickly, if you haven't noticed. The computer age of technology and all that. Twenty years ago the displaced, disgruntled Americans like me moved here to escape all of it, but it has come and found us. Faxes. E-Mail. The Net. Don't kid yourself. Civilization and all that comes with it has found Maine." Jimmy 4 by Four leaned back, lighting his cigar. Coffee Dog sensed his moment, and grabbed the hat back from Jimmy's lap. That was the thing about Coffee Dog—he was patient, biding his time, then striking when weakness was conveyed. When he realized 4 by Four wasn't going to put up a fight this time, he tried to egg him on, jabbing the hat against him. Jimmy, lost in thought, just absently patted his head. "New York has moved to Boston." He concluded, "Which in turn has come to the suburbs, and believe it or not, Brunswick's the suburbs now."

Langdon smiled. "What are you saying? That my business as a private detective is going to be picking up?"

Jimmy pressed his point. "Look at Brunswick and who lives there. Do you know who lives out on Mere Point? The Harpswells? Bailey Island? Its not just fishermen anymore, but rich, influential men who like the lifestyle and plan to rape that very lifestyle to further their aims."

Langdon disagreed with that last point. "Don't you think they're bringing something with them, too?"

"Like what?" Jimmy snorted derisively.

"Money for the economy, culture for the mind, I don't know, but they seem like good enough people. I don't buy into this theory that you have to be a third generation Mainer to be considered a local, to be worthy of social interaction."

"It's not really their fault," 4 by Four began, picking each word with care. He'd given this a great deal of thought. "But the type of people who move to Maine are usually upper-middle class. They believe in the American Dream, progress, computers and all that stuff. They no sooner move in than they notice there isn't a Wal Mart and instead of saying 'oh, that's nice, I can shop at small local businesses', they see opportunity. Bigger is better. Strip malls reign over most of the country and there's a reason for that, its called 'easier'. But that doesn't mean it's better."

Langdon silently watched the signs of Lowell, Lawrence and the rest of Massachusetts whip by. He felt that Maine was changing, too, and agreed that it wasn't all for the better—but for the moment brought the conversation back to the matter at hand. "What did Richam say to you?"

Jimmy answered with a question of his own. "Tell me about the case."

And so Langdon told him all. Including his aggravated assault the night before on the strange little man who'd been following him, and including Peppermint Patti's fresh outlook. Although he did not mention it to Jimmy, surrounding the whole thing was his pain at having lost not just his wife but his daughter, giving him reason to drink, to feel insecure in a world that he no longer understood.

Jimmy listened thoughtfully, rolling his cigar quietly in his mouth before speaking. "I have a friend who works for Casco Bay Power, in the head office. They might be a good person to talk to, if indeed, you are in need of selling your services to a new client."

"Don't you think I should go to DownEast Power first?" Langdon wanted any excuse to go back for another meeting with the mystery lady, Abigail Austin-Peters, who seemed to somehow have unsettled his senses. Perhaps that was the attraction.

"If, and I stress the if," 4 by Four began with a smile, "there is something odd going on at DownEast Power, there's a real good chance that the officials at the plant have to know about it." He savored the last of his cigar. "What is it that you think is happening out there, anyway?"

"I don't know." Langdon was noncommittal.

"Come on, I know you better than that," 4 by Four implored. "You at least have some sort of hypothesis, no matter how stupid it is." Jimmy 4 by Four had done some detective work with Langdon before, most recently for an environmental group hoping to uncover river pollution by Maine factories. 4 by Four had come to appreciate Langdon's instinct and ability, and his stubborn persistence.

"Well, Pepper did come up with one possible scenario, but I'm still not sure about it..."

"Come on, let's here what it is."

"Pepper suggested that perhaps it had to do with nuclear waste."

"Nuclear waste?"

"Sure, why not, these plants generate a lot waste, from low level contamination of gloves and workclothes, to spent control rods and the whole nine yards. What is DownEast Power doing with the waste? Believe me, the place isn't treated like a nuclear silo, the security is minimal." Langdon thought for a second, wondering how many of his suspicions he should voice, before continuing. "It would be real easy for a few key individuals to be paid to turn a blind eye and have radioactive waste taken from the facility."

Jimmy shook his head in disbelief. "You think somebody's stealing nuclear waste?"

Langdon shrugged. "Maybe."

"But why?"

"I don't know, maybe for some sort of terrorist activity."

Jimmy laughed. "So, somebodies going to park a truck full of radioactive waste outside the white house and leave the doors open?"

Langdon shrugged. He wasn't smiling.

"Devious."

Jimmy 4 by Four just shook his head. Nuclear waste terrorism seemed awfully far-fetched to him, but he had come to learn that Langdon had a knack for coming up with the correct solution to a problem, no matter how whacked out that solution might seem. "Don't you think it more likely that there are safety issues at DownEast Power? Perhaps the reactor is damaged, cracks in the fuel rods, something of that nature? Maybe the problem is serious enough to shut down the plant and somebody's trying to cover up that fact. "Like who?" Langdon asked.

"Maybe the boys in the front office for Casco Bay Power decided it would be cheaper to cover up safety violations than to fix them," 4 by Four suggested.

Maybe.

It was good that Jimmy 4 by Four had come along for the ride, for it wasn't actually Philadelphia they were headed for, but Williamstown, New Jersey, about thirty miles outside of the city. 4 by Four gave directions from a hurriedly scrawled scrap of paper, a map spread across his lap.

Williamstown was living proof of the boom that took place in the 80's. Every few miles there was a settlement of condos, all looking as exactly alike as eggs in a carton. It was as if some sort of ultimate socialistic society had been achieved, all people being equal, living in the same exact dwelling; even the cars had little variety, four door Japanese cars of conservative colors. There were no houses, not even housing developments.

This massive concentration of condo dwellers had to be supplied with the necessities of life, so the scant space between each development was crowded with strip malls, generic signs dotting their facades—each and every one promising the fulfillment of a need with as little social interaction as possible. If and when automation replaced humans, this would be the first test ground. It wasn't that the shops that filled these malls were bad in and of themselves. Everything that a person could possibly need or want was here-groceries, donuts, pharmacy, liquor, movies, dancing girls, newspapers, Vietnamese restaurant, books. It simply was what it was.

Langdon was certain that somewhere Williamstown must have an old section of quaint, huge, imposing houses, but they were well hidden from view..

Jimmy 4 by Four mumbled obscenities as he tried to decipher the directions he'd written out only that morning, occasionally distracted as Langdon threaded in and out of the heavy traffic and braked for the stop lights that popped up everywhere. Pedestrians were much safer here in New Jersey than in Maine, for here they were not under the slightest apprehension that traffic might stop. They darted quickly across only at intersections with red lights, and were even then leery of the hulks of metal revving their engines inches away.

"This is it, right here, on the right!" Langdon continued on past the turn, suddenly gripped by insecurity. When he stopped at the next light, Jimmy reached to touch his shoulder gently. "We didn't come all the way to Condo-Mall Land just to turn around and go back, did we?"

Langdon spoke very quickly. "What if she doesn't remember who I am?"

"Missouri? That girl loves you, Langdon. I've seen the two of you together and one of the saddest aspects of my life is seeing the two of you apart. She remembers you alright, and she misses you, and if you don't want her to become cynical and disillusioned at the age of, what is she, three?, then you better go face your wife and daughter."

"My ex-wife." Langdon muttered.

"Not unless you got another lawyer to do the paperwork on that one. There have been no divorce papers even filed, much less settled. Anyway, your marital status isn't really the issue here, is it?" 4 by Four suddenly realized that in his babbling he may have struck a nerve. He sighed. "So it's not just seeing your daughter that has you scared."

Langdon made himself smile, turning it into a joke. "I've always been terrified of facing my wife."

After eying his friend for a moment, Jimmy chuckled. "Sort of like the time we had the poker night, then took an extended break to visit some of the local bars, then resumed until 6 in the morning and you'd neglected to call..."

"She does have a certain bite to her when she's angry," Langdon grinned, "but this time it's not me who's been missing for the past six months. So maybe I'll get the easy side of her tongue."

* * *

Amanda was strikingly beautiful in her anger. "You needed your lawyer along to pick up my daughter?"

Before Langdon could answer, a tiny voice shrieked. "Daddy!!" A small body ran full tilt into his legs and hugging them fiercely. Missouri, tiny and delicate. Full of strength and not bothered by anything but the true existence of her feelings.

Before he could pick her up she was bowled over by the Coffee Dog, who licked her face, enormously pleased. Screaming with laughter she tried to hug the dog that was her friend, her buddy. Coffee did an excited dance, his whole body shaking, just all around ecstatic to see her. "Daddy! We have some serious butt wiggling going on here!" Missouri shrieked in glee.

The dog located the ponytail band holding her hair in place, and somehow managed to whisk the elastic off without pulling her hair. He trotted away with the band in his teeth like some trophy, happy with his achievement. Missouri took off after him like a shot and the two disappeared into the interior of the condo.

For all of his brave talk of facing the music and paying the piper and all the rest of the bull that Jimmy 4 by Four had used to get Langdon to arrive at this grey shingled condo that looked similar to the three hundred units surrounding it, Jimmy 4 by Four proved to be more talk than action as he skulked in the background by the car.

"He came along as a friend," Langdon replied in defense of his now tongue-tied lawyer. "Somebody to help with the directions in this land of traffic, highways, speed tracks and confusing road signs."

Amanda was leaning against the wall by the door, her arms folded across her chest. "Do you want to come in and have some coffee." This was not phrased as a question, but rather an invitation to do battle, like drawing a line in the sand and daring the boy in front of you to cross it.

"Still take it black?" Langdon really couldn't be bothered with putting cream or sugar in his coffee, too much of a pain in the butt.

The living room was small but tasteful, stairs leading up on the right side to a balcony, mood lighting illuminating the walls, the artwork, the curtains. The steady sipping of coffee and the clinking of china was the only noise, Missouri off somewhere playing with the dog, an occasional crash letting them know all was still well.

"So, Amanda, I guess I have to ask," Langdon began after the tension around the small living room had grown to an impossible barrier, threatening to suffocate them all, "what have you been doing with yourself and with E for the past few months?"

Amanda sat back in her chair, the anger that had held her rigid since they'd come seemed suddenly to leave her—and she seemed small and bewildered by a life that hadn't quite worked out the way she'd planned. "I got caught up with a professional golfer. Not that I ever saw him golf. All he wanted to do was go to cocktail parties down in Florida and get pleasantly smashed, and try and seduce any female that crossed his path. He ended up sleeping on the floor by mistake more often than not. I finally drew the line when he began to knock me around." Amanda had always been able to talk to Langdon, tell him anything.

For a moment Langdon felt nothing so much as an overwhelming sorrow for her. He remembered the first summer they'd dated, how brash and happy she'd been, how she'd laughed as she'd scrambled on the rocks by the water ahead of him...

But there was a sobering question to be asked. "Where was Missouri during all of this?"

"There mostly, sometimes with a babysitter..." Amanda threw out the words somewhat defiantly with a toss of her head but trailed off with a look of shame.

"You had my daughter in the middle of all of that trash?" He'd jumped to his feet and started pacing. "When you could have just left her with me to take care of?" He had never been so angry in his life.

"One thing just led to another, I didn't mean it to turn out that way." Amanda was silently crying now, the tears running down her face.

Langdon didn't care. He was still shaking with rage, but spoke now in a quiet, precise tone. "I'm going to take her with me. I don't think you'll be getting her back, not if my lawyer is worth half his money. You'll be lucky to see her again."

Amanda dropped her eyes to the ground and nodded her head once, and then again.

"Mommy, what's wrong, aren't you happy that Daddy's back?" E stood in the door, poised delicately, one hand lightly touching Coffee Dog's head. Coffee Dog stood stock still, trying to understand what it was that he sensed in the room.

* * *

Jimmy 4 by Four drove back with the dog in the navigator's seat while Langdon and E rode in the back, she chattering away with little that made much sense until she dropped off to sleep. When he was certain that she was sleeping, Langdon broke the silence of the ride, "She looked healthy if not happy, didn't you think?"

"Who?" 4 by Four was surprised out of his internal hypnotic driving state.

"Amanda."

"She looked real good," 4 by Four stated with perhaps a little too much appreciation.

"Not just in an attractive sort of way," Langdon spoke cautiously, "More like she was a little more comfortable with who she is."

"Maybe after a drunk who beat her, you're starting to look like quite a catch to her, is that what you mean?"

Langdon couldn't begin to sort through his conflicting emotions towards Amanda. There was something there, he knew—but after the renewed pity he'd felt when he saw her standing in the doorway as they drove away, his anger at the risk she'd put their daughter through now resurfaced. He shook his head, deciding to put this all aside for the moment. "So why do think somebody is harassing me?"

The change in subject took 4 by Four with surprise but he rolled with the flow, "You mean Shakespeare?"

"And whoever he works for, yeah." Langdon's voice was low and muted. "We can discuss the talent scout from the Vikings another time, but right now I mean Shakespeare. The guy calls me up and threatens me before I've even been offered the case. And then he shows up in my apartment and tries to buy me off..."

"You do have a successful track record." Jimmy spoke cautiously.

"Not that successful." Langdon snorted.

"It was only six months ago that your picture was on the front page of the Portland newspaper for breaking that story about the paper mill."

* * *

Jimmy 4 by Four had been approached by an environmental group from Clinton, Maine, "The Family of the Forest!", his name having been recommended by one of his hippy friends. The group's leader was Rasputin Snow, a man who appeared to come right out of some grade B horror flick, his black hair pulled into a long ponytail, his nose flat and crooked from having been broken a time or two, cheekbones that flared under the cracking of time, his body short, squat and sturdy. When he smiled, though, that initial impression of terror was dispelled and was enveloped in the warmth of his face.

There were currently seventeen people in the 'Family of the Forest', including five children, none of whose fathers were known for certain in the commune, and some had even forgotten who the mothers were. The group had been living together since the early 1970's, ever dwindling from its fifty-one member peak. The ravages of time had seen many of its numbers move out to return to mainstream civilization, succumbing to society, families of their own, houses in a neighborhood with white picket fences, or at least houses with indoor plumbing.

In an effort to stave off this inevitable process of reassimilation, Rasputin Snow had organized an environmental group to allow the hippies to flex their considerable talents and intellectual prowess while remaining true to their mission statement of a returning to simplicity and snubbing technology.

Just down the street from the commune of 'Family of the Forest!', there was a paper mill, situated on the river as mills are, and it was Rasputin Snow's contention that this mill had been leaking illegal chemicals, polluting and killing the fish and vegetation and posing health risks to anybody or anything that came in contact with the water. Rasputin wanted Jimmy to get a restraining order preventing the mill from further polluting the river, 'Before we become New Jersey.' He'd said.

Jimmy 4 by Four had accepted the case even though he knew there wasn't much chance of his being paid for his work. Money wasn't everything, and actually had played a very minor role in Jimmy's life since he'd been a slave to that evil god years before in New York City. His first step had been to call Langdon.

Langdon had spent several weeks investigating, trying to crack the paper plant officials, while 4 by Four filed an injunction. The paperwork was stalled, the officials and most of the entire town had clammed up and the case was going nowhere.

4 by Four thought they should take water samples on their own and get them analyzed, but Langdon, with a hint of wickedness in his smile, told Jimmy that afternoon that he had a better idea.

At midnight that same night, Jimmy, Langdon and Rasputin sat hunched behind a tree, smoking cigars, two of them still not sure exactly what was going on.

Langdon finally told them his plan in whispers.

Rasputin and Langdon crept up to the nearby barn while 4 by Four kept watch. With a minimum of noise, they stole a cow. They brought the cow to a salt lick which Langdon had loaded onto the back of his car. The unfortunate beast developed a great thirst—and then they lead him to the slaughter. Sometimes when playing for big stakes, sacrifices have to be made.

Sometime the next morning, a farmer in Clinton found his stray cow within several feet of the river that ran down behind his barn.

The cow was dead.

The newspapers were somehow tipped off.

Before the farmer even knew what was happening, there was a veterinarian present taking blood samples...

And Rasputin Snow and "The Brothers and Sisters of the Forest" were on the scene before anybody could even blink, carrying signs protesting the illegal dumping and pollution of the river...

Goff Langdon had his picture on the front page of the Portland newspaper being quoted as, "I'm just glad that it was a cow and not the farmer's kids that discovered the river was being poisoned."

* * *

4 by Four looked up in the mirror and saw that Langdon had dozed off, escaping into sleep, his arm around Missouri, the two of them leaning together and clutching each other tight, intent on not losing what they had and what they'd been missing.

Chapter six

Langdon woke up in a crowded bed. The whole night had consisted of Coffee Dog, Missouri and Langdon fighting for space and for covers. Missouri, who had won the battle, slept deeply, arms thrown carelessly over her head, a little smile kinking the corners of her tiny mouth. On a normal morning the dog would have jerked upright at Langdon's first movement as if shot from a cannon, butt wiggling, quivering with the thought of being fed. But this morning, due to a lack of quality sleep, the dog took the opportunity to snuggle further under the covers into the warm space Langdon had vacated.

There had been some x-rays taken a few months earlier because it was feared that Coffee might have bad hips, but the x-rays showed no serious irregularities. The truly enlightening part of this whole episode had been a grouping of triangular objects on the x-ray. The coffee Dog had been eating rocks and the proof was right there on the screen! It would seem that rocks don't digest very well... Coffee Dog was not a picky eater.

When Langdon emerged from the shower, his ears were tickled by the suppressed giggles of his daughter, a sound he had not heard in some time. He poked his head around the corner of the door. careful not to expose his nakedness. There had been the time right before Amanda had left that the two year old Missouri had come in to the bathroom as he was getting out of the shower. This was not unusual. This time, though, Missouri had giggled, pointed and said, "Daddy, you have a finger on your belly button." Langdon had been more careful around his daughter after that episode.

On the bed, Coffee Dog was steadily lapping Missouri's face, wiping all vestiges of sleep away as if they were cobwebs infringing on the unsullied bed chambers of some great Queen. Missouri was not the typical child who leapt out of bed at the break of day and was off like a shot, leaving her parents gasping in the dust. Rather, she woke as if she were a college student hung over from the excesses of the frat party the night before, cranky, irritable, whiny and downright snotty. The only way to wake her in the morning had proven to be the face lick method as demonstrated by the Coffee Dog.

"Coffffeeee," she now squealed, the name of the dog rolling from her tongue with delight, for she truly loved him and he her, two beings with no clutter to impede their true emotions.

Langdon reflected that it wasn't a bad way to wake up, smothered with kisses by the one true love of your life. Missouri had started telling people right after she turned two that she and Coffee were married. Well, maybe in a way they were.

"Morning E," Langdon pounced when he felt that Coffee Dog had sufficiently removed her from the danger zone of being a morning crank, "How did you sleep?"

"Daddy, Coffee's licking my face," was all she said.

No matter, move on, for E was not known for answering questions, bored with the mundane pleasantries of life. "What do you want for breakfast?"

"Bagel with cream cheese," E shrilled, "AND SOME JUICE." Forceful. Commanding. Langdon thought that she would do just fine at an all male military school.

"Sorry, we don't have any bagels."

"Toast and cream cheese," Missouri replied without missing a beat.

"Actually we don't have any toast and before you want cream cheese on something else, we don't have any cream cheese either." Langdon surveyed the contents of his refrigerator with disdain. Two pizza boxes, empty, some ketchup, mustard, two very old looking hot dogs and a mostly full case of beer. Predicting that her next request would probably be something other than moldy hot dogs, stale pizza or beer, Langdon subtly moved on, "How about we go out for breakfast and get you a bagel with cream cheese? Just let me make a couple of phone calls first..."

While Missouri wrestled with the dog, Langdon picked up the phone. Jewell, Richam's wife agreed to watch Missouri for a few hours as he knew she would.

"Goff, you know I love that darling girl of yours, bring her right on over." Jewell was of some Caribbean extraction, that amazingly beautiful mix of African, French, Spanish, Native and whatever else, each word from her mouth tinkling like a tiny bell, lilting, wafting, enticing-teasing but not really.

"And Jewell, when your husband wakes up, tell him not to go stirring up things, especially when he has no call to."

"Sure honey," Jewell frolicked, "but my man sure ain't hardly ever wrong about his instincts, you know that."

He did.

The next call was to ensure that Chabal could and would open the bookstore today.

Bowdoin information.

Peppermint Patty.

She also awoke to the phone as if she were a college student stung awake on the morning following a frat party. Through her sleepy response, Langdon managed to make plans to get together with her in the afternoon, to return her Jeep key and talk.

Next came the Widow Dumphy, whose voice was as usual a not-so-subtle purr.

"Just calling," he said, "to see if you were still retaining me to investigate the murder of your husband?"

"Of course," the Widow answered, "And I do notice that you said murder, not suicide, not suspected murder, but plain out murder."

Langdon was not in the mood to play cat and mouse, especially when his role was that of the mouse. "I need some information," he said. He arranged to stop by her house in forty-five minutes.

When he hung up he called for his daughter, but there was no reply. "Missouri!" Coffee Dog came bounding out from under the bed, a strange place for him to be, and so, a dead giveaway, but Langdon played the game anyway. "Where are you Missouri? Are you in the bathroom? Nooo. Are you in the kitchen? Noo." All the while Coffee Dog energetically wagged his tail and stood by the edge of the bed, a low whine emitting from deep in his throat, as if to say - right here stupid!. Missouri finally sprang from under the bed screaming, "Boo!" He was properly frightened, she was appropriately happy, Coffee Dog was sufficiently disgusted and they were on their way to breakfast.

She then ran out the front door, yelling, "Let's play hide and seek again, can we, can we?" She bounced down the stairs, a small nymph happy with her situation, whatever that was.

"Missouri!" He called—but she was gone, giving him a momentary fright. He bounded down after her, his early morning legs crickety and stiff from the previous day's long car ride and from his having slept in a huddled ball on the corner of the bed.

"In the car," Langdon called as he reached the bottom of the stairs, but there was no answer, no sign of life. "Where are you now?" He called. He wasn't sure that he liked this game of hide and seek, not when there were people like Shakespeare around.

"Coffee Dog, find Missouri!" The dog was off with a bound but proved fairly poor at tracking down the girl who giggled at this, much to Langdon's relief.

When they came back down after he'd dressed her and buttoned her coat, she asked if they could ride with the top down. Langdon smiled at this, for his daughter was one of the few people in the world who appreciated driving around with the top of the convertible down in the fall and winter. But Langdon didn't want to get arrested. It was one thing to be eccentric, it was quite another to do that same thing with a three year old. "Not today, honey, not today."

"Where are we going?" Missouri demanded.

"The Diner for breakfast and then out to see Will and Tangerine." Langdon buckled Missouri into the car, climbing over her to his seat.

"Yippeee!" Missouri squealed, happy to be off, happy to be going to the diner, happy to be seeing her friends.

Rosie, the hostess, greeted Missouri with a fake expression of sternness. "Isn't this the girl that pulled the fire alarm here about a year ago?"

Langdon had forgotten about that.

Missouri looked uncommonly shy.

"Everybody had to pile out into the freezing snowstorm, all, that is, except deaf old man Rodgers, he heard the noise but he just thought that somebody had turned the juke box up."

Missouri grabbed Langdon's legs and tried to hide behind them.

"That's okay honey," Rosie laughed, "I'm just teasing you. We needed a fire drill anyway, make sure everything was working and all."

Allison, the waitress, led Langdon and Missouri to a booth in the back—past a glaring couple from away who seemed to have been waiting for a table for some time. Langdon shrugged—there were perks to being a local.

"What are you going to have to eat?" Langdon prodded his daughter who was currently under the table.

"Pancakes!" A voice boomed from the deep caverns below.

Allison brought coffee and an orange juice with a smile. She enjoyed children greatly, and had a minor crush on Langdon to boot. She was a pretty lady, if somewhat beaten by the harshness of being a single mother of two little boys with no child support and the need to work double shifts so that they could eke out a living and make the payments on their trailer. "That man is in here again today." She said to Langdon with a note of warning.

Langdon looked around until he located Shakespeare, reading the paper at the end of the counter, a glass of water in front of him. As if aware of the sudden attention, he looked up, catching Langdon and Allison's gazes as if they were two schoolkids caught by the teacher talking during a test. With a smile, Shakespeare dropped the newspaper and ventured over.

"Good morning Mr. Langdon."

"Good morning Mr. Shakespeare."

"Have you thought over my offer any further?"

"Which offer was that?"

"Mr. Langdon, if you are not going to leave this beautiful state, I am going to have to go take that money out of the stove and then do some damage." From across the restaurant the two would have seemed to be having a perfectly friendly conversation, smiling, with even voices and casual gestures.

Missouri took this moment to peek her head out from under the table and yell, "BOO!" Shakespeare flinched, stepping back off balance, his composure momentarily lost.

"My, what a nice little girl, is this your girl Langdon?" Shakespeare posed the question with syrup coating his voice, dripping, warm and hideously evil.

Langdon didn't answer.

"And what is your name little girl?"

Missouri smiled. "Cinderella!"

Langdon put his hand around his little girls waist and pulled her close, though she squirming to get loose.

"It was very nice to meet you...Cinderella." Shakespeare said with a tip of his head, "I hope you don't lose your...slipper." He slid out of the diner and was gone.

* * *

Jewell and Richam lived in a beautiful ranch style house out on Simpson Point, a quick five minute's drive from town. Even with the close proximity to town, the area was secluded and, best of all, on the water. The driveway was a dirt path weaving through the pine trees which hid the house from the road. Richam had built the house himself, with the help of some friends, Langdon among them. The outside was stained wood with large picture windows facing in every direction. Langdon entered with E in tow through the garage door, not bothering to do any more than give a quick knock before entering. E went skittering across the floor as at ease as in a second home, for she had spent a bit of time here and was friends with Jewell's four year old daughter, Tangerine, and on good terms with the older boy, Will, who was seven. The house's hardwood floors were partially covered by bright, Caribbean style rugs. The furniture throughout was simple but elegant. Plants hung from the ceiling, smothered in the sunlight that shimmered through all the windows.

Jewell was out on the back deck, which was twenty feet wide and ran the entire length of the house. Tangerine and Will were in the spacious, snow-covered yard which was enclosed by a wooden picket fence protecting the children from the ocean, now at high tide, the sun sparkling off the water as if it were a field of diamonds.

Jewell, Tangerine and Will were in the process of building a snow man, the sun having moistened the snow into the perfect substance for such a task. Tangerine and Will whooped with delight, making more of a mess of things than anything else. Jewell was valiantly trying to place a second ball of snow upon the bottom of the snowman. She was dressed in a ski jacket with a bright green headband to keep her ears warm and to keep her rich, dark hair from falling into her face. Black, designer sunglasses glinted on her face. Missouri screamed a high-pitched whoop of a greeting and then immediately grabbed onto Langdon's legs, hiding her face behind him, excited but shy.

"Missouri!" Will yelled bounding over and dancing around her.

"Missouri!" Tangerine yelled, trying to run over as well but falling back into the snowdrifts, her head disappearing, her feet kicking straight up into the air.

"Hello, Goff." Jewell said, leaning over and plucking Tangerine out of the snow and setting her back on her feet.

It did not take long for E to disappear into the white wonderland of the backyard, egged on by Will and Tangerine into a state of ecstatic, squealing delight.

"So, will it be okay for E to spend some time over here over the next few weeks while I work on this case," Langdon asked Jewell, "or should I try to get her into a daycare?" "Of course you're not going to put that child into a daycare, Goff." Jewell was indignant at the thought. "She's more than welcome here. Besides, having her over makes it a lot easier on me. Tangerine and Will get tired of each other. Missouri keeps everybody happy."

"She sure does love coming over here, I know that," Langdon said. "Kids her own age are really what she needs to grow."

Langdon was going to call out a goodbye to Missouri—but decided not to interrupt her hooting and hollering. As he turned to leave, Jewell stopped him for a moment. "You be careful Goff," She said, with a mother's protective tone, "Richam told me a little of what's going on and it sounds like a real powder keg."

Langdon looked at her for a moment before replying. "You tell Richam to stick to bartending and I'll stick to investigating."

"He's worried about you on this one Goff," Jewell replied. "And you know he does not worry easy."

Real or imagined, Langdon felt a chill to the air for a moment. He looked over the yard. Missouri was lying on her back making snow angels, vigorously flapping her arms and legs. Langdon took three bounds through the snow and picked her up, smothering her with a great big bear hug and kissing her rosy cheeks glistening with melting snow.

* * *

The Widow was draped in a multi-covered silk bathrobe that did nothing to hide the fact that she was naked underneath. The robe wasn't transparent—rather, it somehow allowed something to be sensed, known to be true without doubt. For somebody who had supposedly just rolled out of bed, her hair was amazingly collected, her make-up applied evenly, her eyes bright and her manner sharp. She answered Langdon's first question, about her husband's friends. "His best friend was Bob Dole, not the presidential candidate, mind you, just some schmuck that Harold knew from school."

Langdon was glad he'd decided to tape the conversation, because the list of names was endless. Somewhere in the jumbled collection, Langdon just knew there was going to be a bona fida lead. But where? He asked his second question. "I know that this is difficult, but how exactly did you hear about the...suicide...of your husband?"

The Widow crossed her legs gently, then suddenly she was standing, "I am going to get myself some tea. Would you like anything?"

The question truly meant 'anything'.

Langdon politely declined.

While she was in the kitchen, Langdon took the opportunity to survey his surroundings. His attention span was generally limited to one thing at a time, and all of his concentration to this point had been applied to Mrs. Dumphy. The living room had come straight out of a catalogue. Everything had obviously been purchased from tupperware parties, the type of party where a group of women got together to sell each other junk as an excuse to get together.

The carpet was a thick lavender. The walls were a soft but distinctive pink. The room was perfectly square. There were several wall hangings saying things like, 'Jesus Loves' and 'God's Footprints'. Langdon did not quite fit in here. The room was too small for his frame, too frail for his taste, too clean for his boots.

Maybe Harold Dumphy *had* committed suicide.

The Widow swayed back into the room, her silk bathrobe matching the walls, the carpet and the floral displays perfectly. It was almost too much, as if she were in camouflage.

"It was the Chief of Police, what is his name, Gaylord Thompson, or something like that."

"Guyton LeFebvre?"

"Yeah, that was his name. He came over with some other officer, didn't even get his name, just stood there like a lump the whole time."

"What did Guyton LeFebvre have to say to you. Exactly."

"He told me that my husband was dead."

Langdon leaned forward slightly in his chair to stress the seriousness of his questions. "Tell me exactly what he said."

"Well, he asked if I was Mrs. Harold Dumphy, and I said yes, call me Janice, please. And then he told me that he had very bad news for me, that my husband had been killed, and I just stared at him..."

Langdon broke into this rambling abruptly, "Did the Chief use the word killed? Not deceased? or dead? or maybe even suicide?"

The Widow Dumphy looked at him with large eyes, her face serious and sincere for the first time since he'd met her, "Killed."

* * *

It was time to start talking to Harold Dumphy's friends and co-workers, to the people with whom he may have shared information.

When Chabal arrived to open the bookstore, Langdon was in his office, attempting to organize all of the names into lists, family, friends, co-workers, men, women, first shift workers, second shift, the lists went on and on.

"Morning, Langdon."

"Hi Chabal. Did you happen to open the bookstore yesterday morning?"

"Sure thing."

Langdon wondered how she'd known to do that when he hadn't called, and hadn't asked her to come in until noon.

She smiled. "Jimmy 4 by Four called me, told me you'd be gone for the day."

Of course. There seemed to be a whole network of people taking care of Goff, making sure he didn't screw up his life.

"Could you get me Abigail Austin-Peters on the phone?" Langdon snapped, intent on testing this theory of people going out of their way to aid him in his rocky journey through life.

Chabal just laughed, small pealing bell-like sounds of mirth. She turned and left his office, making a face and shaking her head.

With a wry grin, Langdon picked up the phone and dialed Ms. Austin-Peters' private line. "Abigail..." Langdon wasn't sure whether they were on a first name basis, but he was sure that he had too much trouble with her last name. "This is Goff Langdon. I was wondering if I could run a few things by you..."

"I'm awfully busy right now," the lady replied. She was a little too cool to merely be a public relations director; there had to be something more. "But I can probably answer a couple of quick questions from a man who has such a cute dog."

Cute dog?

"I need to talk to some of your employees. It would be a great help if I could catch them at work and pull them aside for a few moments."

"We could probably arrange for that to be done, maybe pick a day sometime next week?" They both knew that sometime next week was not acceptable.

"I was thinking more like this afternoon or maybe tomorrow morning." Langdon held no real hope. He never would have made much of a salesman; he knew and accepted no all too easily. His style was to find another way around the problem—which in this case meant tracking down people and talking to them in their homes.

"Any earlier than next week is impossible, Mr. Langdon. You have to realize that we are dealing with nuclear power here. Its not like we can just pull somebody away from their job without some sort of substitution."

Langdon threw his feet up on his desk and leaned back in his chair, accepting defeat on that one. "Well, then, maybe you can explain to me exactly what it was that Harold Dumphy did for your company."

"Mr. Dumphy was in charge of security."

"Which means..."

He could picture her checking her watch. "I'm sorry, Mr. Langdon, but it would take some time for me to explain exactly what security is for at a nuclear power plant. Or at any other place for that matter. Perhaps you'd like to set up an appointment with our new director of security and go over his job description?"

Langdon was not going to let her off the hook all that easily. "Was Mr. Dumphy proficient at what he did for DownEast Power?"

"Meaning what, Mr. Langdon?"

Getting anything out of this lady was like pulling porcupine quills out of Coffee Dog's nose. "Meaning were you happy with the job that Mr. Dumpty...Dumphy did." Langdon cursed to himself for the slip of tongue, the nursery rhyme ringing in his head.

"I really don't know. Perhaps you should talk to the personnel director." Abbigail Austin-Peter's voice had grown more cold during the course of the conversation.

"Don't worry, I'm starting a list."

"I really have to go now, Mr. Langdon." Snippy, very precise and very snippy, "I'm sorry that I couldn't be of more help to you."

"On the contrary, Abigail, you've been a great deal of help thus far." It was true. Langdon's real reason for calling had been to see if the company would open up the books and do all they could to help, or close all the doors and hope he went away.

Langdon wasn't going to go away.

* * *

Langdon came out of his office to find the bookstore surprisingly crowded. Of course, it was crowded with people he knew well. Richam. Bart. 4 by Four. Pepper was somehow in the mix, chatting closely with Chabal at the counter. All of this spoke of trouble, but there was nothing to be done.

"Is this my birthday?" Langdon cracked, "or an intervention?"

"Your birthday was last month and we got good and drunk and ended up stuck in some mud hole in the woods wondering why your rag top wasn't installed with four wheel drive, you schmuck." Bart wasn't much for goofing around.

"Don't tell me you're all here to buy books?" Langdon innocently wondered aloud.

"Thought maybe you wanted to go have a beer," Richam shot right back, retorting in sarcastic kind, "Or maybe nine or ten?"

"You know I don't drink when my daughter's around. Mr. Butt Yourself In Where It's None of Your Business."

4 by Four smiled. "Kind of like me calling Chabal yesterday to make sure somebody was here to open your bookstore?"

Jimmy's tone was a little too smug for Langdon. "Listen, you yuppie wannabee Indian Zen philosophizing yoga pretzel load of warm fuzz balls, I can get along just fine without your interference."

Pepper had stopped her conversation with Chabal, and was looking at this open season with her mouth agape.

"Now that we have that all settled," Langdon continued, barely pausing for breath, "Are you all here to lend a hand? Or do I have to ask formally?"

Even Bart had to smile at this. It was decided that Pepper was the one most suited to do research on nuclear waste, DownEast Power, reactors, and all that junk that left the rest of them tongue-tied. After all, this was much more fun than the studying she should be doing. It turned out that Richam knew most of the people on the Widow Dumphy's list. Even the minister from Harold Dumphy's church was somewhat of a regular at the Wretched Lobster. Jimmy 4 by Four seemed to be most interested in researching Abigail Austin-Peters, obviously having heard a few things about the lady from somebody, probably Richam.

"If she doesn't talk to me she'll find herself facing the wrong end of a law suit brought against her on behalf of my client," 4 by Four remarked.

"Your client?" Langdon laughed.

"By way of a sort of proxy, of course," Jimmy 4 by Four replied with a faint smile.

"Okay, so you tackle the beautiful sorceress that can repel the ugly demons that reside within the wicked bottle of Turkey. What do you want Bart?" Langdon gave in with a shrug of his shoulders.

"I guess it should be me that talks to Tommy, since he is a fellow police officer. But I'm not going to lose my pension over this. If Guyton Lefebvre tells me to lay off, then I'm going to lay off..." The Bart Man hesitated, drawing out the word 'offfff' with a sort of groaning sound, "and crack him one right up side of the head, that little pretty boy suit that calls himself a policeman. Piece of dog turd is more like it."

Chabal smiled, her eyebrows raised meaningfully, "Well Langdon, that looks like all the bases are covered leaving you without anywhere to go. Maybe you should just go home and take a nap."

"Give us a few hours without your sorry butt getting in the way and this case will be as good as solved." This from Pepper—who immediately put her hand over her mouth, astounded and shocked at what she'd said in front of all these strangers.

Chabal laughed softly in support. Richam, Bart and 4 by Four noted the new voice with measured eyes, taking stock of something that was far too important to decide in an instant.

“Don’t you worry about me,” Langdon finally interjected into the silence that hung like damp sheets on a still August noontime. “I think that I may look up my friend Shakespeare and ask him what he’s doing in Brunswick, Maine. And ask if he would be interested in leaving.”

“If you need me, I’ll be with the lady with two last names,” 4 by Four said. “But I can’t represent you if I’m an accessary, so wait until all the violent stuff is done and you need to be kept out of Thomaston State Prison.”

“Feel free to call me if you need help smashing the fop.” Bart said. He pulled a Subway sandwich out of his pocket and tore half off with the first swipe of his stained teeth.

Langdon grinned, then addressed the group. “Anybody gets anything good, check in with Chabal and let her know what’s going on so we’re not all running around in the dark.”

The group broke up, each going about his or her particular task—Langdon getting the much-needed help that only friends can supply, and each of them getting a chance to live out the fantasy of being Philip Marlowe or Sam Spade.

Chapter seven

Peppermint Patty left the gathering a little bit disillusioned with the whole private detective business. Here she had sucked up her courage to the very zenith of her gumption, shown up out of the blue at The Coffee Dog Bookstore, bantered with Langdon and his friends—and now she found herself going back to the Bowdoin Library to do research. If research were what she wanted, she could be preparing for her term paper on Lenin.

"Hi Patty," the elderly receptionist at the front desk called out. The woman was the exact same woman you'd find working in every library across the country. Thin, white haired, her tiny curls powdered slightly; looking as if indeed a lot of time had gone into the making of this look of plain severity. Glasses perched atop her puff of a nose—thick glasses, but not so thick as to hide her twinkle of friendliness.

"Hello Mrs. Bostwick," Pepper replied, taking a moment to stop and trade pleasantries, "How is it today?"

-Very busy.

"Its that time of year with finals coming up so soon and all."

-Last minute preparations is not my fault.

"The weather sure is nice and crisp this evening though." Pepper was trying hard to find some firm footing for this conversation so that she could move on.

-Maybe you should get outside and enjoy the weather a little.

"No, I don't think I should take any time off, I have a big project due."

-On what?

"Oh, its on Nuclear Power here at DownEast Power."

"If you need any help I have some insights into the plant." Mrs. Bostwick, for the first time since Pepper had known her, showed a bit of enthusiasm.

"I'd love it if you made some suggestions."

"You know, my husband worked there for almost twenty-two years before he died of a heart attack." Mrs. Bostwick added with a sad smile.

"Your husband worked at DownEast Power for twenty-two years?" Pepper immediately realized how rude it was to repeat what the kindly librarian had said, especially when it had to do with the death of her husband. But it seemed that every which way she turned these days there was some connection to DownEast Power.

Mrs. Bostwick continued, "He worked in security. Not really too much to it but the stress of what if must have finally got to his heart. He dropped dead as a doornail one day right in the middle of work."

"I didn't even know that DownEast Power had been around that long." There was a lingering question in Pepper's voice.

"Oh yes, they started building the plant right after the big blackout of 1965."

"The big blackout?"

"There was some sort of electrical overload in the circuits, something shorted out somewhere and all of a sudden the short circuit went whizzing all over New England and Canada, knocking out electricity everywhere, scaring the dickens out of all us. It was as if the end had come. After that nobody trusted the utility companies. They had to come up with something. And nuclear power seemed to be the answer, an unbelievable power source. Cheaper, easier, safer..."

"And your husband worked for DownEast Power from the very beginning?"

Mrs. Bostwick's voice was quiet with just a shadow of sadness. "Until the day he dropped dead as doornail on the nightshift. Had a stroke and it was over an hour before anybody found him."

"Do you live in Woolington?" Pepper asked the elderly librarian, never having been to the town herself, interested in what it was like to live in a town with a nuclear power plant.

"We bought a house there in 1967 and that is where I plan to live out the rest of my days." Mrs. Bostwick said.

"Did you ever think about moving closer to your work?" Woolington was only about ten miles North, but you did have to drive through the traffic created by the shipyard which was often a hassle.

"I couldn't afford to leave Woolington, dear, why my taxes are almost nonexistent, with the plant paying so much in taxes and all."

Pepper wondered how many people braved the dangers of living next to a nuclear power plant just for tax benefits.

Pepper had been working at a carrel at the back of the second floor for only a short while before Mrs. Bostwick found her. She was carrying a stack of articles printed off of microfiche—articles in general that Pepper never would have found. "I thought these might be useful," she said. Before Pepper could thank her, she continued, "I'm going to look for more." Pepper was about to say no, but stopped herself. Mrs. Bostwick was the type of lady who needed to be needed, and was hurt when her efforts were unnoticed or declined. Helping others seemed truly to make her happy, to give her a sense of self. Before her husband had died, Pepper was sure, Mrs. B must have done everything for him, gotten up to make him breakfast, done his laundry, packed his lunch, made sure dinner was on the table when he got home.

After eleven hours of research, the only breaks coming when Mrs. Bostwick delivered books, notes and photocopies and made suggestions, sometimes ruminating about her late husband, chattering away like some angry sparrow, (Reflecting not anger but loneliness), Pepper wasn't sure if she now knew nuclear power inside-out or had no more real knowledge than she'd had before she'd started. All she knew for certain was that she had a headache.

She'd found the type of uranium used at the plant. Uranium-235 was shaped into fuel pellets about a half inch long and no thicker than her finger. Two-hundred of these pellets were stacked into tubes, and 179 fuel rods as they were called were bundled together to make a fuel assembly. These fuel assemblies were then loaded onto trucks and taken to DownEast Power, where they were placed in the reactor, which was housed in the containment building. The containment building, made of reinforced concrete and surrounded by thousands of gallons of water, was built automatically to seal itself if anything went wrong, to prevent any waste from reaching the outside environment. Fission, the splitting of the atom, the ultimate source of nuclear power being the splitting of the atom, occurred at the center of the reactor. Water was the key to creating fission, slowing down the neutrons and so allowing them to collide and split. The splitting of billions of atoms through this process then caused the fuel pellets to get very hot, the first step in making electricity.

Control rods made of materials that absorb neutrons very quickly were kept at the ready to be lowered into the reactor should the fission process somehow get out of hand. The water surrounding the reactor was a further safety check, cooling any pellets that got too hot.

In the next stage of the process, a large pipe moved water past the fission taking place; the water in the pipe was heated in this way, kept from boiling by a careful monitoring of pressure. The water then flowed into a steam generator, where it met water from a secondary pipe system, turning it into steam and sending it into the turbine, a cylinder shaped machine whose purpose is to convert other forms of energy—for example heat and kinetic energy—into electricity. A turbine is shaped like a fan; when steam passed by the blades of the turbine it caused those blades to turn. The shaft of the turbine then turned large magnets, creating a field between them that was electricity.

Pretty simple stuff really.

But it wasn't really her forte.

What she did come to know was the layout of the DownEast Power Plant. She studied the maps and directories detailing the entire complex and the bureaucratic structure attached to it. This had proven to be a much more interesting topic than nuclear energy.

Pepper stood up to clear her head, shaking her tousled red hair, a deep auburn in the sparse light of the deepest corner of the library. "I've had enough of this crap!" She said aloud and with some force.

"What's that dear?" Mrs. Bostwick asked, appearing with another armload of material. Mrs. Bostwick had gotten off duty some four hours earlier but had stayed to help with the project.

"I was asking if you'd like to go have a beer with me." Pepper said, smiling a little sheepishly.

"But I don't drink beer," Mrs. Bostwick tittered. "But you go right ahead. I've been telling everybody all along that Patti Smith is too serious, always working, never smiling..."

The elderly librarian was still talking as Pepper eased out of the room with a small wave of the hand and a wry smile.

Pepper paused suddenly as she went to enter her room on campus—a room she shared with a classmate, Ann Spelling. There was a strange noise inside that it took a long moment for Pepper to place—a grunt, a groan, a creaking. And then a squeal.

Pepper smiled in the darkened hallway. There could be little doubt—the only girl on campus possibly less popular than she had brought somebody back.

The two girls had decided to room together not because they were friends, but because of the simple fact that they had no other option. At some point the year before, the two of them had realized that to live on campus they would indeed need a roommate, and neither of them really knew anybody else. Patti and Ann Spelling had fallen on each other in desperation, in one of those moments that had proven to be so difficult throughout both their lives, in the midst of the feeling of not being wanted or needed. Patti saw images of herself in third grade, sitting alone at a table eating her lunch, while the next table over was filled with chattering voices, flashing smiles, rosy cheeks. In the fifth grade she was the last one chosen for a team in Phys Ed, not because she was the worst athlete, only because she had no friends. It was about this time that she had begun competing in individual sports, tennis and track, activities she'd continued into college. By the time Patti Smith entered high school she had taken to going to the movies by herself, studying to fill her time, reading constantly, and day-dreaming.

Instead of being angry with her roommate for having chosen this night to break out of her social cocoon, Pepper simply shrugged to herself and walked back down the hall. Ann was certainly eccentric and wasn't easy to live with, but she was quite nice in her own way. And there would be somebody else to share that beer with.

Her Jeep once again brought her to Goldilocks, this time on her own. Pepper was somewhat embarrassed to return after having run out just two nights earlier, but she figured, what the hell, this is the new me.

The bartender from the other night immediately asked to see her I.D. She stared him straight in the eye, not challenging him in any way but sure of herself for some strange reason.

"No identification, no entrance." Goldilocks said. He went back to polishing the glass, dismissing the girl from his mind.

"I was with Langdon the other night." She said. "I'm supposed to meet him here."

Goldilocks carefully set the glass down, looking up and reassessing the girl. Pepper smiled a tight smile of victory, relishing her new strength. (Langdon carried a great deal of weight in here.) "Bring me a beer would you," She did not ask.

"You were drinking Geary's if I remember correctly." Goldilocks took this defeat easily, almost as if he were pleased with the girl's backbone. She'd passed a test of admittance that had nothing to do with being 21.

"My name's Pepper," she said as he set the beer on the table before her.

"Goldilocks."

"Thanks for the beer."

She'd been there only about ten minutes when a man who'd been eyeing her from across the room chose to make his move. Somehow Pepper knew that he was coming for her even though she was a novice with men. He had a very powerful body but was lithe in his movements. His face and hands were weather-beaten. There was just a hint of scruff on his face, not too much, just enough to give him the Brad Pitt look. The man took his time, working slowly through the tables, chatting with people as he went. He seemed to know most of the people there.

"Buy you a beer," he said when he'd finally reached her.

"Sure."

His knuckles were scarred, his skin rough and chapped, joints swollen ever so slightly. "Haven't seen you in here before," he said.

"Only my second time."

"You new to town?"

Pepper suddenly didn't want this man to know that she was a Bowdoin student, a rich kid from the hill, somebody that had had it easy all her life, who spent thousands of dollars a year to read books and go to parties. That she had a Jeep Cherokee with no payments to be made. That her Christmas vacation was going to be spent in Paris and her spring break in the Caribbean. "I just moved to Topsham a couple of weeks ago."

"Where you from?"

No use in trying to hide the South even from this man whom she would guess had never been out of Maine. "Texas."

"Well, I'll be, all the way from Texas." The man was in his early twenties, his manner smooth and easy. "What brings you all the way up to Topsham?"

Pepper noticed the man was missing a tooth—a common Maine trait. The man indeed looked as if he'd seen a few scuffles in his time, and had probably enjoyed them all immensely, and probably won more than he lost.

"Are you going to tell me what brings you so far North?" His eyes smiled way back in his head, his teeth, or most of them anyway, bared and wolfish.

Pepper realized this was flirting, bar style. And then she realized that the man was still waiting on her answer. She said the first thing that popped into her head, "I got a job working with Harper Truman."

The man whistled low in his throat. "So you work for the Governor."

"Yep. Can I get you another beer?" From his surprised look, Pepper realized that it wasn't her role to be buying HIM beer.

But his recovery was quick. "Sure," he said with a shy smile, "My name is Josh Martin."

"Patti Smith. Friends call me Pepper."

"So, Pepper, if you don't mind me calling you that, what do you do for the Governor?"

"I'm a sort of personal secretary," she said. She was hoping to change the subject—but he'd seen his opportunity.

"I've got some grievances that you might bring to his attention," he said. "The clamming licenses are getting more and more abundant and the times and places are getting smaller and fewer."

"You're a clammer?" Pepper didn't even really know what a clammer was—probably somebody who got clams and sold them, but she had no idea how this was done.

It was no less than three more beers in the telling. Josh Martin had his arm around Pepper as he continued to talk about clamming, embellishing—making his job romantic-and to a girl from Texas, it sure was, just like being a cowboy was romantic to somebody from Maine. The truth of the matter was, the profession of cowboy and clammer both had to do with brutal hard work. But for some reason, probably due to western movies, cowboys had become strong romantic figures—John Wayne and Clint Eastwood and Roy Rogers—while clammers had been left behind. No star had sufficiently taken up their cause. Pepper could just imagine Brad Pitt taking the role of the man she was talking to, working his clam flat, saving up for a lobster boat or something like that, fighting the bad guys or the establishment, clam raiders encroaching on his turf, threatening his way of life. He'd be deadly with a clam rake, a poetry spouting clam digger who bothered nobody except when pushed. With a Ford Truck instead of a horse.

The bar had become increasingly noisy as they'd sat there, Pepper's lips now almost brushed the ears of the clammer as she talked. "I'm supposed to go out to DownEast Power tomorrow for the Governor," she said. "I'm ashamed to admit I don't even know how to get there. Are there a lot of security clearances and things like that?"

"Phssst. Security," he said. "I hit the clamming flats out there sometimes when the tide is low and I'm right there. There's been times when I've looked up and realized I'm practically in the middle of the entire complex. I could probably take anything I wanted and nobody would know the difference."

* * *

Bart walked away from The Coffee Dog Bookstore angry. He had shown up to help out, but hadn't realized he'd be one of the many. That damn 4 by Four, what a stupid name. And that bartender, the tall black guy, Richam or whatever the hell his name was. What the hell had that college kid been doing there, anyway? It certainly seemed that if anything were going to get done, Jeriamiah Bartholomew was going to have to do the doing. Bart emerged from the basement location blinking in the blinding sun reflecting off the snow. The day was crisp, clear and beautiful, the kind of day Bart lived for, the reason he'd chosen to stay in Maine,

-clean and pure-

Untarnished beauty.

Not even Langdon was aware that Bart wrote poetry. It wasn't the grand things of life that Bart lived for, it was something ineffable, the small things—the smile of a baby, the sun glinting off the snow, a woman playing the guitar in the park, a man swimming in the icy grip of a river. The essence of things was what Bart was after. For seven years now he had been trying to express the feelings of grandeur that filled him on days like this, his appreciation for what was real and should be protected. Nature in all its pristine beauty. No Broadway play could equal a day like this. No fancy restaurant could beat a simple picnic at Popham Beach. No museum could quite equal a quiet trip through the forest. Bart had been to the city, to Boston, New York, Philadelphia—and had left happily. It wasn't for him. Sometimes he feared that the city was creeping his way, trying to find him, to taint the place where he'd been born and raised. This murder/suicide thing for instance—it had all the stink of some big city corruption, Boston or New York trying to take over his town.

A murder in Brunswick, Maine?! A murder shoddily covered up to look like a suicide? The Chief of Police somehow involved? It was too much. It had to be stopped. Before it was too late. Before Brunswick became North New Boston.

It was a short walk across the street back to the police station, Bart passed by the receptionist with a casual wave of his hand and a gruff 'Hallo'. The file cabinet was centrally located, several officers standing around chatting, Bart just ignored them as he pulled the file for the Dumphy case—or tried to. It was missing.

Bart carefully flipped through the files, checking to see if it had stuck to another folder or been filed out of order. Finally he gave up the search as a coldness descended upon the room, chilling his fingers, gripping his bowels in an icy embrace. Bart raised his eyes to find himself alone in the room with Chief Guyton LeFebvre.

"Looking for something Sergeant?"

Quiet. Too quiet.

"Yeah, I'm lookin' for the Dumphy file. Only there ain't no file."

"The Dumphy file?" The question hung heavy in the air.

Anger had gotten the better of Bart. After all, he wasn't much for subtleties. "Ya know, Harold Dumphy, the guy that got murdered and we called it suicide."

"Perhaps you should come into my office, Sergeant?" Guyton LeFebvre was a few inches over six feet, his shoulders stooped as many tall thin men's shoulders are, giving him a look like that of a vulture. Much of his hair was gone, receding gracefully if prematurely. The lack of hair on his head was offset by a short-bushy mustache, which drooped over his upper lip and got into his mouth whenever he ate or drank anything. His eyebrow were just as bushy. His face was bony, the skin pulled tight over harsh features. At this moment, one of his eyebrows was raised in question, as if professing an ignorance of whatever it was that Bart was talking about.

Bart, not about to be had, stormed into the haven of the Chief's office. "The facts are simple. There was evidence suggesting that Harold Dumphy was murdered. You ordered the case closed. And now the file is missing."

"The case is more delicate than you think, Sergeant." The Chief began. "I would appreciate if you'd give me the benefit of the doubt on this one."

"I talked to Tommy."

The Chief raised his bushy eyebrow again. "He had a stern directive to keep this all to himself."

"I plied him with a few drinks."

"A weakness that doesn't belong in civic duty," Guyton LeFebvre tut-tutted with a mock sympathetic shake of his head, "Perhaps you should realize that your anger is jeopardizing your friend's career."

Bart stared morosely at the Chief. It was time to keep his big yap shut, and listen.

Guyton LeFebvre eased around Bart, who was standing in the middle of the room, shutting the door firmly, enclosing the two of them in solitude. He moved with small sliding steps, his shoulders jerking slightly. He had been the Chief of Police in Brunswick for nine years now, brought up from Beverly, Massachusetts. For this reason Bart had hated him from day one. The Chief should have been chosen from Brunswick's ranks, or at least from Maine. Guyton LeFebvre was just another instance of the creeping urbanization that was decaying the foundation of Brunswick's fabric, city values and attitudes attempting to change what had always been.

"Okay, Bart," the Chief said, settling comfortably in his chair. "I'm going to let you in on some privileged information that is not to go past this room. Understood?"

Bart merely grunted.

"Yes, it looks like Harold Dumphy was murdered. There is currently a Federal investigation. A private investigation. The Feds are in on this one Bart, they took the case from me and told me keep the publicity down."

"So you called it a suicide to keep the papers quiet?" Bart was incredulous.

"Basically."

"Call me crazy, but isn't that illegal as hell?"

The Chief didn't answer, but smiled a little smugly.

Bart pressed on. "And how about immoral? What about the feelings of the Widow? Do you know that she can't even collect on his life insurance policy?"

"You've got to give me some time on this one, Bart." The Chief wasn't very good at looking earnest. "I know I've made some mistakes but I can put them back right if you just give me a chance."

"I'll have to think this one over." Bart spoke quietly and then eased out of the room, out of the office, out of the building, headed home.

* * *

Jimmy 4 by Four returned to his second-floor office, small in size but with huge picture windows overlooking Maine Street, giving the illusion of spaciousness. His thoughts were filled with the picture of Abigail Austin-Peters he'd created in his mind, a sketch he'd pried from Langdon and Richam's lips. If he'd known that Richam had never even seen the woman and that Langdon had been rocked when he met her, 4 by Four might not have put quite so much stock in this image. These days, 4 by Four didn't have many bad habits. There had been the time when he'd been addicted to work, then the spell when he'd smoked a lot of grass and some hash, and had dabbled with acid—never anything stronger. With the advent of the eighties he'd turned to alcohol; Bart was his drinking buddy on many nights neither of them could remember. But this was merely a phase he'd moved out of after a few years. The habit that had consumed the last seven years of his life was women. Jimmy wasn't one for the casual fling, but enjoyed building short relationships and then moving on. The movie 9 1/2 weeks had been a strong influence—9 1/2 weeks was the perfect duration for any male-female relationship, as far as he was concerned. Intense but short lived. During the span of 9 1/2 weeks everything was new, everything exciting; there were no expectations, no commitment. He realized that a therapist might provide some explanation for his lack of desire for a serious relationship, but he wasn't particularly interested in that insight. Jimmy 4 by Four was happy with who he was, with what he was. He felt no need for answers.

4 by Four picked up the phone with intense concentration. He believed that first impressions were important. "Abigail Austin-Peters, please."

Her receptionist put him on hold for twenty minutes. He didn't mind. He was in no hurry.

"This is Ms. Austin-Peters?" The cool voice he finally heard on the other end of the line held a question, an accusation, but also the promise of danger.

"Ms. Austin-Peters," he began, "this is Jimmy 4 by Four. I've been retained for the case concerning the...suicide...of a former employee of yours. A Mr. Harold Dumphy. I was wondering if we could get together and discuss a few details. Relating to DownEast Power's legal perceptions of this case."

"I'm not sure that I'm the person you need to be talking to. Legal issues aren't my forte. I could put you in touch with our lawyers." Her voice was crisp, bordering on icy cold.

"What I'm more interested in is the policy DownEast Power has followed in this case, Ms. Austin-Peters. Maybe you could give me some insight on what DownEast Power has done and plans to do with regards to my client." His tone was both formal and pleasant. There was plenty of time to get to a first name basis once they'd met in person.

There was a faint edge of impatience in her voice. "My job is public relations, Mr. 4 by Four. I'm not sure the actions of a former employee are of relevance."

He kept his voice pleasant. "I believe that Harold Dumphy was still an employee at DownEast Power when he died. Under somewhat suspicious circumstances. I'm trying to sort out what pressures from your company may have led to the violent actions he imposed upon himself."

There was an extended pause, meant to make 4 by Four uncomfortable. But he was in no hurry.

"If you want, you can schedule an appointment with my receptionist to see me." Definitely cold.

4 by Four knew that this meant sometime next week. That was not good enough. It was time to get tough. "What you're telling me is that DownEast Power has washed its hands of Harold Dumphy—a man who killed himself due to the stress of his job. Is this something the local paper would be interested in, or can we get together and settle this matter without a lot of needless exposure?"

"That isn't what we want at all. But I'm a busy woman. If you could just set up an appointment..."

"Tell me that The Bath Daily News wouldn't make a headline story out of this if the proper buttons were pushed and I will gladly set up an appointment." He let this sink in for a moment before continuing. "Or we can get together over dinner tonight and discuss this like the rational adults we are."

Blackmail.

Hard and simple.

Meet cold with cold.

Her pause this time was much longer than the first. 4 by Four was impressed that the lady on the other end of the line didn't feel the need to complain about his lack of ethics.

Her voice could have shredded steel. "Where, then, would you like to meet?"

It didn't matter. He had won round one.

Chapter eight

Langdon had a few more things to do after Pepper, Richam, Bart and 4 by Four left the bookstore. After all, he did own a business, and while Chabal's hands were quite capable, he couldn't neglect all responsibility. But first there was the Coffee Dog to take care of, now restlessly padding up and down the aisles. With impatience Langdon grabbed his leash and took him out to the alley behind the store, to the prime bushes there in which he often did his business. Langdon picked it up, as he always did, scooping the little round turds into the plastic bag he carried, turning it inside out with his hand, grabbing the pile and then pulling the bag through and tying the top, lofting a sky-hook into a nearby dumpster. This dog of his had the sort of metabolism that every overweight person in the world dreamed of, consuming huge amounts of food with relish and almost immediately dispensing with the remains in a pile on the ground.

With a whistle Langdon headed back into the bookstore, having made this trip several times a day for quite a while now. Idly he noticed that the bushes there did seem a little bit more plush.

Langdon then called his distributor to order books off a list he'd compiled from a trade magazine. He was disheartened to find out that the street date of the latest James Lee Burke paperback had been delayed yet again. He then called the Mysterious Press which was the best mystery publishing house in the world-and one that he did a lot of business with.

His sales representative at the Bath Daily News wasn't in, so Langdon left a message for him telling him he had some ads for him to pick up.

He ordered coffee for the store, then called the latest artist planning an opening at the Coffee Dog in early December, a local guy who did rock collages.

Done.

Time to get on with it.

Running a bookstore wasn't exactly rocket science.

"Chabal," he called from his office, "can you change around some of the tables, come up with a couple of new writers in the spotlight, maybe throw Marcia Muller into the display window." He wandered into the main part of the store, taking his time, in no hurry for what he knew was to come, "We should be getting an Ingram order today. Request sheets are in the folder..."

"I think I can figure it out, Langdon."

"If anybody calls with anything important, I've got my beeper with me. Emergency is 911, otherwise I'll get back to you when I can."

"Right-O Boss Man." She went back to straightening books on the shelf.

"Do you think that if you get a chance you could try to track down who I should talk to at Casco Bay Power about the case? You know, if the Widow dumps me and I need a client."

"Can do."

Langdon was procrastinating and Chabal knew this, not allowing herself to be drawn into any conversation or discussion, doing everything but push him out the door.

"Goodbye, then," he said.

"Goodbye."

A few browsers came into the store at that moment. After only a few months of selling books, Langdon had been able to pick out potential buyers from perpetual browsers, something about their attitude. With a wave of his hand he slipped out the door, Chabal's concern followed him like a cloud, but she'd known better than to express it. Langdon wasn't looking forward either to seeking a confrontation with the whip thin man who called himself Shakespeare, but there wasn't any other way, it was time to take the bull by the horns and shake everything up a little. So far, all Langdon had gotten was a lot of bullshit.

Langdon whistled for the dog, a raspy, shaky whistle—not commanding enough in itself to garner Coffee Dog's attention, but when the dog saw that Langdon was indeed leaving he leapt up and came charging after. He wasn't the type of dog you could leave behind with a promise to be back soon.

First stop—The Diner.

* * *

"Hey Rosie, how's it been?"

"Goff Langdon," the hefty waitress replied, "What a sight for sore eyes. I haven't seen you in here for a few days now...almost no reason to get up in the morning if I'm not going to catch a glimpse of your bod."

"I was in this morning Rose," he said. "At eight-o-clock."

The corners of her mouth turned down in a frown. "I must have just missed you, had to go out and buy some food stuff. But that's a little late for you. Decide to go into early retirement or something?"

"Actually, I'm working on a case," Langdon answered with a smile, knowing full well that this was gossip central and there was no chance of keeping any secrets in a place where the regulars were grilled interrogation style over the slightest fluctuation in their schedule.

"Anything I can help you with, Langdon, you just let me know." Rosie leaned on the counter, her large breasts taking a momentary respite from their ongoing battle with gravity. Her short, pudgy forearms also spoke of a strength that couldn't be attained in any gym.

"Cup of coffee, beautiful, and maybe a few questions answered."

She grinned. "Coffee will cost you fifty cents but the rest might cost you plenty."

It was now late morning, a good time to catch Rosie with a moment to spare. Only a few regulars sat at the counter. All the booths were empty, waiting for the lunch time rush.

"The other day when I was in, there was a man who didn't belong here. A stranger, had my newspaper."

She nodded. "Wasn't he a strange one. Queer as a three dollar bill."

"You know anything about him?"

"Like what, does he prefer little boys, that sort of thing?"

Langdon was getting impatient. "Cut it out, Rosie. Has he been in since the other day?"

"Comes in every morning, just like clockwork, eats dry toast, black coffee, reads the paper, leaves a good tip. Better than you ever do, cheapskate."

Langdon knew better than this, for if nothing else, he was a good tipper. "You know where he's staying?"

"No idea hon," she said. "You're the only one I've ever seen him talk to, except to order, that is. What in hell where the two of you talking about, anyways? That's been the main topic of conversation around here for the past couple of days."

"You ever see two dogs pissing on a post?" Langdon smiled at Rosie with affection, just a tinge of teasing in his voice, "Well, the two of us were just testing each other to see who was tougher by pissing on a post."

"Okay, I'll bite, who was tougher?"

"Can't really tell by pissing on a post, now can you?"

Langdon was interrupted from this banter by an arm sliding around his throat—clenching tightly, cutting off his breathing passage. With a quick twist Langdon fell from the stool and turned all in one motion, effectively breaking the hold, his arms gripping the man's legs, ready to ram his assailant into the ground. Just in time he pulled up.

"Shit Langdon, I'm just joking around," Danny T. said. He was a regular at the Diner, a friend of Langdon's. He was an enormous man, no other word for it but fat, but good natured and with a mind that was every bit as agile as his body was not.

"You think I'm going to give a break to a guy that owes me money and then sneaks up behind me and puts me in a headlock?" Langdon said. "I thought you were bumping me off to save yourself five bucks." Langdon's casual dismissal of his overly violent reaction didn't fool either Rosie or Danny T., but they pretended to be fooled for his sake. If Langdon didn't want to tell them what was going on, well then it was none of their business.

"Double or nothing on Vikings-Bears this weekend then," Danny T. said. "If I can't kill you then I might as well take your money."

Langdon grinned. "Bears don't have a chance against my Vikings, Danny T."

"The fact that when you were about four years old, you liked the color purple and started to root for the Vikings because they had purple jerseys and were known as the purple people eaters doesn't mean that they're any good. The Bears are going to the Super Bowl this year." Danny T. spat out in mock anger.

"Double or nothing it is then," Langdon said.

He started to leave, tossing a dollar up on the counter for his coffee. But he stopped by the door to call back as an afterthought, "Hey Danny T.. You know anything about the strange fop that's been hanging out here?"

"The one you got in a pissing contest with?" Danny T. asked. "I got some junk you might want to hear about that one."

Langdon took a few steps back towards the counter. "I'll give you seven points in the game this weekend if it's good."

"I sure could use some food," Danny T. whined, staring forlornly at a passing platter of eggs and bacon.

Langdon returned to the counter, threw down ten dollars and grabbed a few pre-made sandwiches from the rack, not bothering to wait for his change. "Let's go." Danny T. followed him out the door—but Coffee Dog did not. Coffee was behind the counter, hurriedly licking up scraps of food that had spilled—onions, peppers, toast crust, it didn't matter what it was, if he could chew it, or at least fit it down his throat passage, then down the hatch it went.

As Langdon watched impatiently from the door, Rosie began lobbing small pieces of bacon to various corners of the Diner. Coffee Dog bowled over several patrons in his quest to get the goods. Luckily, the dog was a regular here, and far from offending any of the sparse crowd, the three men and two women in the place soon joined in the fun, throwing bits of their own food to all corners of the Diner. They howled with laughter as Coffee desperately tried to get it all, running frantically from one spot to another. Finally, Keith Lemiuex flung an entire sausage, which spun across the floor and came to rest at Langdon's feet. When Coffee came in hot pursuit, Langdon collared the dog, snapping his leash on and dragging him out under a hail of food particles from the frenzied diners—who were about to realize that they were still hungry and quite out of food.

"Coffee, don't you understand dignity?" Langdon had two hands clutching the dog's leash, and was leaning away as if he were pulling a reluctant draft horse in a harness. If Coffee Dog had suddenly decided to come along easily, Langdon would have toppled over and crashed face first into the snow—but there wasn't really the slightest chance of that. Coffee wasn't going to leave that bonanza of food behind without a stiff fight. "They were laughing at you, not with you!"

Coffee didn't care.

Langdon knew enough to put the seat all the way back for Danny—his own legs could barely reach the gas pedal and brake, but there was no other way Danny T. would fit. As Langdon started the car, Danny T. ripped into the packaged sandwiches like starving man. He made no pretense about his love for food, no apologies for his weight. He loved to eat more than anything else in the world. Why should he feel bad about that or attempt to diet?

Once the car was mobile, Langdon made the mistake of interrupting Danny T.'s eating with a question. Danny T. didn't even give Langdon the satisfaction of a sidelong look as he continued to savage the sandwiches.

The day was a real corker, the early December sun filling the sky, glinting off the fresh snow on the ground, clear and crisp. Langdon headed back to Maine Street. If there were anything of interest in the small town of Brunswick, it could usually be found on this strip of real estate between the college and the river. Langdon waved to Jack Turgeon as the tall gaunt man crossed the street in front of him, and beeped his horn at Alice Renquist walking along the side of the road with several friends. Whatever else this was, it was Langdon's town, the place where he belonged. Langdon knew people here, was liked, respected, felt comfortable. Brunswick was his home. It was too bad that Amanda couldn't understand that. Sacrifices are an important function of any relationship, but there are some that can't be made without stripping away the fabric of the soul. Sure, Langdon loved his wife—but if she fit him into the mould of some southern town, taught him manners, dressed him up, took him out to the opera—well then he'd no longer be Langdon.

Amanda couldn't understand many things about Langdon, such as his friendship with the man currently sitting in the passenger seat of his car. Okay, so the man was fat, his clothes were unkempt, and sometimes he smelled pretty bad. Danny T. worked at Cumberland Farms. Didn't have a car, didn't even have a license. Lived with his mother. But there wasn't a mean bone in the man's body. There was always a smile plastered on his face and a kind word on his lips, a hand to help you if needed. His mind was agile and Langdon was convinced that if he'd wanted, the man could have been something more, could have gone to college, taken computer classes, gotten a better job. But then he would no longer be Danny T.

* * *

Danny Terio was a square built boy of seventeen years old, no fat on his body at all, but big all around, big enough so that it was hard to find clothes that fit him properly, because the only part of him that was not big was his height, not being much over five feet tall. He gave the strange impression of being nearly as wide as he was tall. He stood on the bow of the fishing boat, happy with life, not that life had offered him much so far. He lived in Harpswell and had grown up on fishing boats, having stopped going to school when he was fifteen and having quit when he was sixteen, there was nothing in school that would help him with his chosen profession, that of working the boats and maybe one day owning his own fishing boat. In his minds eye he had already earned the money and purchased the boat and was now busy fixing it up and painting the name that he had chosen, "Dawn Surprise", for that it was what he enjoyed most about fishing, the surprises that each new dawn brought, the beautiful colors in the sky, in the water, the wind in his face, the adventure to be had. His reverie was interrupted by a sudden shout of fear or pain, he was not sure which.

"Aaaahhgg."

Danny Terio spun around and saw his friend, Bobby, caught in the net and being sucked into the winch.

"Shit, Danny help me!" Bobby screamed in terror. He was wrapped into the fishing net and being pulled steadily inward, there being many a man on the waters that had lost a finger, had a hand crushed or had died from the powerful force of the winch that knew not the difference between the fishing nets and human flesh.

"Shut the motor down!" Danny yelled, his voice balling in his throat and expelling from his mouth like the whoosh of an air gun. The man in the engine room couldn't hear him, the noise was too loud...

Bobby leaned backward, the tough net holding him in its firm grip, his arm inches from the grinding gears, face white with terror...

The engine room was too far away, maybe he would be able to save Bobby's life but his arm would certainly be chewed to pieces...

A machete for cleaning and chopping the fish was on the deck and to this Danny went with firm decision, grasping the machete and swinging it in a large arc, an arc that spoke of much practice, flashing in the light of day, for Danny had spent his entire life on fishing boats and he was familiar with machetes, winches, nets, boats and everything about fishing. The machete swished through the air with no thought but rather instinct. It was the sort of decisive action which created heros in wartime, it was a swing that Hank Aaron would have been proud of, practiced, without thought and incredibly efficient.

The huge blade severed the net, toppling Bobby over backward as the tension was suddenly gone, hurtling him into the deck, shaken but not scarred. The severed end of the fishing net was sucked back into the water, pulling free from Bobby now that it had been cut mere inches from where it had entangled him, disappearing with its load of fish into the murky blackness below.

"What the hell is going on here?" The Captain and owner of the boat stood glowering over the two boys, who were flush with victory over potential death and certain crippling injury.

"Bobby was caught in the net and was being pulled into the winch and I cut the net and saved his life, sir!" Danny stuttered and spat the words out, excited, scared of the gnarled figure of the Captain who rarely smiled and knew nothing but work.

"You cut my net?" The Captain now spoke quietly, a rage simmering below the surface, eyes murky with hate.

"Yes, sir, I had to or Bobby..."

"Shut up boy!"

"But sir..."

"Get off my boat." The words were final.

Danny Terio heard them and knew no explanation would do.

"You are fired."

Danny Terio began to get mad himself at the injustice.

"Not only are you fired," the mean spirited fisherman spat out, "but I'm going to blackball you from every boat on this coast, you won't work on another boat in your life. Nobody cuts my nets!"

Danny Terio merely stared in horror.

After the Captain had stormed off, Bobby stood up from the wooden deck, rubbing his shoulder that had been wrapped in the net, a mottled bruise already appearing on the skin surface through the deep tan from sun and wind. "You shouldn't have pissed my dad off," was all Bobby said, going back to work and leaving Danny Terio spent and lifeless by the now silent winch and the severed net, flapping in the sea breeze.

* * *

"So you're looking for the guy that took your paper the other day at the Diner?" Danny T. finally asked when he'd licked the wrapping from his last sandwich clean. Langdon had turned off of Maine street and was headed toward's Route one. "Seems to be a lot of trouble just because he took your paper."

Langdon smiled. "I had an ad in the classifieds that I wanted to check, 'Former Private Detective looking for quarterback job with National Football League team, preferably in Minnesota'."

"The way Moon is throwing the ball you have a chance there partner, maybe you should give it a go." Danny T. said with just a touch of malice. He took his football very seriously, second only to food. "Besides, he's almost forty years old. I think the retirement age at Cumberland Farms is forty, let alone the NFL."

Langdon was planning to take Route One to Cooks Corner, Brunswick's token strip mall area. A block before the on-ramp, a dog—with no owner in sight—ran along the side of the road, barking furiously, causing Coffee to perk his ears up. Langdon swerved widely just in case the dog decided to pursue what he obviously considered to be an invasion of his turf. As the car pulled away, Coffee made faces taunting the dog out the back window. This was false bravery, pure show, because Coffee was safe in the car and knew it.

"What do you got for me?" Langdon asked now that the food was finished and they were on Route 1, safe for the moment from distractions.

"Your man, the fop, he's been around asking a lot of questions. I don't think he understands the small town mentality. He acts like he wants to blend in, slip into the background, but he sticks out like a sore thumb and then he goes and starts asking all these questions. So people are watching him, waiting for his next move."

"What questions?"

"Seems he's interested in Janice Dumphy, you know, the widow of Humpty Dumpty, the guy that fell in the river? He also has a lot of interest in DownEast Power. Didn't Humpty Dumpty use to work out there?" Danny T. rambled on in this fashion, finishing each statement with a question, taking his time and enjoying his moment in the spotlight.

"That's the case I'm working on." Langdon began, choosing his words carefully. Client confidentiality didn't mean much when it came to the rumor mill Danny T. traveled in; to give the confidentiality of the case any degree of emphasis would have sent the fat man out that much quicker to spread the news. "The widow Dumphy has hired me to investigate her husband's death." Langdon was trying to think of ways to use the rumor mill to his advantage. He planned to leak out a smokescreen of information to his friend. "In other words, of course this guy is interested in Harold Dumphy, of course he's asking questions about DownEast Power. Tell me something I don't know?"

Danny T. seemed hurt by this retort. This wasn't the way things were done when juicy gossip was to be passed; passing on gossip was like eating a steak, drinking a good beer. Foreplay was needed, otherwise the moment of enjoyment was lost. "Maybe a big shot like you don't need what I've got to say? If you have all the answers, what am I doing in your car...eating your food?"

Langdon felt a little like someone on a first date who'd pushed things too quickly. "I didn't mean to press you Danny T. I just got a lot on my mind. And my time is running out. If you got something for me, let's have it, if not, I have to get about my business."

"Okay, okay." Danny's tone was still a little hurt. "I'll skip the lead up and get to the point. You know Randi Petersen?" Danny T. waited to see if he had Langdon's full attention before continuing, "You know, the live-in nanny who takes care of the Governor's kids while him and his wife run things in Augusta?"

"Yeah, I know who she is. She comes in and buys books all the time for the kids. The Governor comes in every month or so and pays up on his bill, or rather his wife does." The Governor, Harper Truman, and his wife, Karol, lived right in Brunswick. They seemed like real regular-type people for being the biggest celebrities the region had to offer.

"Well, Randi was in to the Diner the other day talking to one of her friends when the fop, what's his name, came in."

Who could forget the name Shakespeare? "Shakespeare?"

"Yeah, that was his name, what she called him anyways, what the hell kind of name is that? French or something?"

Langdon begin to seriously question Danny T's. intelligence at this moment, but it sure did sound like he had something brewing on the kettle, so Langdon just muttered that he thought it was English.

"English?" Danny T. was astounded. "Well, I'll be, I remember reading something by him in school but none of it made any sense so I figured it must have been French class."

"Get to the point," Langdon almost screamed, barely keeping his voice down to a shrill hiss. He wondered if what he wanted was going to be worth all the beating around the bush.

Danny T. turned his gaze to face Langdon, his eyes brown and mournful. "This guy Shakespeare comes into the Diner and Randi turns to her friend, not that I was eavesdropping or anything, I just happened to be sitting at the booth behind them..."

"Get to the point," Langdon was fairly itching in his seat, patience long since gone.

So Danny T. finally told him. Randi had apparently been up with the kids watching a movie, about to get them ready for bed, when the doorbell rang. She'd answered the door, wondering who it could be at this time of night. It was a very elegantly dressed man, standing with his back to the light, hiding his face in the shadows. When asked what he wanted, he had merely said, 'I need to see the Governor.' She'd told him that the Governor had gone up to bed already and had asked not to be disturbed. But the man was insistant—and when she told his name—Shakespeare—to the governor, he'd come to the door in his bathrobe almost immediately, waving away the security guard. The two men had talked quietly on the stoop for several minutes, and then Shakespeare had left.

Danny T. fairly wiggled with an excitement, similar to Coffee Dog's when he was about to be fed. "Pretty good stuff, huh Langdon? This guy has late night dealings with the Governor. Talk that can only be done after dark on his doorstep. The same guy that's been digging into Humpty Dumpty having a great big fall. The same guy that's been asking all sorts of personal questions around town about you and Amanda and Missouri?"

"What?!" Langdon slammed on the brakes. Traffic piled up quickly behind them, but Langdon didn't care. "Shakespeare's been asking questions about Amanda and Missouri and you're just now getting around to telling me!"

"Not so much Amanda, mostly Missouri." Danny T. stuttered—eyes wide like saucers—shocked at Langdon's violent reaction. "Why?"

Langdon didn't answer, clutching wildly for his cellular phone. His fingers madly hit the buttons. He somehow hadn't quite realized that there was more in danger on this case than himself. The phone rang, once, twice, and then a third time. The answering machine kicked on. "Hello, you have reached the number

729-4431, if you don't recognize my voice, then you have the wrong number, if you do recognize..."

Richam's voice droned on as Langdon silently cursed to himself—but the voice was then suddenly interrupted by a clicking noise, and finally Jewell. "Hello, hello, hold on a second, I've got to shut this stupid machine off." She was out of breath, rushed, causing Langdon to feel an endless anxiety as the clicking noises continued.

Silence.

"Jewell, are you there, is everything okay?" Langdon shouted into the phone frantically hoping for a response.

"Goff, is that you?" Her voice was calmer now. "What's going on?"

"Is everything okay there?" Langdon managed to bring some semblance of control back to his voice, though his heart was beating crazy in his chest.

"Everything's fine. I was just out back and didn't get to the phone before the machine went on..." Jewell spoke in perfect clipped English tones that made one think she was a elementary school grammar teacher. "Is something wrong? What is all that ruckus?" The cars behind Langdon had been laying on their horns for the past thirty seconds or so.

"I'm just in a traffic jam," Langdon said, throwing the car back in gear and driving on. "Have there been any visitors, anything strange there?"

"Nothing out of the ordinary, Missouri fell off a stool trying to climb up on the counter, but she's fine."

"Do me a favor, would you Jewell. Go look out front and see if you see anything or anybody out there."

Jewell must have sensed the urgency in Langdon's voice, because she didn't bother asking why. Langdon could hear her steady breathing as she moved to the front of the house, to the one window from which the road could be seen.

"There's a car parked across the street." Now her voice was anxious. "What's going on?"

The anxiety that had slowly been settling in the pit of Langdon's stomach surfaced once again in a minor explosion. "Jewell, listen to me carefully, do not hang up the phone, go get the children inside and make sure all the doors are locked. Do not, I repeat, do not, let anybody in the house. I'm on my way and will be there in five minutes. After you get the kids inside, get back on the phone and tell me everything's okay." The phone went silent and then Langdon heard Jewell yelling at Will, Tangerine and Missouri to come inside and then yelling at them a little louder in a tone that would brook no argument. Langdon handed the phone to Danny T. and bent to the task of breaking every traffic law in existence to get there as quickly as possible.

He barely made the light at Cook's Corner, flying through the yellow even as the red began to take its place. The car in front of him had planned to stop—Langdon had to swerve into the left turn only lane to get around him. Danny T.

was white as a sheet, looking strangely like the Pillsbury Dough Boy except without the shit-eating grin. "You're going to get arrested before you can get wherever you're going."

Langdon talked as continued hurtling down the road—more to keep himself sane than to impart any real information. "You know this man Shakespeare we've been talking about? Well, this guy's about the only suspect I have in what I believe to be a murder case. You following me so far?" A slight nod of the doughboy's head. "Well I had a bit of a run-in with him the other night. The police have closed the case as far as he's concerned, and he's home free or so he thinks, until I come nosing along. This leaves him with two choices as far as I can see. He can lay his head low and hope that I don't find anything or he can scare me off of the case."

"And you don't scare easy," Danny T. squeaked from the passenger seat where he'd managed to raise his knees to brace against the dashboard. One arm lay rigid against his thigh while the other clutched the car phone grimly.

"I didn't think I did either, Danny T. I didn't think I did either."

"So this guy is after Missouri to get to you."

"The thought had crossed my mind," Langdon muttered, lips tight with concentration—fear—anger—hatred.

"Well, then, you might as well slow down. If Shakespeare is trying to scare you through your daughter, well then, he ain't going to hurt her or there'd be no way left to scare you. He might let you think he was going to hurt her. But if he's half as smart as you think, then he's not touching your little girl."

It was at moments like this when Langdon realized that perhaps Danny T. was just a tad smarter than he let on—even if he couldn't pick a winning football team to save his butt. It very well may have been this observation from Danny T. that saved their lives on this day—for as they came screeching around the curve more affectionately known as Blind Can Alley there was suddenly a moose standing in the road in front of them. Langdon swerved the steering wheel hard—hitting a moose was like running dead-on into a brick wall. If they'd been traveling any faster, the car would have rolled and a rag top doesn't serve as much protection when your car suddenly turns into an out of control bowling ball. As it was, they managed to escape with only Danny T's. screeching leaving any lasting injuries. The car went over the snowbank at a pretty good angle and skittered over the drifts in the field that luckily lay along the road. Lady Luck must really have been present, because the road bent back—allowing the car to bang down with all four wheels momentarily touching pavement before it went careening off into the snowbank on the far side. The back end caught on the snowbank with one last whiplash jerk and then they were once more under control.

Even with the concern Langdon felt at that moment for his daughter, the opportunity was just too good not to make a nonchalant seeming comment. "Ya know, Danny T., you can have your four wheel drive jeeps, your trucks, whatever—I'll take this old beater convertible every time. The way it handles in the snow is a sight to see."

Danny T. croaked something that scarred Langdon's ears, the last part of it fortunately ending in a silent contortion of Danny T.'s face as his throat muscles, tired from his recent screams of fear, failed to make themselves heard.

At this moment Danny T. realized he still held the car phone and decided that it would be more useful airborne, so he chucked it at Langdon's head. Once again Lady Luck was present—for the phone was still plugged in, the cord acting as sort of a bungee, the phone just reaching the bridge of Langdon's nose before it was snapped back into the dashboard. When Langdon went to pick it up it crumbled in his hand, smashed to bits. Not that big of a deal, Langdon thought, they were almost there.

If Langdon had known at that moment, Jewell was on the other end trying desperately to get his attention, he might not have been quite so carefree about the loss.

Chapter nine

Inside the house, Jewell Denevieux ordered the children upstairs. Missouri not understanding the seriousness of the situation, hid under the kitchen table and then ran through the downstairs of the house laughing, teasing—a pain in the ass as only a three-year can be and still get away with it. But at this moment Jewell wasn't amused. A rip thin man had slid out of the car across the street and was looking toward the house with a long appraising glance. Langdon was no longer at the other end of the line.

"Will, go into Mommy and Daddy's room with the girls and lock the door. Now!" Will, at seven, was old enough to understand the time to rebel and the time to obey. Nervously he herded the two girls in front of him, his tiny body making slight jerking motions as he walked down the hall.

"Damn that Langdon," Jewell muttered.

"What was that, Mom?" Will hesitated with a question on his lips, looking very adult in his position of responsibility as he paused momentarily at the door to the bedroom, searching with his eyes for the answer that this whole thing was just a joke but somehow knowing better.

"Nothing, honey. Get in the room and lock the door. Don't come out until I come and get you, no matter what." At that moment, there was an almost indistinguishable knock at the front door, so quiet that it could have been snow falling gently from the eaves or a bird landing on the ledge.

Richam kept a pistol from back in his school days, when they'd both been caught up in the unrest in the Dominican Republic. The pistol was large, old and unused, and probably wouldn't work—but by the time Shakespeare knocked again, Jewell had it cocked and ready.

"What do you want?" Jewell spoke hurriedly through the door, gasping as if out of breath.

No answer.

"What do you want!?"

A calm, quiet voice. "Please let me in, I have a very important message for you from Goff Langdon."

Jewell took a deep breath, pulling her cheeks in to her nostrils and then letting them out again with a steady stream of swishing air. When there was no air left to breathe out, she unlocked the door—swinging it open with a jerk, the door banging into the wall with a crash. She stood in the open door with her hands clasped around the ancient pistol so tight they turned white at the knuckles, the bones threatening to burst away from the skin. She pressed the steel barrel of the pistol lightly against the skin that happened to be attached to the forehead of Shakespeare. He seemed more than a little surprised as if he'd been counting on cowering submission so completely that he hadn't considered any other option.

"Don't move motherfucker!" Jewell felt for a moment as if she were in some bad B movie.

"Listen lady," Shakespeare said with an unconvincing smile, "I dont have any money on me, I'm not the legal representative of your divorced husband and I'm not the neighborhood crack man. So move the gun away from me before I call the police!" Shakespeare's calm voice belied his claims of innocence—your average person would show a little fear when a gun was pressed to his head.

Jewell held the gun steady. "You told me what you're not, now tell me what you are before my finger slips and I find out I just killed the AllState man!"

Just then the door upstairs cracked open and Will poked his head out. "Mom, Tangerine and Missouri won't listen..." He froze as he processed that his mother was holding a gun on a complete stranger.

What happened then was as if slow motion in fast forward.

Jewell turned her head towards Will in surprise...fear...and total knowledge that she had just blown it...

Shakespeare came uncoiled like some desert snake, his left hand snapping up and over, removing the gun from his forehead...

Will opened his mouth in a silent warning to his mother...

Jewell was spun sideways from the force of Shakespeare's blow, her hair crazy on her head spinning in the wind, her figure stark against the bleak background of the day—Terror—for her children screeching through her like a runaway train...

Will saw what was coming next and found his voice and his legs in the same instant, lunging forward and screaming...

Shakespeare wheeled as if he were a spinning top, his right arm slicing through the air with a sickening crack to Jewell's jawbone...

And then the actions of life returned to their familiar speed. Will huddled over the inert figure of his mother, cradling her head in his arms, tears streaking his face, anger ravaging his features...

Tangerine and Missouri came silently to the bedroom door and stood watching as if two angels presiding over the actions of mankind...

And a car came to a screeching stop in front of the house...

Shakespeare turned to face the driveway. Langdon was charging across the walkway like a mad bull.

Langdon had been pumping up for the vicious blind side, the blitzing linebacker who comes from the back side and takes a chunk out of the opposing quarterback—but Shakespeare, with a sixth sense that was far superior to any cat or snake of the jungle, turned with a snarl ripping the corners of his mouth to the point of bleeding, teeth bared as if some vile creature from Hell—and smacked

Langdon with the butt of his palm. The blow drove upward through Langdon's nose, snapping his head back like a dog door.

"Bastard," Shakespeare spit at the inert figure as Langdon's head roared with the commotion of a freight train coming through town.

Langdon struggled to his knees. Blood gushed from his nose, spattering the white snow with drops as if the sky had opened up and begun dumping buckets of red rain. He had to protect his daughter.

With a snakelike move Shakespeare struck again, his pointed boots punching into Langdon's ribs. Langdon didn't feel the blow itself at all—but for some reason all the air inside him was suddenly gone, and he found himself toppling over onto his back.

As if a turtle out of water Langdon struggled to roll over again, to get his hands underneath him, idly wondering at the redness of the snow, the blackness of the sun, the dull roaring in the air.

"What we have here, Mr. Langdon, is a failure to communicate," Shakespeare ranted, his eyes wild in his head, spittle flying with each hard bitten word, a man that perhaps had been pushed too far. "I tell you to do something and then you do the exact opposite. This is a failure to communicate." Shakespeare was pacing as he spoke, delivering a sharp kick to Langdon each time he passed by, to the chin, to the back, to the kneecap .

At this point, Coffee Dog—shaking his collar free from Danny T.'s hands—came streaking across the short distance like a bolt of brown lightning. The dog ploughed into Shakespeare, knocking him off his feet. Shakespeare pointed the pistol he still held in his hand at the dog. With a supreme effort Langdon rolled over the intervening space and jostled Shakespeare's aim. Langdon had imagined delivering a knock out blow that would have ended the fray, but in his weakened state the jostle was the best he could do. It was enough for the moment, making the banana-shaped man miss, the bullet whizzing off aimlessly.

Shakespeare slugged Langdon again, sending him into a world where everything was black and white.

Tangerine had lead Missouri back to the bedroom before the beating of her father began in earnest. There Tangerine pulled out the phone and hit a series of buttons in imitation of what she'd seen her parents do countless times. The first button she hit happened to be the redial button. Tangerine wasn't surpirsed in the least when her father answered the ringing phone. After all, it was he that she'd been calling.

Danny T., throughout all this, had been cowering in the front seat of the car, attempting to hide his huge bulk from sight. He finally ventured to peer out the driver side window, this being no small feat as he'd found himself stuck between the seat and the dashboard and had only gotten loose with a vigorous effort. When he saw Langdon's battered form being kicked repeatedly, his fear was replaced with a deep flowing anger. He searched grimly for a weapon in the car, finding nothing. His eyes came to light finally on the keys still in the ignition.

Richam answered the phone in the bar and there was no reply. He was about to hang up when he heard..."Daddy?"

"Tangerine, is that you?" Richam smiled to himself, thinking all the while that Jewell was probably standing by, having dialed the phone and then put the receiver to his daughter's ear.

"Daddy, there's a very bad man here. He hit mommy." Tangerine spoke very clearly before a sob rippled up through the phone and reached Richam's ear with all of the impact of a freight train.

And then Missouri began screaming in the background.

Richam was stunned for no more than a split second, but in that time several things happened. He heard the screeching of tires in the background. Tangerine began babbling incoherently, and then there were several sharp stinging sounds that could only be gunfire. He was over the counter and out the door before the echoes on the phone had died away.

It took Richam nine minutes to reach his home. What he found there was a scene of exactly the kind he'd moved to Brunswick to avoid.

Langdon's car was resting silently against the living room window, the glass in both the car and the room gone, glinting brightly on the ground—shards of glass beautiful and deadly in their arrangement of disorder.

Jewell was sitting on the ground with the children clutched to her, dazed and bewildered. Missouri trying to pull free to go to Langdon, who was on all fours in the driveway being pulled to his feet by Danny T. Coffee Dog was licking Langdon's face, frantically trying to clean him up.

The mist that had cloaked Langdon's consciousness for the last few minutes began to clear, and he felt a moment of stabbing panic before his eyes came to rest on his little girl. Tears streaked her face as she twisted away from Jewell and ran to her daddy. And Langdon knew that there was nothing more important in the world than the safety of this two-and-a-half foot thirty pound human being.

He made his decision then and there.

The sound of police sirens filled the air. The blue lights squealed up the driveway and two uniformed officers sprang from their car, followed by Guyton LeFebvre.

* * *

Langdon made three phone calls from the house.

"Chabal," Langdon gasped hoarsely into the phone, "I need you to meet me at the hospital to help take care of Missouri while I get checked over?"

She would be there.

"Jimmy, you need to contact Amanda for me and tell her to come get Missouri."

For a lawyer, he was strangely compliant.

The last call was to Langdon's brothers. Lord and Nick Langdon were twenty-four year old twins living out in Colorado. "Lord, is that you? I need your help, you and Nick, can you come give me a hand."

The booming voice of the older of the twins by eleven minutes echoed in Langdon's ear, merely a question for more details.

"They threatened my daughter, Lord, they threatened my little girl."

The phone went dead.

Lord and Nick were on their way.

Then there would be hell to pay.

* * *

By the time Langdon was done relating the events of the past few days to the chief, they'd arrived at the hospital and had been sitting for at least fifteen minutes in the parking lot. If Langdon had known that the Chief knew most of the story already, he wouldn't have been so eager to unburden himself. But at the moment Langdon was weak, tired, and frustrated, and after all Guyton was the police.

Langdon hoped that his story had nothing to do with the chief's death on the following day.

Chapter ten

"Nick, wake up, we gotta' go."

"Whamffmnat?" Nick was currently pressed face down into a pillow, trying to sleep away the hangover from the previous evening which had actually lasted until about 4 A.M.

Lord's eyes went flat and hard as he passed on the message. "Goff just called, said he needed our help."

Nick Langdon went cold all over.

Chills seized him in their icy embrace, fear sticking in the pit of his stomach like a scalpel-tearing, piercing, ripping.

Goff had never asked his brothers for help before. He'd taken care of them, helping them every step of their lives. Kept them out of jail. Gave them rides to places when they were younger and couldn't drive. Helped them with their homework. Beat the shit out of some guy that threatened Nick with a knife at a party one night. Loaned them money he never expected to be repaid. In fact, bought them the Volvo they still drove. Goff Langdon was Lord and Nick's older brother, but he was more than that. He was their teacher. He was their friend. He was their advisor. He was their trust fund. Goff had been forced to be a father to the two of them when they were growing up and had managed to pull off this feat without ever causing resentment. In fact, Nick and Lord worshiped their older brother.

"He call from Brunswick?"

"That's where we're going."

It was only after they had cleaned out their bank account that Nick casually asked Lord if Goff had mentioned why he needed their help.

"All he said was that they threatened his little girl."

The speedometer noticeably wavered upward.

"Did you load the guns?"

The twins had few real allegiances in life. They bought nothing that couldn't be left behind at a moment's notice. Their apartment would probably not be theirs when they returned, for they rented it by the month and the month was almost up. They had bothered only to pack the few clean clothes they had and, of course, the guns. They hadn't bothered to call into work. They had a few friends, but none they bothered to leave messages for when they left. For all intents and purposes, Lord and Nick Langdon were about to disappear from Denver, Colorado without a trace.

When they reached the airfield, they found it mobbed with police—or, to be more specific, two police cars, an ambulance and three fire trucks. It wasn't hard to guess that their friend Crazy Larry was involved.

In front of the burning husk of a plane that somehow didn't look as if it been in a crash, Larry stood arguing with a man who appeared to be the fire chief.

Larry was, at the moment, bare-chested with wild black hair and thick black horn-rimmed glasses. He wore tight blue jeans with the knees ripped away and a large hole in the butt. He didn't appear to be wearing any underwear. His naked torso was thin with no definition whatsoever, his arms like pencils sticking out of a scrawny yet hairy chest. Thick sideburns curled around the light gristle of his face, giving prominence to his already dominant nose.

When Larry spotted them, he waved Lord and Nick over. "This buffoon," he yelled, "is trying to tell me I can't burn up my own plane if I want to. What? You want me to get a fire permit or something? What else am I supposed to do with the damn thing, won't run, can't be fixed, costing me money. You want the thing, take it, but don't tell me I can't burn the thing if I want to."

The fire chief shook his head in disgust and walked off for a moment to answer a call on the radio in his truck. Lord took advantage of this interruption to tell Crazy Larry that they needed a plane, now.

For the briefest speck of time a sliver of sanity crept into Crazy Larry's eyes, and he cast an appraising glance at Lord and Nick Langdon, a look that took in their appearance, delved into the core of their emotional state, probed their very essence. "OK," was all he said, walking quickly away with just a shrug of his shoulder to indicate that they should follow.

When the chief called to them from his truck to stop, Crazy Larry raised his arms to the heavens and uttered a long thunderous moan.

He spoke: "Christ, my Lord, has spoken to me and told me of the devil that would appear dressed in shiny black and attempt to interrupt the doings of the work that I do on this Earth. And he told me what I should do to destroy the devil and send him back to Hell from whence he came..."

This was enough for the Fire Chief, who shook his head in baffled disgust again and turned back to his radio.

Crazy Larry walked onward, giggling peals of insidious laughter that shook his body like small seizures, rippling up through the surface and erupting onto his face every few seconds. "The religion thing scares them away every time."

Nick and Lord had only wanted a plane from Larry, not the pilot to go with it, but Larry had other ideas. "I'm not going to face that mob over there," he said, pointing to the assembled law enforcement a short distance away. "And I hate to miss an adventure."

There was really no other choice. A slight nod was all the answer Larry needed. They quickly hopped into the silver gleaming plane they'd been standing next to, and Larry started hitting switches, banging buttons, pulling levers. Nick barely had time to sit down before they were taxiing down the runway towards a large group of police, fire and rescue vehicles, several of the men running anxiously towards the plane and waving their arms like tiny bees in the path of some eagle bearing down on them.

* * *

Chabal was waiting at the doorway to the emergency room with the rest of Langdon's sad-looking group of friends. Danny T. was sitting in a forlorn heap on a bench, next to Richam and Jewell, each of them clutching a child. Chabal was shocked at Langdon's appearance, but didn't utter a word. Langdon carried his daughter, who was sleeping deeply, and was followed by the Coffee Dog, limping along like a mangy wilderbeast. Chabal chattered to keep herself from panicking, "After I talked to you, I realized I had no idea which hospital you were talking about, so I gambled and picked this one, because I tried to call you back, but you weren't home, and you..."

Langdon raised a hand, calming her, or attempting to. "Its okay, Chabal, everybody is okay."

"Can I help you?" The receptionist behind the counter inquired, interrupting this conversation.

Blood streaked Langdon's face, blood clotted his hair, and was spattered over his shirt; his broken nose was supplemented by several gashes in his scalp that were still bleeding. He was hunched over from his cracked ribs and there wasn't a part of his body that didn't hurt or wouldn't be bruised by morning. He looked at the receptionist with a deadpan expression and replied, "Yes, I was wondering if this was where I would get a job application?"

After a moment frozen in time, Jewell began to chuckle at this, and then Chabal giggled, a twittering sound like a small bird, and the very upset Richam released his tension in a huge guffaw—and then the whole group of them was standing there laughing, huge, gasping chuckles and long pealing squeals.

This is where Jimmy 4 by Four found them. Langdon sobered enough to give the stern receptionist—who hadn't so much as cracked a smile—his name. She evidently determined that he wasn't an emergency and could wait to see the next available doctor. Langdon turned to his bewildered-looking lawyer. "Did you get through to Amanda?"

"I left a message for her with her sister." Jimmy eyed the bedraggled-looking crowd. "What's going on Langdon?"

"Jewell and the kids had a run in with our friend Shakespeare, and me and Danny T. happened along. Danny T. scared him off by running into the side of the house with the car. I'm still not sure why he did that, but it worked."

"He was shooting at me," Danny T. spluttered. He had finally done something brave and bordering on heroic, and now here Langdon was belittling his gallant charge of the enemy lines!

"Mister Langdon?" The receptionist called. "Is that your dog?" Her voice implied that dogs were NOT allowed in a hospital waiting room.

"I have no idea whose mangy mutt that is," Langdon told her with a straight face, "but I wouldn't go near it, look at the beast frothing at the mouth. I bet the thing's got rabies!"

Coffee Dog looked at Langdon with the eyes of one violently betrayed.

Langdon smiled back at him. "Chabal, will you take Missouri and Coffee Dog home with you?"

Jimmy 4 by Four shook his head. "Home isn't such a good idea right now.

"Where, then?" Langdon said.

* * *

The house was a summer home, belonging to a fairly prominent author Jimmy 4 by Four had done some divorce work for. Langdon had been involved in that case as well, taking pictures of the man's wife doing intriguing things with a certain local fisherman. Because of those pictures there wasn't much of an argument during the divorce. The novelist, who spent most of his time in Montana, appreciated this outcome and knew well how to return a favor.

4 by Four took the battered group of friends to his house when the doctor had finished checking over Langdon and Jewell. Though the doctor had pronounced them both unfit to leave, they'd ignored him. Langdon gasped in pain and awe as he attempted to carry Missouri into the house. His body was beginning to feel as if it had been run over by a steam roller. He consoled himself with the thought this was probably how the forty year old Warren Moon felt every Sunday after the game. Professional football might not be all that it was cracked up to be.

Richam whistled a long, piercing wolf whistle that echoed quietly in the empty rooms of the house. "Man, oh man, I do believe we all might just stay in hiding for the rest of our lives." The house was more mansion than summer cottage, as the ample six car garage had implied, two empty bays next to the Saab convertible, the Hummer, the jeep and the boat. They stood now in a huge hardwood living room with a gigantic stone fireplace anchoring the far end, the rest decorated by sparse but tasteful furniture. An immense cast-iron chandelier hung from the ceiling, casting a soft glow of light. 4 by Four was busy pulling the curtains on the huge bay windows that overlooked the ocean.

"Don't want anybody to know you're here. This area is full of rumors. Everybody and I mean everybody in Harpswell knows all the gossip and is ready to spread the story with some enlargements. So, keep the shades pulled, don't go outside, remember, fishing boats will be able to see you on their way out to do their rounds. Stay inside and keep the shades drawn."

Harpswell was one of the peninsulas of land jutting out into the Atlantic ocean from Brunswick. The ocean on either side of the half-mile strip of land made almost all of the houses there at most a stones throw from the water. There was only one road out.

Richam, Jewell, Missouri, Tangerine, Will and Langdon merely nodded their heads at Jimmy's warning as they wandered further into the palace as a collective group, almost as if their ankles were chained together, silent in the face of their prison warden for fear of reprisal. Just off the living area, down a short hall, was the recreation room—which housed a pool table, a ping pong table and a bar that was fully stocked. The walls were filled with authentic fishing rods and paintings of boats. A small glassed-in room adjoining the rec room held a hot tub with a fine view of the choppy waves of the Atlantic.

"Stay out of the hot tub," 4 by Four growled, following close behind them, "I've got to get back to town, I'll call you later. The phone is still hooked up, I checked it, but don't call me, I'll call you."

"Thanks, Jimmy."

Coffee Dog was doing his best at bounding around but was obviously a little sore from the day. Before the uptight receptionist had been able to kick him out from the hospital, one of the doctors had come along, a real dog lover, and had taken him under her wing, putting some goopy stuff on the abrasion on his shoulder and taking the dog down to the break room to get some food. This was better service than the rest of them had gotten.

Richam took it upon himself to cook the group a huge but simple meal of pasta from the pantry, he being the only one not entirely wiped from the day's events. Of the children, only Will was still awake to eat any of the food, but he ate hungrily, as did as did Richam, Jewell and Langdon. Coffee Dog, of course, having just eaten, still managed to find enough space for the full plates of the two sleeping girls.

Langdon and Jewell cleared the plates as Richam got the children ready for bed. "Jewell..." Langdon attempted the beginnings of an apology, "I'm sorry to have gotten..."

"Let's not talk about it right now Langdon." There was no room for argument in her voice, no reason to think that the morning would find his apology accepted. Langdon had put her kids in danger, and whether that was his fault or not, it was unforgivable.

Langdon understood.

* * *

If there were one thing Langdon had learned by being a parent, it was that kids were amazingly resilient and needed no more than a normal night's sleep to bounce back from just about anything. On mornings like this, this fact proved both good and bad. It was definitely good that it didn't appear that Missouri was going to need any therapy to help her address the events of the day before. At 7 a.m. she was doing a war dance on the bed, hopping up and down, her face smiling and happy. She screeched like an Indian preparing for battle. This also happened to be the bad part, for Langdon just plain didn't feel like getting up.

"E, its kinda early. How about you climb back under the covers and sleep a little more?"

"Iiiieeeee-yi-yi-yi-yi-eeeee!" This obviously meant something like 'die paleface'.

"Don't jump on me," Langdon shrieked as the child suddenly turned into a human cannonball, taking the last bounce high off the side and descending onto his cracked ribs. Langdon managed to deflect this descent slightly, sweeping his arm and catching the little warrior a glancing blow.

But this was taken by E as a declaration of war.

Suddenly it was a fight to the death.

With amazing quickness E rebounded and smacked her dad a blow to his shoulder—which he discovered must be bruised as well. Langdon's grunt of pain was taken by E as acting out his part in the 'fight'.

Before Langdon could pin this whirling devil down she delivered two or three more blows to his damaged body. Langdon was breathing hard, taking short gasping breaths. A sweat had broken out on his brow. There was really no way to explain cracked ribs to a three year old.

"Let go, Daddy!" Missouri whined as she struggled to free herself from his grip.

Langdon smiled weakly and tousled her gleaming straw hair. If Missouri didn't understand the concept of cracked ribs, bruised bodies and human weakness, especially in daddys, then there could be no such things.

"Listen kid, I gotta' take a shower or I'm gonna' be grumpy all day long. You stay here and play until I get out, okay?"

Missouri's face suddenly became very serious and then in her best Snow White imitation she said, "You must be Gruuuummmpyy." Giggling hysterically, she threw herself face down into the bed.

The bathroom held the largest bathtub Langdon had ever seen. There were twin shower heads and jets for whirlpool action. Langdon quickly changed his mind about the shower and eased his aching body into the whirlpool's twisting jets. Some rock-like fragments sprinkled into the heat of the water dissipating and soothing his muscles. Langdon gave it about ten minutes, which was about as long as he figured he had before Missouri lost interest and wandered off into the house.

As the tub drained around him, Langdon took a cool shower to wipe out the last of the cobwebs. As he toweled himself dry with the large, soft, fluffy towels he had found in the cabinet, he decided this sort of life was something that he could get used to.

There was a brush, lather and straight razor on the top shelf behind the mirror. Whoever this novelist was, he sure had class. Maybe Langdon would have to stock his books in the store, even though he didn't write mysteries but rather fictional accounts of modern day cowboys on road trips discovering the meaning of life. In the closet, Langdon found some clothes that, while they didn't quite fit, did manage to stretch over his limbs without tearing. And they were clean, not ripped and bloody. A definite improvement.

"Okay, you little monster, let's go find the kitchen and some food," Langdon growled at Missouri as he emerged from the bathroom. While he didn't feel quite as recuperated and vibrant as his daughter did, at least he felt alive and like less of a terminal hospital patient.

Missouri and Langdon were the first to arrive at the kitchen, but Jewell and Tangerine weren't too far behind. The two young girls went racing off through the house while Langdon poured Jewell a cup of the coffee he'd made. Langdon started making homefries while Jewell disappeared with her coffee to set some boundaries for the girls.

4 by Four had thought to stock up on bacon, eggs, potatoes and toast while the others had waited in the hospital. As Langdon sat down to this huge breakfast, he thought about how much he liked his lawyer, the transplanted New Yorker with the funny name and eccentric personality. He had class if nothing else.

Richam poked at his plate with his fork, his brow furrowed. "Dang Langdon, these grits got mushrooms, onions, green peppers and more hot red pepper than I've eaten in my life. My kids won't touch this stuff. We got any cereal?"

Langdon looked at Richam and then shifted his gaze to where Will and Tangerine were hungrily shoveling homefries drenched with Ketchup, slurping it all down with orange juice.

"What time was 4 by Four going to come back by?" Jewell asked as she methodically picked through her food, leaving three bites for every one she took, "Are we just supposed to wait around until we hear from him?"

"He called while you were off with the kids," Langdon answered, noticing that Richam had entered the fray and was now working his 'grits' as if afraid his kids were going to finish up and start on his. "He said he'd be out around ten, and that he had a surprise for me."

"So what's the game plan, anyway, we retire here for the rest of our lives?" Richam wanted to know. "I could easily get used to that."

"The game plan is—" Langdon began with a distracted eye on his daughter. "Missouri, you leave Tangerine's fork alone." He continued. "4 by Four is going to..."

"More juice. Pleeeeeaase, Daddy," the little angel with wide eyes asked.

"Be out here around 10," Langdon continued as he rose to get more juice for E." And then we'll have to sit down and talk out what we all want to do. I'm certainly sorry I got you all into this mess. But I'm not so sure it would be safe for you to go back to your house."

"Daddy, Coffee Dog's bothering me," E whined. Coffee Dog, indeed, seemed to have recuperated from the day before and was now hungrily searching for any scraps of food that Missouri might drop—helping her to drop them by nudging her arm as she tried to eat.

"Coffee, come over here," Langdon commanded. He turned his attention back to Richam. "I have looked into obtaining some help in terms of safety but I can't say when that will get here..." Langdon didn't think it would take long for Lord and Nicky to arrive, but they did have to arrange transportation, getting time off of work, getting somebody to watch their place for them. Langdon should have known better where his two brothers were concerned. "But why don't we just wait until 4 by Four gets out here with some information for us?"

They all heard the car in the driveway. As it was a little early for the lawyer to be there, Jewell rose to peer out cautiously from behind the drawn shades. "A police car."

Nobody moved.

"Why's everybody so quiet?" Tangerine wanted to know in a loud voice.

"Shhhhhhh, hon," Richam replied unnecessarily.

"Its Bart," Jewell reported from the window. "But who does he have with him?" And then as Richam and Langdon moved to the window at the same time, Jewell put names to faces. "It's Lord and Nick. And some crazy looking fellow."

Sure enough, it was Bart, Lord, Nick and some crazy looking fellow name Larry.

Chapter eleven

It was Friday morning at around 8 a.m., and Chabal had just gotten her kids out the door and onto the bus when the doorbell rang. Of course she answered it, swinging the door wide—long before she remembered the ordeal Jewell, Will, Tangerine and Missouri had been through less than twenty-four hours earlier. Before her stood a man with a banana shaped head and an incredibly dour expression, face all pinched and creased with unhappiness.

"May I come in, Ma'am!" Shakespeare entered the house without much of a question in his tone, herding the woman in front of him. With a gentle nudge he closed the door behind him.

He slowly forced Chabal down the hall into the living room, easing forward, moving like a snake. "Nice house you have here. Been here long?"

Chabal shook her head in the no.

Shakespeare suddenly shot out his hand and caught Chabal on the shoulder with one of his heavily veined, hairy hands. "You are able to talk, now, aren't you honey? Because I have a message that I want you to convey to Langdon. And if you aren't able to talk I might have to find some other way to convey it. Like carving it on your skin." His free hand was suddenly grasping a long, tapering knife.

Chabal had stopped breathing but somehow was able to mutter that carving a message would be unnecessary.

Shakespeare pressed the point of the blade into the hollow of Chabal's throat, the icy blade pricking the skin, causing small drops of blood to bubble to the surface and drip slowly down her white blouse.

"Tell Mr. Langdon he can keep the ten-thousand dollars I've already given him. Give him this envelope which contains two airplane tickets to Hawaii. My boss doesn't want DownEast Power to be closed due to some small cracks in the equipment. That is not how business is conducted." Shakespeare had momentarily lost control, saying more than he'd intended. To cover himself he jabbed the knife into Chabal's soft skin, bringing a small squeal of pain. "Tell him that if I see him in Brunswick again that I'll start killing his friends and family. Tell him that if this had been tomorrow and he'd still been here, you'd be dead and most of the available evidence would point towards him as the killer. Tell him that after I've killed all his friends, his wife will be next. And then his daughter."

4 by Four found Chabal sitting in the chair in her living room a few minutes later.

Tears cascaded gently down her delicate features.

Her body shook ever so slightly.

But her eyes were steady with resolve.

"Chabal, honey, what happened?" 4 by Four asked, carefully wiping the blood drops from her throat with a damp cloth he'd found in the kitchen.

"I have a message for Langdon," Chabal croaked in a hoarse, cracked voice. "A Mr. Shakespeare stopped by."

"What message?"

"I think that had better wait until we get the whole group together."

"Everybody's out at the house in Harpswell, even a few surprise visitors."

"Who?" Chabal wanted to know, asking, but not really listening. She was still seeing Shakespeare in front of her, knife pressed against her throat, the evil leering man just the drop of a hat away from killing her, knowing that it could have gone either way and that Shakespeare had restrained himself from killing her with the most supreme effort.

Jimmy 4 by Four considered telling her that if she were going to keep secrets so was he, but this wasn't a time to be petty, "The twins. Lord and Nicky. Bart picked them up this morning from some airstrip in Lewiston."

"I hope those boys catch up to Mr. Shakespeare and do a number on him." Chabal spoke distractedly, but with a hint of malice. She couldn't get the image of Shakespeare out of her head. "Jimmy, will you come upstairs with me while I change my blouse?"

Jimmy 4 by Four had never been in Chabal's bedroom before. He now stood uncomfortably looking at pictures of her husband on the bureau while Chabal changed behind him. "Does your husband know any of what's going on?"

"We don't talk about anything important anymore, just day to day details." Her tone was brusque. "I don't ask about his work, he doesn't want to hear if some man breaks into our house and threatens me with a knife."

"I don't believe that."

"It might be closer to the truth than I want to believe," Chabal said in a small voice, then changed the subject. "I have a message to deliver."

As they walked out to the car, 4 by Four told her they needed to stop along the way and pick up Pepper. "She shouldn't be part of this." Chabal spoke with finality.

"Probably not. But its not our decision to make."

"She's just a kid!" Chabal was tight around the eyes, sharp with her tongue, adrenalin still pulsing through her veins.

"Langdon really thinks she could help the case. And he seems to be infatuated with her."

"Langdon is having a mid-life crisis and has a crush on some college girl, and that makes it okay to endanger her life?"

"Why don't we just pick her up and let her make up her own mind?"

Chabal shook her head. "I'm going to talk her out of this one."

* * *

When 4 by Four, Chabal and Pepper arrived at the summer mansion, Langdon was in the bedroom attempting to comb some of the congealed blood from his hair. He quickly put down his comb in surprise when Chabal entered his room without knocking. One look at her face and Langdon instantly felt the terror that she had recently been exposed to. Her eyes were bright and feverish, her movements quick and jerky. He pulled her into his arms wishing he could take it all away. What was he doing to his friends?

She sobbed against his chest for a few minutes and then calmed herself, trying her best to relate what had happened and what Shakespeare had said, word for word.

Langdon asked only one question, repeating what Chabal had said. "My boss does not want DownEast Power closed due to some small cracks in the equipment'?"

She nodded once, not sure of the meaning, but sure of the message that had almost been carved in her skin.

The kids were introduced to the kid's room, replete with toys (the novelist had several children)—which insured they wouldn't be heard from again. The adults gathered in the recreation room, lounging in its comfortable arm chairs and various couches.

Nick Langdon couldn't understand what it was they all had to discuss. He'd come to Brunswick to beat the living crap out of Shakespeare, and that was that. With surprising grace Nick began to twirl, toss and catch the bowie knife that had been taped to his leg.

Lord Langdon sat in a walnut chair pulled close to a coffee table, scribbling into a notebook. Lord had already gotten the basic run down of what was going on from Goff—Shakespeare, Harold Dumphy, Maine Yankee. He'd penned the basic facts of the case into the notebook, and was now doodling with hypothetical situations, potential pitfalls, possible outcomes.

Jewell and Richam sat pressed tightly together on a love seat, holding hands. Jewell was sipping tea and Richam occasionally took a short nervous pull off the coffee he'd braced with just a tad of Jack Daniels.

Pepper and Chabal spoke in strained voices from their chairs on the far side of the room. Chabal was still trying to convince Pepper that it was time for her adventure to end. Pepper wasn't a confident person but was sticking to her gun's on this, shaking her head emphatically. She was involved and was going to see this thing through.

Bart stood morosely in the doorway drinking his second beer. This room held all the people in the world Bart counted as friends and as family. The only living relative he possibly had was his dad, who'd been in the navy and thirty years before, on the last day of his stint at the Brunswick base, had met his mother at a bar and engendered Bart. Neither Bart nor his mother had ever tried to track him down. They didn't even know his last name. Bart's mother had died a year earlier of liver trouble. The people in this room were everything to Bart, and—though he never showed it—he knew how to appreciate that better than most. Jimmy 4 by Four shot a game of pool, taking his time with each shot and knocking each ball in with steady precision. They were all waiting for Langdon to begin.

As Langdon stood, conversation immediately dropped away as if it had never existed, leaving the room in absolute silence.

Langdon began without preamble. "Some guy known as Shakespeare has threatened Jewell, her kids, my kid, and pistol whipped me. This morning he came to Chabal's house with a message for everybody here." Langdon nodded his head towards Chabal.

A very shaken Chabal looked around the room at her friends, weighing her words carefully before speaking. "Some little man came into my house and said that if Langdon didn't take a plane to Hawaii, all of our lives were in danger. He made his point with a knife." Chabal spoke as if reciting a lesson for school. "But I say fuck him."

Nobody in the room had ever heard Chabal even say Hell.

Bart shook his head emphatically in agreement.

Nick let out a little whoop of encouragement.

Jimmy 4 by Four grinned broadly.

"Is that what your husband says too?" Langdon had to know.

"I haven't told my husband about any of this and don't plan to."

Richam pressed Langdon's point. "How about your kids, Chabal. Have you consulted them on whether they want to risk their lives for Harold Dumphy?"

Chabal answered him right back. "I think Harold Dumphy's death was a horrible thing. But this is about more than Harold Dumphy. It's about something we can't back away from now and still face our kids and tell them to always do what's right. Life is full of crossroads. I'm going to continue on the way I am and not let some little pissant foreigner dictate right and wrong for me." Chabal spoke heatedly, but without once moving any part of her body.

"I've risked my life for causes that I believed in before," Richam retorted with a breath of hot air. "Causes I was willing to die for. And then when my side won I found out all those ideals were an empty bag. All that matters is reality. And reality is that some man with a gun slugged my wife and has threatened to kill my children if we don't stop. Chabal knew of Richam's past, but continued to press her point. "Turning your back on problems is not a lesson to teach your children."

"Survival is the most important lesson," he shot back.

"Survival means more than breathing and talking." She said.

"We don't even know what it is we're supposed to leave alone!" He said.

Richam and Chabal now stood in the center of the room glaring at each other. "I'm sorry," Langdon interjected with sincere apology in his voice. "This whole thing is my fault. But the die is cast. It's time to either leave town or get nasty. If you wanted to take Jewell and the kids out of here while we settle things I'm sure nobody would blame you."

"First of all," Jewell interrupted, "Mr. Langdon, don't you think somebody had better ask the 'little woman' what she thinks before you have Richam pack her up and 'take her out of here?'"

Langdon smiled and said very sweetly, "Excuse me ever so much for being such a male chauvinist, but as you well know, I can't help it, being a redneck from Maine and all."

Jewell smiled at this in spite of herself, but then pressed on. "Well, I don't know what they teach you rednecks in Maine, but it's one of the great 'black myths' that the African male tells the female what is what. Just like any other ethnicity, we African/American women let the man huff and puff and make a lot of noise and then we make the decision for him." Richam seemed about to object, but Jewell stared him down. "That damn man of mine was nowhere to be found while some European sensitive sort of gentile was terrorizing his children and beating his wife. So he gets left out of the decision entirely." She paused for a moment as if for effect, and then addressed the room. "And that decision is that Brunswick is our home."

"So, you're in for the long haul?" Langdon said.

Jewell nodded. "Next time I pull the trigger and then I ask the fop what he wants."

"So, what exactly is the issue here?" Nick Langdon wanted to know.

"We don't really know," 4 by Four replied with candor. "Langdon was hired to investigate a suicide that might not be a suicide at all, but a murder, and suddenly the world seemed to turn upside down."

"Right before my run-in with Shakespeare yesterday I found out some new gossip that should prove to be very interesting," Langdon interjected. "Danny T. tells me that Shakespeare knows the Governor and has had at least one late night rendezvous with him."

"Harper Truman?" Jewell was incredulous.

"The very same," Langdon said with a faint smile. "Perhaps our Governor isn't quite so squeaky clean as we'd like to think."

"He's a politician," Bart growled.

Lord spoke, summing up everything he'd been told since he'd arrived a few hours earlier. "So what we have is a suspicious suicide of a man who worked at a nuclear power plant. A nuclear power plant representative who seems worried and evasive. A police chief in the middle of a cover up of some sort or another.

A foreigner named Shakespeare who makes threats and holds after-dark rendezvous with the governor. And pretty much nothing to connect any of these things to another. Is that about right?"

Langdon nodded his head, amazed at his brother's knack for clarifying a situation.

Nicky's focus was on another matter. "This Dumphy Widow is a pretty hot number and seems pretty loose about who she does?"

Langdon nodded.

Nicky nodded back as if filing away a very important fact.

"You have no connection between any of this as far as you know?" Crazy Larry piped in from the hot tub in the alcove off of the recreation room. He'd been lying there nearly submerged, stark naked, for over an hour now.

"Actually," Chabal spoke as if just remembering something, "I did find out something that might start to tie a few loose strings together. I was playing around on the Net at the bookstore yesterday and came across some interesting information."

"Since when are we on the InterNet at the bookstore?" Goff Langdon asked sharply. Chabal ran the bookstore much more than he did but he'd never quite gotten used to that fact.

"I've been meaning to tell you about that," Chabal continued without breaking stride, "but first let me tell you what I found out."

He shrugged and she cleared her throat.

"When our fine governor first graduated from the University of Maine Law School, he disappeared into the Maine woods. Where he opened up a practice in the town of Madison with two other lawyers, Jordan Fitzpatrick and Jonathan Starling."

"Mill town, paper town, something like that, isn't it?" Richam mused out loud.

"So, what does this have to do with anything?" Goff asked with calm patience, raising his eyebrows at Chabal.

"If everybody would just shut up for a second, I'll tell you what I know so far." Chabal glanced around the room to see if there would be any further interruptions, "I was looking through some of their old cases when I came across the name Starks, which struck some sort of bell in the foggy recesses of my mind," she recounted. "And then it came to me, Starks is where the Flower First party headquarters is, up there in the middle of nowhere."

"What is the Flower First Party?" Nicky was shaking his head in amazement at the waste most people seemed to make of their time when there was plenty of beer to drink and when there were plenty of woman to chase.

"Flower First is the environmental group Governor Harper Truman shaped into the political force that paved his way into the Blaine House," 4 by Four stated with growing anticipation.

"So what's the big deal?" Lord wondered aloud.

Jimmy jumped in, his warm brown eyes glinting with excitement. "Have any of you heard of the more aggressive sector of the Flower First Party?"

Chabal nodded at 4 by Four, letting him know he was on the right track.

"What's going on?" Crazy Larry suddenly chimed in, now standing behind Richam and Jewell, water dripping from his naked body onto the hardwood floor beneath.

Jewell turned, suddenly coming face to...with a very naked Crazy Larry, "What in the world are you doing you crazy sonofabitch!" Jewell screamed, plucking a pillow from the couch and socking Larry squarely in the midsection—missing the offending organ but knocking the wind from him with a solid 'whoooshhh'.

Richam, realizing the cause of his wife's shock, suddenly went into waves of deep, convulsive laughter. Chuckling deep in his throat and straining unsuccessfully to disguise his mirth, Goff attempted to bring back order and focus to the discussion, "What you're saying, Jimmy, is that there's an offshoot branch of the Flower First Party. I've never heard of it."

"Sure you have." Jimmy said. "You just never put a name to the group, but wrote them off as fanatics or vandals. Don't you remember hearing in the news about the tree spikers?" 4 by four warmed to the task of addressing the room, pacing as would in a courtroom. "Those crazy guys, no offense Larry, but those environmental terrorists who drove spikes deep into the trees so they couldn't be seen..."

Goff broke in, remembering, "And the spikes, or the action of spiking, prevents huge tracts of land from being cut because the chainsaw blade could easily bounce back off the unseen spike and chew up an arm, leg, face or body pretty damn easy." He continued, "I remember a few years back there being a big hubbub about some lumberjack woods guy getting his leg cut off because of one of those spikes."

Jimmy nodded. "All the Terror First group had to do after that was call up any company that was about to cut a lot and claim the trees had been spiked, and nobody wanted to go in and cut."

"They accomplished their goal without actually spiking?" Lord said.

"And the poor lumberjack that fell by the wayside?" Langdon remembered being horrified by the story.

"Well, he was just an unfortunate casualty in the drive towards a better earth, and what's one life when compared to a healthy mother earth?" 4 by Four sounded almost as if he might be a card-carrying member of Terror First and Flower Second.

"Well, I haven't heard of any tree spiking incidents for some time now. Is the group still around?" Pepper asked. Chabal nodded, taking the floor back. "They're just not so much in the news anymore. That incident a couple of months ago in Rumford—vandals pouring sugar in the gas tanks of the skidders and sand in the oil?" Chabal held their attention as if she were a puppeteer, "Terror First." All of them had read about the vandalism in Rumford, even Lord and Nick; it had been headline news, picked up by the national wire services. The action had resembled Edward Abbey's Monkey Wrench Gang, ruined millions of dollars worth of equipment and halted, if only temporarily, the logging operation on a parcel of land that was deemed to hold environmental significance, one of the prime habitats of some fairly rare bird. "The sudden resignation of the man in charge of bringing the cargo port to Searsport Island? Terror First." Chabal continued, her face flushed with excitement.

The cargo port at Searsport Island had been a source of huge controversy, environmentalist groups fighting the building of a cargo port on a pristine, beautiful island off the Maine coast. The port had been proposed by several logging companies, as part of a solution to their problem of what to do with the wood chips, or more exactly, excess wood, produced by logging. Only so much of the wood they cut was good for paper. The paper companies had been searching for a way to make money off the excess scrubwood, as well. And of course a process was developed to turn this junk wood into wood chips and then put it back together into a cheap plywood. The paper companies had developed some customers for this product in Japan and Europe, and were then faced with the problem of how to ship these wood chips to their customers. They chose Searsport Island for a distribution port, and went about getting the proper permits and such—before they ran into a brick wall.

The cargo port would have destroyed the natural beauty of the small coastal island; the harbor would have had to be dredged to make room for the hulls of the gigantic ships that would be transporting the chips; and pollution was a factor as well. The paper companies had made a mistake when they chose Searsport: the population of the surrounding area was wealthy, educated and had connections. For the time being the opposition to the cargo port had stalled plans. It had been widely assumed that it was the local opposition, with the help of the Sierra Club, had won the day—but Chabal's implication that bribery and blackmail had played a part in the paper companies' defeat made perfect sense.

But Jimmy 4 by Four was now skeptical. "I followed the whole Cargo Port controversy very closely, and never heard any mention of Terror First," he said. "And I never saw a mention of them in relation to the Rumford vandalism."

Chabal was insistent. "I'm assured by a friend of mine in the State Police that this is the work of Terror First—which is, like we've said, a militant offshoot of the Flower First Party. Which is the party the governor of our state started years ago with his two law partners. Jordan Fitzpatrick and Jonathan Starling." Chabal paused, letting the silence of the moment build up the huge finale she'd planned.

But Crazy Larry scooped her crowning moment with a wild guess, "And now Jordan Fitzpatrick and Jonathan Starling are in charge of the organization known in certain circles as Terror First." Larry, still naked, was now perched delicately on the armrest of the couch. Jewell and the others had chosen for the moment to ignore his state of undress.

"That's what Jackson Brooks with the state police tells me," Chabal nodded, a little miffed that her thunder had been stolen. "Both Starling and Fitzpatrick seem to have dropped off the face of the earth—which seems kind of strange. One law partner runs for governor and the other two disappear."

"So this is just hypothetical?" Goff Langdon asked. "I mean, there's no proof of any connection between the governor and Terror First?"

"Jackson Brooks was pretty nervous about coming out and saying anything directly," Chabal said. "But he did raise some questions about some of the governor's background."

"Such as?"

"He was a pretty radical environmentalist for several years, very active in blocking legislation and creating protected areas, him and his partner Jonathan Starling."

"What about Jordan Fitzpatrick?"

"To tell you the truth, Jackson didn't really have any information on him. It seems he joined the firm of Starling and Truman right before they closed the practice down and Truman began his campaign for governor."

"We all seem to be missing the same thought here," Lord broke in, frowning with thought, "Okay, let's take it for granted that the Governor has some connection to this extremist organization, Terror First. So what? Maybe he does, maybe he doesn't. Any way you look at it, its still a pretty big jump from that to murder."

"Don't you get it?" Richam explained, but slowly, as if the words were helping him understand the situation as he spoke. "Terror First is involved in some sort of vandalism at DownEast Power. Harold Dumphy discovers it, they have to kill him..."

"And then they call the Governor to cover the whole mess up for them. And he exerts some pressure on the Chief or maybe the Chief is in on it as well!" Jewell was excited with the whole thing, as if it were a Sunday cross word puzzle she'd cracked.

"And you think Shakespeare is some member of Terror First?" It was a good thing Langdon wasn't alone on this case; for he was struggling far behind in the wild connections being drawn.

"He don't strike me as no tree lover," Bart chimed in. He was still paying attention even though he continued to knock down the beer. "If this whole fantasy you all got worked out holds water, then Shakespeare must be a hired gun."

"He's got a real city boy attitude." Goff Langdon agreed.

"We seem to be missing one key ingredient here." Pepper suddenly jumped into the conversation, standing up and excitedly walking to the center as if giving some sort of presentation. "Why would an environmental organization, no matter how extreme, vandalize a nuclear power plant? I mean, the whole kick about nuclear power is the potential for accident. Otherwise it's safe, not causing much pollution. Why would an environmental group, no matter how extreme, create a situation with potentially disastrous consequences. "And if there were a problem at DownEast Power, why would Abigail Austin-Peters be covering it up as well?" 4 by Four was reminded suddenly of the exciting public relations director.

"That, my friends, is what we're going to find out." Goff Langdon spoke in a tone of reassurance to ease the tension, "First, what happened exactly to Harold Dumphy. Second, is DownEast Power involved in all of this or are we just jumping to conclusions. Third, why does the Chief seem to be covering something up. Fourth, why does Abigail Austin-Peters seem to be nervous about something. Fifth, is the Governor involved, is he a member of Terror First. Sixth, who in heck is the Shakespeare guy terrorizing us. And lastly, do we still have a client in Janice Dumphy?"

It was time.

Chapter twelve

The meeting broke up with no emotional rousing speeches or surge of energy. People began to drift about their business. 4 by Four and Bart were headed up to Madison to see what they could dig up on Terror First. Jewell would stay at the house to watch the kids, with Richam standing guard. Nicky and Crazy Larry were off to find Shakespeare and chase him out of town—a task with which both men seemed immensely pleased. And Chabal was command central at the bookstore.

Pepper was left sitting on the couch. "What about me?" At once both afraid that she'd been overlooked and angry. The anger won out. "You're not leaving me out of this thing. I'm the one that got the ball rolling for you in the first place. I'm not a kid and can make up my own mind. So are you going to include me or what?"

Langdon looked at Pepper with genuine surprise. She was a crucial part of his plan. He'd just hadn't gotten around to telling her yet. "You're going with me," he said. "We're going to snake out a few snags in this thing and see if we can't get a better hold on what's going on."

"Oh, okay." Pepper suddenly looked sheepish. "Where do we start?"

Langdon wanted to say goodbye to his daughter before they left. She was in the playroom wearing a blanket wrapped around her waist as a skirt, and her shirt bunched up on her head as a turban. She wore nothing else.

We were playing dress ups, it would appear.

"Daddy, play with me," she squealed. "You can be the prince and I'll be Snow White!"

Before Langdon quite knew what he was doing, his entire persona of hard boiled private detective came tumbling down. He soon had a blanket draped over his shoulders as a cape and a hair net on his head as a crown.

"Dance with me, dance with me!" Missouri screamed jumping from one foot to another, busily pushing the shirt up over her eyes. Will had put the stereo on, and it belted out some classic Rolling Stones.

Tangerine was giggling hysterically as Missouri and Langdon tumbled around the room in an energetic dance, a cross between square dancing and slam dancing, singing out of sync to 'Jumping Jack Flash'. Will, it would seem, was totally disgusted with the whole business and spent his time reading a book, a 'Goosebumps', scowling all the while.

Pepper waited patiently in the doorway. She looked like she may have wanted to join in but didn't know how. This was the story of her life.

Leaving would prove to be no easy business for Langdon. Here he was with his daughter for the first time in months. But this was the biggest case of his life, a murder case at that. Somebody had been killed. And his friends were counting on him.

Missouri wasn't very happy when her dad stopped dancing and told her he had to go. Her tantrum and tears tore at Langdon's frazzled nerves. His very first priority in life was his daughter, no doubt about it. But how could he be a successful father by walking away from his problems? It wouldn't be setting a very good example to run away now. Leaving his daughter behind, in danger, was the hardest thing Langdon would ever do in his life—but it was the course of action he must follow if he wanted to be the sort of person he could be happy with, if he wanted his daughter to grow up into a mature, caring, giving and resourceful adult.

Langdon also knew the spirit of his three year old girl, and knew that two minutes after he left she would be again playing happily. If nothing else, the girl was resilient. Langdon whistled for the dog as Pepper and he walked out to the garage, not knowing what the day would bring.

* * *

One of the regular patrons of Richam's bar owned a motel out on Pleasant Street in Brunswick, and this is where Langdon and Pepper were headed. Richam had set them up with a room under an alias. This would be the base from which they'd try to present Pepper as a Time magazine journalist doing an expose on the power plant, to see what they could stir up.

Of course, Langdon's separation from his wife and resulting single lifestyle, withdrawn and celibate, had created a loneliness within him of which he wasn't at the moment unaware. He was after all checking into a motel with a young woman.

Many conflicting thoughts hurtled their way through Langdon's battered mind as he checked into (or rather snuck into) a motel with a nubile college student with an athlete's body and a crush on him greater than his weak resistance could ever hope to withstand. Langdon was terrified for his daughter's safety out in Harpswell, grateful for the support of his friends, ecstatic to have Lord backing his action once again, confused as to what was going on, filled with lust for Pepper's rock hard calves and proud body. Above all, Langdon missed his wife.

They didn't have to check through the main desk, as Richam had arranged for the room, number 13, to be left unlocked with the key in the top drawer of the night table between the twin beds. Langdon had taken the Saab convertible, now parked in the space in front of their room, from the summer mansion so as not to be traced or found. A small fridge in the room held a bottle of wine, with a card attached stating that any friend of Richam's was a friend of Jack's (the motel owner, presumably).

They'd stopped on the way at Pepper's college room to pick up some clothes, but had opted against paying a visit to Langdon's apartment as it was probably being watched. Not that they expected to remain anonymous for long. This was small town Maine after all.

Langdon looked longingly for a moment at the bottle of wine. It had now been two full days since he'd had a drink. This was a fairly long time, since he hadn't missed a day over the past several months and usually started well before it grew dark. It wasn't that Langdon had a drinking problem—he had no problem with drinking. The demon alcohol simply added a dimension to his life of routine.

But for now, far removed from his normal life, Langdon could do without a glass of wine.

"Pepper, you might as well take the bureau. I don't have anything to put in it anyway." Langdon was aware of a burning in the air that caused a thin sweat on the back of his neck and made it hard for him to breathe. "Are you taking the bed by the window?"

"Sure."

Talkative girl.

"You all set with what you need to do?"

"Sure."

Langdon wasn't sure whether this silence was an attitude on her part or simple shyness, but it certainly was annoying the hell out of him. "Why don't you run it down for me just to make sure."

Pepper shot Langdon a barely concealed look of irritation. "I'll read through this paperwork you've given me. But basically my name is Cassandra Greer, I work for Time magazine, and my editor is John Lavoie." A friend of Langdon's from school who truly worked, if not as the editor, close to the editor, at Time magazine. "His phone number is blah, blah, blah. And I'm in town doing a story on nuclear power in the environment."

Langdon still had to call his friend John Lavoie at Time and fill him in, a call he wasn't looking forward to. But there was no time like the present.

"John Lavoie, please." Langdon stood with the phone in his hand, wondering if John Lavoie would even remember him.

"Mr. Lavoie is in a meeting, can I have him call you back?" The receptionist on the other end of the phone replied without missing a beat, making Langdon think that this was a standard answer whether John was in a meeting or not.

"This is a friend of his from college, Goff Langdon..." Langdon gave the receptionist several seconds to say something like, 'Oh, here comes Mr. Lavoie out of his meeting, I'll put him right on,' but that didn't happen. Langdon gave her the motel and room number grudgingly. He probably wouldn't be here when and if his friend called back. Coffee Dog stood by impassively. Were they going to get on about their business or stay in the motel for the afternoon? Either way was fine with him. His wide brown eyes were in no hurry.

"Well, then," Langdon said. "If you're all set I'm going to run out and do some errands, I'll check back in with you in four or five or hours and see what you've come up with." But Langdon couldn't quite make himself move.

"I'll be fine by myself," Pepper spoke quietly. But a bit of a warble cut in to her voice indicated some sort of distress.

"Lord is in room 24 if you need him, don't hesitate to call." The motel was just off of a busy street, shaped in a U with the opening facing the street and a parking lot in the middle. Lord Langdon had taken up surveillance on the second floor. "And there's one more thing I didn't mention to anybody else..."

"Yes?" Pepper was suddenly rigid with anticipation.

"When Shakespeare paid a visit to Chabal this morning, he said something about his 'boss not willing to have DownEast Power closed down due to some leaks in the equipment'."

"So?" The anticipation went out of Pepper as if a release valve had been thrown wide open.

"Well, we seem to be operating on the premise that Shakespeare has been hired by governor Truman, or the 'Terror First' organization, or the both of them. But that doesn't quite make sense now, does it?" Langdon was giving his thoughts a chance to air, wondering how they'd sound when spoken aloud.

"Who else would care enough about what happens at DownEast Power?" Pepper was skeptical. "I mean, we're not just talking murder here, we're talking a murder that the police themselves are covering up! Who beside the governor has the power to do that?"

"It might be worth a talk with the chief executive officer of Casco Bay Power, to see if we can turn over any stones with creepy crawlies underneath." Langdon said without any real conviction.

"He doesn't care if DownEast Power shuts down." Pepper argued. "He'll just pass the cost along to the customers. Besides, some suit with a plush job isn't going to be hiring goons like Shakespeare."

"But the governor would?"

"Why don't we just take this one step at a time," Pepper replied with little interest, "Let's not complicate this thing more than necessary."

"Okay, then," Langdon said—not quite convinced, but ready to go with the flow for the moment.

"Get the heck out of here Langdon." She said, a little more sharply than she'd intended.

He smiled. "Bye to you too." He left on those words—but it was her eyes he'd remember, round with flickering lashes, burning with life and the passion of being twenty years old.

Pepper watched Langdon from the window as he drove off. For the first time in her life she'd become a participant and not just an extra. She rather liked the feeling of warm blood rushing through her veins, pulsing just below the surface. All of her senses were heightened, it seemed. She could still hear the heavy breathing of Goff Langdon standing quietly next to her, could smell his after-shave lotion and the nervous perspiration between them and above all the desire.

As he'd left the room he'd touched her arm lightly, sending small tremors of tingling anticipation through her.

Though to him she'd seemed composed and stoic.

Langdon put the top of the Saab convertible down and squealed out of the parking lot. Even if there were some bad guys around, wasn't Lord himself watching over room 13 and Pepper? To double check this last, Langdon reached for his cellular phone, which had recovered from the day before. Coffee, behind Langdon in the back seat, growled low in his throat, at what he didn't know. For just a second Langdon glanced over his shoulder wondering what the deal was, but then a gap in the traffic opened allowing him to pound the accelerator. At the same moment Lord picked up the phone and said, "Yes?"

"What about Hello?" Langdon pounced, smiling to himself. Even with all the mess they were in the middle of, Langdon suddenly felt on top of the world, a knife edge slicing through to his destiny. "You sound like some damn Butler." Loosen up a little.

"Goff, you're the one who's married, with a child, in the middle of a murder investigation, threatened—and you tell me I'm too serious. I'm living in Colorado with my twin brother drinking beer every night and chasing girls, a different one every night, letting my body and mind deteriorate as fast as possible. And you tell me I'm too serious?"

"Yeah, but look at me now," Langdon nonchalantly drooled the words out as he pulled into the breakdown lane (which on Pleasant Street pretty much meant the sidewalk) to pass a slow-moving truck, "I'm shacked up in a hotel with a college girl, out driving a Saab, breezing through town with the top down and not a care in the world." Langdon came to the stoplight and saw the mall in front of him. He idly wondered if perhaps the bookstore wouldn't do better business in there, more toney, more foot traffic. "Anyway, keep an eye on the place at least until I get back."

"I'll survive." Lord Langdon was all business, speaking in a cold-clipped voice. In life there were times to screw around and times to get down to business, and this was a time to get down to business.

Langdon started to reply and then realized the phone had gone dead. There was nothing further to talk about, and Lord knew Langdon only wanted to continue the conversation to calm his nerves and procrastinate.

There was still a nagging concern in the back of Langdon's mind—tingling—but he couldn't quite figure it out. He gave Danny T. a ring. Danny had decided to return home and stay out of the entire business after yesterday's episode with Shakespeare.

"Hallo," The cautious voice of a timid man trapped in a huge body answered after seven rings.

"Danny T., hey, can you do me a favor?" Langdon knew he was asking a great deal.

"I don't know, Langdon, I don't think I want to be seen or connected with you for a little while. At least until this whole thing blows over."

"Its easy, Danny T., real easy, all I want you to do is dig around a little and see if you can come up with anything for me on Johnson T. Halperg." Langdon gunned the car through the yellow light connecting Pleasant Street to Maine Street.

"Who is Johnson T. Halpberg?"

Like any good salesman, Langdon knew half the battle was won if he could get potential customer asking questions. "Chief Executive Officer of Casco Bay Power," he said.

"They own DownEast Power, don't they?" Danny T. said as if he were sorry to be bringing up bad news.

"Controlling interest anyway. See what you can find out about him, who his friends are, if he has any hobbies. What he was doing the night Harold Dumphy was killed..."

"Cut it out Langdon," Danny T. whined into the phone. "I don't want any part of this thing."

"You can't let them scare you Danny T. You gotta' keep going. If you don't then they win and you lose."

"Who is they?" Danny T. said morosely.

"The world, Danny T., the entire world."

After a long pause Danny said he'd see what he could do.

Langdon decided now was the time to pay a visit to the Chief of Police. He called ahead first, letting his fingers do the walking. "Hello, is the Chief in?" The answer was no.

Langdon took a wild shot in the dark. "Tommy, is that you?" Langdon barely knew Tommy and had no chance of recognizing his voice, but he had nothing to lose. And after all this mess, there was a good chance Tommy had been demoted to desk duty.

The voice on the other end was cautious. "This is Corporal Tom DePaola."

"Tommy, this is Goff Langdon. I need you to do me a favor." Langdon was now parked outside the police station, pulled up behind a long row of cruisers. "I am working on the Harold Dumphy case. I really need to reach the Chief."

"I'm sorry, Mr. Langdon, but I'm not aware of any Dumphy case. And I have no idea where the Chief is." Tommy spoke with just the slightest warble affecting his words to give away the emotion he was attempting to keep under wraps.

"Come on Tommy, cut the suicide crap and talk to me!"

There was silence on the other end for a full twenty stretched seconds. Langdon knew the power of silence well. Tommy finally bit. "What is it that you want to know?"

Langdon arranged to meet with him at Hog Heaven in twenty minutes.

* * *

It had been some time since Langdon had gone to Hog Heaven without a six-pack in the car, but this was the new Goff Langdon—business owner, detective and father of a three year old girl. Langdon seemed to have entered an arena of life and death, and the slightest mistake could mean that Missouri would grow up with no father.

Instead of buying the six-pack he wanted, Langdon stopped quickly at the Jenny Station and bought a box of expensive cigars.

In the parking lot of Hog Heaven, he ordered food and lit up a cigar.

Tommy slid into the passenger seat cursing. "Damnit Langdon, I thought I told you to not draw attention to yourself!?"

This took Langdon totally by surprise. What in heck had he done? Langdon paused with the stogie held in mid-air, smoke curling in small swirls around his hand. "What?"

"What!? What do you mean what?" How many convertibles do you see here with their tops down and the occupants smoking a cigar?" Tommy was speaking low and hard, each word clipped like the end of the cigar, clean and concise.

Langdon raised his eyebrows. "What's the problem?"

"Its twenty-two degrees. It is nine degrees below freezing!"

"Ten."

"Ten. Whatever! It's cold!" Tommy shook his head. "Look, let's just get this over with before Chief Guyton stops in and wonders when we became cigar smoking buddies."

"Tell me about the...death...of Harold Dumphy," Langdon said.

"Murder! Just say it. You know it. I know it." Tommy was on edge, the whites of his eyes dominating his face.

"Tell me about the murder, then." Langdon never would have possessed this calm if he'd been drinking. Calm was absolutely what Tommy needed to massage him through the conversation.

Langdon attempted to blow a smoke ring. “The murder, Tommy, tell me about who killed Harold Dumphy.”

“You got any booze Langdon?” Tommy said. “Don’t mess with me now, I know you got some booze. I just need one drink to calm down.” Tommy continued nervously, looking around him as he spoke.

Silently Langdon went to the trunk and retrieved the recently purchased fifth of Jack Daniels he kept in case of emergencies. And the Jack Daniels had a further purpose—Langdon was on the wagon, but he knew well the power of alcohol in loosening the tongue when he was trying to get information. He held the bottle away for just the briefest of moments. “The murder, tell me about the damn murder!”

“That’s what I’m trying to do, don’t you understand. I want to work together on this. I can’t take the deception any longer.”

Chapter thirteen

Bart had taken his cruiser to his garage and started up his Cadillac for the drive to Madison. The Cadillac wasn't much of a car, rusting away at the edges and then some—with a large hole in one of the rear passenger doors grown from what had once been merely a dent. The car was brown, but yellow paint streaked the driver side door where Bart had had the misfortune of making first contact with a nice young lady when her car had slammed into his on an icy corner, their eyes locking for a split second before their cars did likewise, a helpless look, a plea for forgiveness. The jarring impact had been much like the relationship that had followed, a relationship long since ended. There was something sexual about a car crash, a heightening of the sensations, a helpless dependance, a tingling of fear and excitement, and it was this emotion that had sustained their relationship for several months.

There was a tail-light out, and the front bumper was mangled from being used as a braking system when pulling up to curbs .

Tires.

The four tires were all brand new, top quality and inflated to exactly the right pressure.

Leather.

The car's interior could never have been guessed at from it's outside. The interior was black leather, soft and lustrous.

Seatbelts.

Had been removed as they only seemed to get in the way of Bart's bulk.

With the seat pressed all the way to the back, his huge hand on the wheel and his foot gently resting on the accelerator, Bart didn't feel in the slightest bit cramped—a feeling of loose comfort he didn't often find in his normal day.

The Caddy was his baby, his pride and joy, his comfort zone; but so as to not wear out the pleasure it gave him, Bart only drove it when he was going on a trip out of town. And Bart didn't very often go out of town, all that he needed in life could usually be found in Brunswick.

With a smile, Bart pulled out of the garage and onto the street, the car humming quietly—like riding on air.

* * *

Back at the house, Larry donned a sheepskin coat over his shirtless chest, a coat that he'd borrowed from the rich author's closet. The coat, he thought, was perfect—it hung down to his knees, or about five inches further than the twin pistols that criss-crossed his waist. He still wore his lizard skin cowboy boots. His jeans were caked with dust from Colorado, and his head was now covered by a black skull cap, pulled tightly over his ears against the chill he wasn't used to in the air. He was busy checking himself in the mirror as an impatient Nicky fumed behind him.

"There's lipstick and eye liner in the bathroom if you want to put your 'face' on before we leave," Nicky muttered in exasperation.

"I got to make sure I fit in with these Mainers before I go out," Crazy Larry replied with a casual smile. "It wouldn't do to be out of place on a job like this."

Nicky was about to mutter an oath in return when the room was suddenly invaded by whooping Indians—in the form of Missouri and Tangerine, chased by Will, who was shooting a cap gun.

"Uncle Nick, save us from the bad man," Missouri shrieked in mock terror.

Nicky swung around with his pent up wrath escaping from his face like heat from an ice cube, scaring Will with its intensity before Nick was able to adjust from reality to the game. There was a strained silence until Nicky became the child he still was, and eased the tension with a boyish grin. But all this had proven too much for Will, who turned and fled. Tangerine was also nervous for a moment, only Missiouri maintaining her happy smile. "Thank you Uncle Nick, you got the bad man!"

"That's what I'm here for, honey, I'm here to protect you from the bad man," Nicky muttered with unease. "Now you be a good girl while I'm gone."

Nicky and Crazy Larry left the house with a brief goodbye to Richam and Jewell—who were having a serious husband-wife conversation in the kitchen while Will morosely read a book close by, fearful of being too far away from them. In the garage Nicky slid into the driver seat of the Hummer and started the tank-like vehicle while Larry slid the rifles into the back. And then the two of them headed off in search of the elusive Shakespeare.

* * *

Back at Hog Heaven, Tommy weighed his words carefully before speaking. "They're blackmailing the Chief."

"What?!" The further Langdon got into this case the more it seemed to come right off the shelves of his mystery bookstore—suicides, murders, corruption, mysterious strangers and now blackmail. These sort of things just didn't usually happen in everyday life, and certainly not in Brunswick, Maine. "Who's blackmailing him?"

"He wouldn't tell me." Tommy said, seemingly relieved for the moment to be unburdening himself. "Only that they had him by the balls and if I refused to go along with the suicide ruling, they were going to hang him out to dry. Take his job, his family, maybe even send him to jail."

"What for?"

"Huh?"

"What for are the bastards threatening to blackmail him with?"

"He didn't say, wouldn't say. Only something about certain sexual indiscretions."

Unless the indiscretions were pretty blunt there was no chance of the Chief's going to jail—but an affair with the receptionist would certainly cause some difficulties with his wife and three children, and would probably lose him his job as well. Hell, in places like Washington D.C. you could smoke crack on a regular basis and still get elected mayor—but that wasn't the case in coastal Maine. "What certain sexual indiscretions?"

"He wouldn't say Langdon. And I didn't press him. It's none of my business."

"Where is the Chief, Tommy, where is he right now?" It was time to go after one of the larger pieces—and while the Chief wasn't the king or the queen, he was at least a bishop or a rook in this game of chess Langdon seemed to be playing against a faceless opponent.

"At home. I talked to him just before you called."

"What about?"

"He just called to apologize for everything. Said it was all a mess. Said he hoped I could forgive him."

"He called to apologize?" Langdon yelled the words unintentionally, drawing stares from the cars around them even though everybody else had their windows up.

"Yeah, sure," Tommy nodded in agreement, "Said he was sorry to have interfered with my case."

"Get out!...Wait! Where does the Chief live?"

Tommy told him.

"Get out."

Tommy did as he was told. As he always did. Without a question.

Langdon went screeching out of the parking lot. Men like Guyton LeFebvre only asked forgiveness when it was all over. Langdon had never particularly liked the Chief. LeFebvre was a man who ran things by the books, making sure to dot all the i's and cross all the t's, a very conservative man in principle and belief, a man who believed in authority and relished brandishing it whenever possible. For all that, Langdon had always considered him an honest man. And a strong man. Men like him didn't call up on the phone begging forgiveness—not unless they were trying to absolve themselves of sin.

Langdon went squealing onto Pleasant Street, almost running down a jogger in the process. The light had been red, so Langdon had cut through the laundromat parking lot and jumped out over the center median. It was a small miracle that he made it, somehow managing to skate between an oncoming oil truck and a minivan carrying a full family. Coffee Dog had been jarred out of his nap by Langdon's reckless driving and had climbed into the front seat—where he put his feet up on the front window to catch the rushing air full in the face. But he was unable to keep his balance with each vicious turn, so Langdon clung grimly to the collar with his right hand to keep the dog from toppling out of the car. With his left hand, Langdon spun the wheel like the captain of some ship out in the middle of a storm. When Langdon hit the River Road he decided to see what that Saab could do and opened the car up, rushing past several slower moving cars taking the corners grimly.

Tommy had told Langdon a gray cape, three miles out on the left side of the road. But there were two of them. This never happened in any of the mysteries Langdon read—but as he was about to choose wrong he caught a glimpse of the unmarked cruiser in an open garage.

Coffee was the first out of the car, his adrenalin pumping from the wild ride, jumping around, wanting to play, just plain ready to go. For Langdon's part, he felt silly standing in the driveway in the middle of this srene, peaceful setting, having risked life and limb to get there.

A faint wisp of smoke rose from the chimney, coming out dark against the white backdrop and turning light as the tendrils reached the coming of night. A look at his watch told Langdon it was only 3:51 p.m. though the sun was already disappearing. A bike with pink tassels and training wheels lay next to the car in the garage, a promise of warmer days. The curtains were drawn tightly shut except for those in the kitchen. Langdon now peered through the kitchen window, feeling unsure of himself, needing to prepare himself. Either he was here to prevent a suicide, to find a body, or to grill the Chief on his sexual indiscretions and the blackmail. It would be hard to hide his relief that the Chief wasn't dead, thus losing the edge he'd need to force a confession.

All thoughts were suddenly wiped clean from his mind by a single sharp gunshot from the inside of the house. Langdon put his shoulder down and charged the kitchen door—only to trip over Coffee who thought he meant to play. Langdon stumbled, almost catching himself then hitting the bottom of the two steps of the stoop with his toe. He sprawled flat—his toe feeling as it were broken—coming to rest gently against the door. The door in turn popped open under the slight pressure, obviously not having been locked or even shut properly. It was a good thing Coffee had slowed Langdon up or he may have gone right on through the house and out the back wall.

Langdon collected himself for a brief moment—and in that time Coffee must have sensed or smelled something, for a low whine started deep in his throat, piercing the solitude with warning, fear and unease.

Langdon drew the large pistol out of his jacket, holding it in front of him like a fishing rod. He'd carried a gun only once before in his life, when he'd been hired to enforce a no trespassing sign against some deer poachers. And on that occasion he had forgotten to load the gun. This time it was loaded, with an extra box of shells in his pocket. But the chances of Langdon being able to hit anything smaller than a house were rather slim. As in most of life, it was a bluffing game.

Langdon was in the kitchen, a very nice kitchen with black marble topped counters. He slowly eased himself through the room, towards the opening to the dining room. There was nobody in the dining room, which had dark grey walls and a pine green carpet. Langdon's eyes were drawn further down that room to the opening which turned out to be the living room and then a long hallway adjacent to it. Coffee followed on his heels, reminding Langdon vaguely of Scooby Doo, bumping against him whenever he paused.

Langdon realized that it was too quiet for there to be any danger; if there had been anyone else in the house he'd have heard a hum, a rustle, breathing. He worked his way down the hallway, pushing open doors as he went, coming at last to the study—and to Guyton LeFebvre's body.

Guyton had placed his gun in his mouth and blown most of the back of his head off, splattering the walls with fragments of brain. Langdon froze for just a moment—more to think things through carefully than in reaction to the death in front of him. Langdon had always been able to deal with crisis situations, putting the tragedy in little compartments, breaking it down and not dwelling on the utter horror of the overall situation. Langdon's grief would come later, sneaking up on him in some hidden form of anger, frustration and sadness. but in the moment of crisis itself, Langdon seemed to see things with certain clarity, to function more efficiently.

Langdon stepped over to the body, careful to not disturb anything. He checked for a pulse, just to be sure. But he could already feel the coldness approaching, the stiffening of death.

There were two large filing cabinets in the room and a desk, and these drew his immediate attention. There was nothing Langdon could do for the Chief except perhaps flush out his blackmailers. The first filing cabinet held only personal information—taxes, bills and budgets. The second file cabinet was empty except for a few paperbacks, Zane Grey westerns.

Langdon saved the desk for last—and this is where he found the suicide note, which seemed somehow long and rambling, filled with apologies to LeFebvre's family and friends with no real reason given for his doing what he'd done. At that moment, Langdon noticed the smoke. Almost invisible strands of black smoke squeezed out of a small metal trash can standing next to the desk. A small fire ticked the bottom of the trash can, burning whatever it was that the Chief had been trying to destroy in order to leave with is honor intact. Not there was any honor in suicide.

It was then that Langdon heard the sirens. They were a long way away, but Langdon knew they must be headed here. Somebody else must have heard the gunshot, or perhaps Tommy had gotten nervous. In any event, it was time to get out of Dodge. Langdon grabbed the burning embers with his bare hand, his eyes watering with pain. What Langdon did next, he did not out of pain or panic, but because he didn't always think things through clearly. He was standing next to a dead man with smoking hands and a reason for the murder—but he left.

He went out to the Saab with a low whistle for Coffee to follow, jumped in the car and headed off away from the sirens. Langdon thought about fingerprints—he'd been careful, he thought, not leaving any except possibly those on the front stoop where he'd fallen.

What Langdon could not know was that when the police arrived a few minutes later a man would be waiting in the driveway with a good description of Langdon and with his license plate number. The man would relate the series of events around Langdon's arrival, with one exception. According to the man, the gunshot had ocurred a few minutes after Langdon entered the house.

* * *

Langdon knew only that it was possible a neighbor may have taken down his license plate number. Because of this he decided it was time to ditch the car and move the home base. The car could be traced to the rich author and traced to his summer mansion. He dialed the house. "Richam, it's Langdon. Are things okay there?"

"Everything is pretty calm. The kids seem pretty comfortable here."

"I hate to be the bearer of bad news, but you need to move."

"Now?"

"Now."

Richam was pissed, but there was nothing he could do about it. Safety was the issue here. "Any ideas?" He said.

"Not really." Too much was happening too quickly, all of it overwhelming Langdon. "Call Chabal at the bookstore, see if she has any ideas. Then call me back."

Langdon had now circled around and was coming the back way into Brunswick. He detoured onto a side road and veered sharply down a plowed driveway he knew lead to the vacant house of a friend of his. His friend spent the winter away from Brunswick but still paid for his driveway to be plowed, every storm—why, Langdon couldn't guess.

But this is where Langdon ditched the Saab, taking the phone, the charred papers, his dog and his gun. From here it was four miles into town. It was a bit of a risk to walk, but Langdon knew a bike trail that would take him most of the way.

If Langdon had known that his name had already surfaced as a possible suspect in the murder of Chief LeFebvre, he would have been more cautious. As it was, Langdon was more worried about being spotted by Shakespeare and his cronies than by the police.

Coffee was oblivious to the entire situation. A walk through the woods was his idea of a good time, running this way and that, kicking up snow, digging up smells and peeing on every available bush. Langdon had walked about two miles, and was passing fairly close to the backyard of a house when his cell phone rang.

"Yes." Langdon wasn't giving out anything.

"We've found lodging."

"Good. Where?"

"I'm afraid to say over the phone," Richam was quiet and elusive. "The police are looking for you in connection with the murder of Guyton LeFebvre."

Looking for him? Somebody must have seen him there. "The MURDER of Guyton LeFebvre?" Langdon asked as the wrongness of Richam's words finally sunk in. "Don't you mean the suicide?" Langdon found himself standing stock still in a grove of small poplars, the breath from his lungs puffing a cloud into the absolute pureness of the surrounding air. His heart was hammering.

"The death of the Chief is no surprise to you." Richam stated the obvious, to make sure there was no mistake.

"I heard the gunshot. I saw the Chief. He shot himself. He was being blackmailed for sexual indiscretions. There, now you know everything I know. How about you tell me something!" Langdon spat out the words in frustration, angry at the fickleness of fate.

"I don't know anything. Only that the police have already spoken to Chabal. They told her they were 'seeking you for questioning in connection with the murder of Guyton LeFebvre'."

"They probably tapped the phone of the bookstore and are coming to pick you up right now." Langdon spoke with panic in his voice.

"The police can only get wire taps that fast in the movies, maybe even in the cities. But certainly not in Brunswick."

"What about Shakespeare?"

This brought a pause on the other end. "We're out the door right now. Jewell and the kids are in the car already. If you need to know where we are just ask the Lord and he will guide you." The phone went dead.

Langdon started walking again.

Langdon broke into a jog.

Langdon ran at full speed which was at most a shambling gait which would not have gotten him a tryout with the Vikings. Langdon had never been known for his foot speed, and on this day his cracked ribs and bruised body didn't help.

The pain was intense, softened only by Langdon's fear that this case was completely out of control, endangering Langdon's family and friends. And now the police were after him. Langdon felt like a puppet, a twitch of the puppeteers strings ensuring that he went the proper way, a direction mapped out for him without his knowledge.

It was full dark by the time Langdon reached the motel. The path ended several hundred yards before it, but Langdon had managed to grope his way through backyards without attracting too much attention. He approached the motel from the rear, working his way cautiously to the back of Lord's second-floor room. He climbed the fire escape, picking Coffee up with effort—his ribs screaming in protest—and boosted the dog over his head.

Langdon wasn't quite sure he had the right room. He found himself staring through the window of an empty bathroom. Why hadn't he just come in through the front door? Of course the bathroom window was locked. Exasperated, he tapped quietly and then more loudly on the pane—not quite sure who'd show up inside.

An icy rain began to pelt him, as a wary Lord Langdon peered his head into the bathroom. Langdon tapped again, gently, and flashed him a nervous grin. Lord was holding a big game rifle leveled at his head. As Lord recognized his brother, the gun wavered and was reluctantly lowered. Lord leaned forward to unlatch the window, and pushed it up with a squeaking of fresh paint. Coffee Dog was the first one in, scurrying through with the simple joy of being out of the pelting rain.

Langdon almost got stuck crawling through the tiny opening.

"Goff." Lord merely nodded his head with a faint smile tucked away in the corners of his eyes. "Funny place to run into you. Coming through the servants entrance." This was a gentle prod at the fact that Langdon's ex-wife, Amanda, had grown up in a mansion in Atlanta that had a separate door for the servants. Langdon had often felt that that was the more appropriate door for him to use but somehow had always been welcomed through the main entrance, even with his often uncouth, uncultured, and unrefined behavior. Lord and Nicky had come to visit once when Langdon was staying there and had in fact, spent most of their time in the servants quarters, playing poker and drinking beers with the hired help and having, Langdon was sure, a much better time than himself sitting perched delicately on antique furniture sipping white wine and making conversation on the plusses and minusses of the neighbors new flower bed.

"I finally found my place in life, Lord, I know who I am." Langdon cracked in return.

"Well, from now on," Lord smiled, "I'll make sure to install doorbells on all my bathroom windows so as to not keep you waiting when you visit."

Langdon was now ready to get back to business. "No action?"

"Pepper hasn't left the room since you left this morning," Lord stated with a wide yawn stretching his face, "The Domino's guy knocked on the door at noon. She paid, he gave her the pizza. He left, she closed the door."

Pepper was to have spent the day making phone calls inside, but it still surprised Langdon that she hadn't gone out for a walk or to buy some soda. She must be having success on the phone, getting good information. Langdon sure hoped so, because so far in this investigation there hadn't been any good news.

"How about you," Lord wanted to know, "Anything exciting on your end of things?"

Where to begin? Langdon gave him a brief rundown of the day's events—stopping after he mentioned finding the Chief's body. A though worked its way up through his thick skull, and he patted his pockets—finally finding the last burnt remains of the evidence the Chief had been trying to destroy. It was a note and the corner of a picture. The picture appeared to contain the Chief's nude back; even though the edges were charred, the back of his head and one shoulder were recognizable. His head was resting lightly on a woman's bare stomach, his body covering hers. One of her naked breast rested on the top of his head, but the other breast and her face missing, casualties of the fire.

"That's some solid evidence for you," Lord chuckled. "Call me when you get around to the police line up."

Langdon glared at his brother, then went with the joke, "I suppose you'd like to be in charge of finding this 'mystery' woman?"

"That might be something a little more up Nicky's alley." Lord deadpanned. But then a flash of concern crossed his face as he wondered where Nicky was at that moment.

Goff stared at the picture, something tickling the edges of his mind. "Don't laugh, but I think I know who that woman is. I can't quite place her, but something's familiar."

Lord waited for a few moments, giving his brother free rein so as to not distract him. but it was no use, Goff just couldn't be sure what it was that was familiar about that body. It wasn't as if Goff had had the opportunity to see a lot of naked woman in his life, much less recently. Maybe it was a customer at the bookstore...

With a shake of his head Goff carefully spread the crumbling note out on the small motel table:

ebvre,

can see by the enclosed photographs of have been caught in some fairly compromising It would be a shame for your wife to find out about your affith this woman and to actually have to view some of the more exotic experiences you have had. It would also be oe interest to a police investigation into a recent mur have these pictures. I think that it would be best for those involved, the police, your wife, yourself, Mrs. f you were to drop the Harold Dumphy investigation a off as the suicide that it was. I have copies of t tures and will not hesitate to see them get int if that becomes necessary.

-your friend L

"It figures the name of the woman is missing," was all Lord had to say about the note. His brow was furrowed and his lips were pursed.

"It appears that the woman was married, though," Goff muttered half to himself. "I assume that would be the Mrs. the note referrs to."

"And look at this part here," Lord said, pointing carefully at a piece of the note. "It seems to be saying that the identity of the 'mystery' woman would be of interest to the police in a recent murder investigation."

Goff nodded, staring at the note, trying to make sense of it all.

"You have a lot of murder investigations here in Brunswick?" Lord wanted to know.

"Not that I know of," Goff muttered.

"Because that certainly looks like 'a recent murder', there that part there, that's been burnt off. So—the Chief is being blackmailed to cover up a murder he himself is involved in?" Lord was putting things together as he went, trying to make the pieces of the confusing puzzle fit together.

"It sounds like a woman is involved in all this, the 'mystery woman'," Goff Langdon said with his lips pursed, knowing full well the strange things that men will do for sex, for love, to satiate some inner need, "It's funny how a woman can make a bad man good, but at the same time, a woman can destroy a good man."

But he couldn't make sense out of any of it for the moment. Langdon sat on the edge of a twin bed, then leaned back on his sore arms. "Did I mention to you that I'm the chief suspect in the Chief's 'murder'." He said, realizing he hadn't quite filled his brother in on all the day's details.

"What was your motive?" Lord retorted.

"It seems that a neighbor gave a rather good description of me."

"So—turn yourself in, explain that he was already dead so you just poked around and took a few things and continued on your way. You didn't think he'd mind." Lord was smiling.

Goff just shook his head, not quite as amused as his brother seemed to be by the situation.

Lord studied him for a moment with concern. "What you need to do is get some rest and relaxation. It wasn't that long ago that you were checking out of a hospital all stove up, probably didn't sleep a wink." He smiled again, trying to lighten the moment with humor. "And now you've gone and shot somebody."

Goff was sure he was a pretty scary sight, battered, pale and with dark rings around his eyes, in need of a shower, a shave and fresh clothes.

Lord teased him again. "What you need to do is go down to that motel room and have Pepper take care of you."

Pepper! "Aren't you supposed to be watching her room?" Goff blurted out, suddenly remembering the danger they were all in, especially this young college student from Texas—who had presumably spent the day on the phone stirring up the hornet's nest.

Lord didn't reply, merely hurried over to the window, which had a chair pulled up in front of it.

The air was still, and the room was quiet. There was just a hint of light coming out from under the door, a faint orange glow in the window, maybe just the light by the bed, or from the bathroom.

Relieved, Goff sat back down on the bed closest to the window as Lord took up his post again.

Lord summoned up the brass to spit out the question that had been nagging at him since he'd arrived from Colorado. "What's the deal between you and this college girl anyway?"

"Just friends." Goff spoke a little too quickly. A lie detector would have gone wild with that answer.

Lord wasn't going to let it drop that easy. "She worships the ground you walk on."

Goff shook his head. "She thinks I'm a bumbling idiot. But that's okay with her because she doesn't have a lot of friends."

"Goff, you've always been oblivious to the world around you. But this girl thinks you're Sir Lancelot come to rescue her. If you're in the same room with her, she watches you like a hawk, blushes when you speak, and giggles at your bad jokes."

Goff was still hoping to change the subject. "She's attractive, young, athletic, and fun to talk to. That's all."

"She's over eighteen. I think you should go for it," Lord said.

"You've been spending too much time with Nick," Goff said with a chuckle. "Life isn't just about getting laid."

"Take her out to dinner, buy her flowers, go to a movie, hold hands and blow in each other's ears for all I care. But you have to move on and enjoy life a little." Lord was quite animated. This was obviously a speech he'd been holding in for some time.

"What do I need to move on from?" Goff sincerely wanted to know, needed to know. "He'd felt of late as if he were in a kind of limbo.

"What is it that you want in life, big brother?" Lord spoke quietly, wanting to help.

It struck Goff suddenly with frightening clarity, the thought he'd been drinking for months to avoid. "I miss Amanda," he said. "I want her back."

Lord was silent for a few minutes, considering what Goff had said. Finally he said, "Then maybe what we need to do is figure out how to get her back."

Goff buried his face in his hands, but Lord pressed on. "It's like solving a drinking problem. The first step is admitting you have a problem. Then you can work on the rest." Lord spoke slowly and carefully. "Now that you've come to terms with your emotions, you can work on repairing, resolving, appreciating what you have and what you have had."

Langdon rose and touched Lord's arm briefly to thank him for listening. All of this was too much for him to process at the moment—and before making any grand plans for his own redemption, he had more immediate concerns. "I better go down and find out what Pepper dug up today," he said. And then he headed back out the bathroom window and down the fire escape.

Chapter fourteen

The road flew away beneath them, the landscape slid past in a motionless blur. The huge Caddy sucked up the pavement like some hungry beast on the prowl...

Bart and 4 by Four were quiet for the moment, contemplating the empty beer cans in their hands—the last of the six-pack they'd gotten in Topsham before entering the highway. It was only mid-morning but the beers had gone down easily and now they were out, still several miles from their exit in Waterville. 4 by Four was silent; it was his misjudgment that had caused the shortage. Although he'd only had two of the six, he had traveled with Bart before and should have known better.

The car hovered in the passing line at a steady ninety-five miles per hour. So smooth and velvet soft was the ride, they could have been going fifty. "So, what's the game plan?" Bart broke the silence, letting 4 by Four off the hook for his disastrous mistake. "We go up to Madison, Athens and Starks and just poke around until we find something?"

"Hey, I'm just the lawyer. You're the cop. I'm just along to advise you against it when you're about to break the law, and then try to get us out of jail when you don't listen."

"Does Flower First still have their office up there?" Bart frowned. "I seem to remember something about them having their headquarters in Augusta, maybe another down in Portland."

Jimmy 4 by Four shrugged. "All I really know about the area is that a couple years back, I went to 'Hempstock' up there in Starks. But I don't remember much about it. I just brought my tent and stood around in the woods and got really stoned."

"You can be a real knucklehead sometimes," Bart growled as he steered the car off at the first Waterville exit. This wasn't their exit—but Bart had determined that the extra two miles until the second Waterville exit would take way too long. "You want me to go in this time?"

Fortunately the first convenience store they came to was a drive-through, so Jimmy was saved from making another gross miscalculation. Bart pulled up to the window and ordered. "I'll take a twelve pack of Lite, some ice, better throw in some chips...salt and vinegar...how about some donuts, you got any cigars, yeah I better take a couple boxes of those and throw a lighter in with that too." 4 by Four never would have thought to get all this.

By the time they had reached Madison it was eleven o'clock in the morning, and they'd drunk a case of beer between them, 4 by Four who was feeling the effects pretty strongly, but Bart showed no outward signs of even having had a single can.

Their first move was to check the phone book at a payphone on the town's main street—but there was no listing for Flower First. There were no law firms for Fitzpatrick or Sterling. "What we need to do is find some old codger and pump him for information," Bart said. "Every town has one, some guy who doesn't have a penny to his name except what he spends on alcohol but knows more about what's going on, past and present, than anyone else."

"Should we check the phonebook?" 4 by Four mumbled with sarcasm. "Look under the O's for old codger, or maybe C."

Bart just stared at 4 by Four with contempt, long enough to make him feel uncomfortable. Then he spike like one overcoming a minor distraction. "Why don't we see what there are for drinking establishments in this town?"

There were three bars. The first one was closed. The second was too expensive. The third was just right.

It was called, simply, 'The Pines.' This was handpainted on a four by six foot piece of plywood leaning up against the wall near the door. The door hung slightly askew on its hinges but seemed to work fine, swinging open with barely a screech. Bart stepped in and immediately headed off to the left, habit pushing him away from the door's outside light. Thus, it was 4 by Four that the seven or eight people inside the bar inspected as he stood framed by the doorway, a nervous grin fading from his face as he attempted to gather his bearings. Finally he took the easy way out and sauntered over to the bar to ordered up a couple of beers.

After several minutes Bart came over and sat down—drawing the attention of the two men playing pool. It was hard for his bulk not to draw attention. "Ya got any menus?" He barked. The chubby woman bartending waved her hand behind her, a broad sweeping gesture that encompassed most of the room but did also happen to pass over a chalkboard, faded and unclear, but readable with effort. "Hell, I'll take four bacon cheeseburgers and some fries, you want anything 4 by Four?" 4 by Four, for his part, was not going to eat anything served in this place, not even a bag of chips. "Better bring us a pitcher of beer," Bart continued, "and hey, buy everybody in here a shot of tequila, these people do drink tequila don't they?"

When the bartender was safely out of earshot, 4 by Four muttered to Bart, "You notice anything missing in here?" Bart shook his head in a puzzled way, and he continued, "Like teeth. I think we're the only two in here with a full set!" This was true, but Bart couldn't quite understand what this had to do with anything.

One of the pool players approached them through the bar's dim light. He was fairly young, maybe twenty-five—and he did prove to have a full set of teeth, flashing a smile to prove it, "Either of you guys want a game?"

At that moment Bart's food arrived. He raised an apologetic hand and gently pushed 4 by Four out towards the man.

"Five bucks a game?"

4 by Four felt pressured. He nodded, and the man let him break.

"Where you from?" The man said.

"Brunswick. My name's...Jimmy." 4 by Four decided to leave his full name out.

"I'm Jere. Good to meet you." The young pool hustler pressed Jimmy 4 by Four's hand just a moment longer than necessary. Jere wasn't really that good a pool player but approached every stranger for a game because none of the regulars seemed willing to play him for money. 4 by Four wasn't aware that the reason for this wasn't that Jere was unbeatable, but that beating him usually led to a fight.

"Nice shot." 4 by Four complimented Jere on what was a fairly easy cut. "You live here long?"

"Just since I was born," Jere joked with a wink, thinking this was a strange question indeed. Nobody moved here to Madison. You were either born here or were just passing through.

"Hey Gail," Jere suddenly shouted as 4 by Four was about to shoot at the eight ball. "Send over a couple of shots of Jack Daniels and a couple of beers would you?"

Distracted, 4 by Four missed the shot—and Jere won the game with an easy tap of the eight ball.

4 by Four glared in irritation at the young pool hustler. But Jere was all innocence. "Why don't you give Gail the five bucks you owe me for the drinks, and we'll play again?"

"How about we play for $10 this time?" 4 by Four asked with an edge to his voice.

The two rough-looking men sitting at the closest table hooted, "This guys gonna kick your butt, Jere, you better look out!"

"Sure, $10 is good with me," Jere smiled his naive young smile. He popped his Jack Daniels to the back of his throat with relish.

If 4 by Four had less than ten beers in him, he might have noticed that the game had become the center of attention in the bar, and might even have noticed that people were edging away from the pool table. But as it was, he noticed none of this and easily whipped his opponent.

"How about double or nothing?" Jere said.

"No, I think I'll take a break," 4 by Four said, suddenly tired of the game, full of beer and in need of some solid food.

"Come on, just one more game." Jere wasn't smiling now.

"No, really, I'm done in."

"You gonna' take my money and then quit?"

This was the first inkling the lawyer from Brunswick had that he'd misjudged Jere's good nature. "Look, tell you what," Jimmy said. "We'll call it even. You won the first game and I won the second."

"You think I need some kind of charity from some fancy dressed out of towner?" Jere had now moved to within less than an inch of Jimmy's face, his body twitching in anticipation. "One-hundred dollars. What do you say?"

This was either an elaborate hustle of some ind and Jimmy would find himself out a hundred bucks—or he'd win again and Jere would lose even more of his good humor. Jimmy 4 by Four internally prepared himself to be hit and then said no.

Jere pushed him with his forearm, a gentle shove. "I think you're a panzy." Another shove—gentle—persistent—and then another, harder. "Hey boys, look, we got us here a queer." He grabbed 4 by Four by the scruff of the collar.

4 by Four knocked his hand away with a slap and the room froze. "You shouldn't have done that," Jere snarled.

Even though 4 by Four was prepared for anything, the swiftness with which Jere suddenly stepped forward and threw his first punch took him completely by surprise. But somehow the blow never arrived. Where Jere had been, there was only empty space. "Let go of me!" Jere screamed from across the room. He was sitting at a chair pressed against the wall, writhing and contorting but somehow unable to move. "I'll kill you, you bastard! Just let me go."

It was then that 4 by Four realized Bart was sitting across from Jere pressing the small bar table into Jere's midsection. After a few minutes, Jere quieted down and Bart let him go.

Jere stood up and took a roundhouse swing at Bart—and Bart knocked him out cold. In a crowd of old drunks the young man was a decent pool player and a fairly tough character.

The bartender, who'd shown no interest in them to this point, now filled a pitcher of beer and waved to Bart with a coy smile filtering through her heavy face, "This pitcher is on the house," She said. "I've been waiting a long time for somebody to give Jere the business."

"Thanks," Bart said with an interested gaze back. "I appreciate that." He turned to Jimmy. "4 by Four, come over here." He grabbed Jimmy by the arm and pulled him to a back table, whispering into his ear on the way, "I think I found our old coot." While 4 by Four had been playing pool, Bart had been subtly talking around until he found the person he was looking for.

"This is Jonathan Starling." Bart waved to the seated man. "Mr. Starling, this is Jimmy 4 by Four."

4 by Four was struck dumb. Even full of beer and confused by the incidents of the past few minutes, the name Starling registered with him. This was one of the original founders of 'Flower First'; along with Jordan Fitzpatrick and Governor Harper Truman.

But while Truman had gone on to become Governor, this man had definitely taken a different path. It had been at least ten days since his face had seen the better side of a razor, gristled and bristly, spattered with tobacco juice and saliva. His black hair was cut short, and obviously he himself had cut it, perhaps with one of the butter knives here. The man was thin, frail, beaten. Every once in a while he coughed from somewhere deep in his body, hacking, choking and clearing his throat with difficulty. With each sip from the bottle of Jack Daniels on the table in front of him, a brightness flared up in his eyes, briefly, like a shooting star, a hint perhaps of the man he'd been. But then the eyes would gloss over and return to the bleary look of the eternally hopeless. Jonathan Starling was dressed in a large green army surplus jacket which hung from his body like a sail filled with wind around a tiny mast.

"Mr. Starling used to be a lawyer here in Madison." Bart spoke with a delicate care, caressing the old codger's story without giving away the fact that Starling's past associations were what had brought them to town in the first place.

"Is that right, Mr. Starling?" 4 by Four asked with wonder. "I'm a lawyer as well. Do you still practice?"

Jonathan Starling stared angrily at 4 by Four. "Of course I don't practice you son of a bitch. I'm a drunk, and you know that as well as I do. So don't patronize me or I'll kick the living shit out of you."

This was just not 4 by Four's day. His face flushed a pulsing red and he bit back a biting reply. They needed this man—and besides, it was hard to insult a man who knew he was a gutter drunk with no future and no possibilities. "I'm sorry, Mr. Starling, we seem to have gotten off on the wrong foot. What was your specialization?"

"I was just telling your friend, the jolly green giant, that I used to be an environmental lawyer." Jonathan Starling had that keen ability of bitter old men to be able to insult at least one person with his every sentence. "As a matter of fact, I used to be in a practice with the Governor himself." With this he took a good haul off the bottle, clearing his eyes for a moment and allowing Jimmy 4 by Four to see deep into the soul of a man tormented by countless demons. "Go ahead, ask anybody in here, they'll tell you. Truman, Starling & Fitzpatrick Law Associates, right here in Madison. Right out of law school, full of piss and vinegar, ready to make a difference in the world, ready to kick some ass and shake up the system."

4 by Four suddenly realized with horror that the man in front of him was probably only forty years old. The man appeared to be at least sixty, gnarled and twisted with age, but perhaps it was just pain and poor living. "What happened?" 4 by Four wasn't going to make the mistake of patronizing the man again.

"Ya' know, I probably could use something to eat, sop up this whiskey. Why don't one of you buy me something to eat?"

"Whatever you want," 4 by Four was foaming at the bit but tried not to betray his excitement. "I'll go get it cookin' right now."

"Not here, Mr. Eager-Beaver. Even an old drunk like me wouldn't eat the slops this place serves." Three pairs of eyes viewed the several empty plates and cardboard cartons strewn in front of Bart. "Place across the street called Riverside has some pretty good barbecued ribs. And the fahitas appetizer with hot sauce will knock you right out of your socks."

Bart grinned, "Sounds good to me, I'm hungry again already. Let's leave this shit-box behind and go get some real grub."

"Riverside it is then, I sure could use some food," 4 by Four said with an authority he didn't feel.

Jere still hadn't moved as they headed to the door. Nobody seemed to pay him any mind, no friend came over and carried him off. It was as if Jere had simply been added to the furniture. Bart walked over and checked his pulse, but as he'd guessed, it was fine. Jere would merely wake up feeling like he'd had too much tequila and would go back to being his old bully self. But from now on there'd be a hidden smile in the faces of those he bullied.

The chubby bartender gave Bart a big wink.

Outside, daylight, cold, precise and piercing, met them with an awkward but welcome greeting. It was as if they'd traveled down into Hades and returned with one of the lost souls, some Herculean feat which was sure to carry repercussions with the Gods.

At a later date there would be Hades to pay. But for now, a sparkling diamond had been found, a chip they most certainly meant to play.

Chapter fifteen

Chabal sat behind her desk in the bookstore, tapping her long nails against the hardwood surface. Thelonius Monk played on the stereo in the background. A nice grey-haired lady was slowly wandering the aisles, not that here was many aisles to wander, looking at a book here, a book there. She'd been browsing the store for over an hour now. Chabal was of the opinion the lady could have read an entire book by this time, but maybe she found her enjoyment in the looking. Life seemed to work like that, Chabal mused—true appreciation could often be found more in the striving for than the actual having.

Chabal's husband was an accountant down in Portland, good with numbers, gentle of manner, sensitive to her needs, wants and desires. He cooked two nights a week, helped with the kids whenever he was home, was a thoughtful lover, provided a comfortable living and a nice vacation every year—and frankly she was bored to death. At some point she had come to work for Langdon in the bookstore, and she fell in love. Chabal wasn't sure exactly why.

Getting Langdon to take out the trash required at least four reminders. He often showed up to work unshaven, his hair uncombed. He often forgot to say hello and goodbye. He lived in a trashy apartment and drank too much. He ate horrible, fried and fatty food. He was a sexist or at least liked to act like one. But the man sure added an element of excitement to her life. Of course, Chabal was perfectly comfortable with her crush from afar, enjoying her desire without having to act on the fantasy. She was a mom with three kids and a nice husband, and her family wasn't something she was about to throw away.

There wasn't much to do in the store on this day. Chabal had cleaned and made displays and done all of her other busy work, and was now waiting for either customers or the phone to ring with an update from the field. Of course the females had all gotten left behind, she thought. Pepper was stuck in a hotel room, Jewell was stuck with the kids and Chabal was stuck with the bookstore while Nicky and Larry got to chase down villains, Bart and Jimmy got to take a road trip, Lord got to do some high-tech surveillance, and Langdon got to roam the town.

"Can I help you ma'am?" Chabal asked the elderly lady for the third time, knowing she shouldn't, knowing she was verging on driving away a potential customer—but come on already, pick a book or don't!

Chabal had always been feisty, the result of having four older brothers, all jocks, all huge, football players and wrestlers who liked to fight and didn't cut her much of a break even though she was a girl and tiny at that. She was eleven when she'd first fought back, dashing her mother's hopes that there would be at least one civilized being in her family, her hopes for dresses, tea parties, and a more genteel existence disappearing when Chabal had charged across the top of the dinner table and tackled her older brother—inadvertantly sticking a fork into his cheek—leaving him screaming in terror while Chabal calmly finished her meal.

The elderly lady took this moment to come to the counter to purchase an Agatha Christie, $3.99, big sale—just as the phone rang. It was Richam.

"What do you got?" She said.

"Easy there, Chabal, remember I'm not one of the ones out on the front lines."

"I'm going crazy here," Chabal sputtered, "I need to know what's going on."

"You're the command center," Richam said soothingly. "Everybody is depending on you for information—like this news of Langdon's being wanted for the Chief's murder."

Chabal was not to be placated so easily. "What do you got for me?" She repeated.

"The women and children have moved to Fort Andross."

"Fort Andross?!" Chabal was shocked. "Where are you staying?" Fort Andross was a big old mill on the river, full of various businesses, restaurants and storage units. Not quite a comfortable lodging for the children.

"I have a friend who's a painter," Richam said, "has a studio loft here. Four-thousand square feet. Of course the place isn't zoned for residential living—but he has a full bathroom facility, beds and furniture. He sometimes works late or spends a lot of time here. Great view, top floor, if anybody's interested. People would have to come up the fire escape after six or call me to let me know they're coming so I can let them in."

"Anybody else know where you are?"

"Lord knows."

She frowned. "How are the kids doing with it all?"

"Will's a little quiet, ever since the other day with Shakespeare. But Missouri and Tangerine are having a great time. It's the best sort of adventure and game they could ever want. This studio was made for kids, it's like a big playground. We're going to have a kick ball game in a little while." He sighed. "But I don't know what to say to Will. I had to grow up when I was his age but I had hoped to keep him from that."

"Can you see the bookstore entrance from where you are?" Chabal wondered, thinking it would be nice to be able to wave to Will and the girls when she left in a few minutes.

"Just a second, I'll let you know," Richam muttered, carrying the cordless phone with him across the expanse of floor to the windows facing Brunswick. It was just starting to get dark, the shadows lengthening with streaks of sunlight filtering through, casting odd illusions on the town below. "Yeah, Chabal," he said. "Not only can I see the bookstore, but I think I have some news for you."

"What's that?"

Richam was watching four policemen, climb out of two cruisers parked in front of the bookstore. "You're about to have some visitors. The police. I better get off the phone. Call me back, 798-4884, don't write this number down, memorize it! Let me knows what happens."

Chabal stared at the phone in wonder, and slowly set the receiver down just as patrolmen Gary Stout and Max Van de Wetering entered the store. The other two officers had remained outside, one in front and one out back.

"Hi Gary. Max. How have you gentlemen been?" Chabal said, doing her best to manage a pleasant smile.

"We're here on business, Chabal." Gary Stout was a young man, new to the force, fresh out of the academy. But he'd grown up in Brunswick, a star athlete, a well-mannered young man who seemed at the moment a little uncomfortable with his position of authority.

"Is Goff around?" Max asked with a little less sensitivity. He was a veteran of twenty-five years on the force and had the extra fifty pounds to prove it. He'd hung on to his position by the sheer fact that he knew too many people and been around too long to be fired. The old boy network was his saving grace. And unfortunately, his seniority placed him in charge of this matter.

"No, I haven't seen him all day. What do you want him for?" Chabal was all innocence, flashing a flirtatious smile at Gary Stout and ignoring Max's glare, purposefully snubbing him.

"It's serious." Gary Stout said, looking down at his feet.

"He's wanted for murder," Max spat out, afraid the rookie would steal his thunder.

"I already told your officers all I know about Langdon and the Chief of Police," she said. "And what I told them is that I don't know anything." Chabal spoke brightly, at ease with the situation.

"He's wanted for questioning in regards to the death of the Chief," Gary Stout began with caution.

"But he's also wanted for the murder of Patricia Smith!" Max said sharply.

"Patricia Smith?" Chabal was stunned for there seemed to be death all around her, but who was Patricia Smith?

Max continued in a clipped voice, enjoying this part of his job. "One Patricia Smith, Bowdoin College student, was found dead forty-five minutes ago and Goff Langdon was discovered with the body. At which point he fled and is now wanted in connection with her murder."

The name finally clicked. "Peppermint Patti?" And Chabal's whole world came crashing down around her, all the order to the universe disrupted with this single concise blow.

* * *

Langdon climbed back out of Lord's small bathroom window and onto the fire escape, scraping his back in the process. On the bottom tier of the steps he heard voices and froze. He'd been about to drop down to the ground to sneak into Pepper's room, but instead he flattened back against the building, clutching Coffee Dog closely to his body. Coffee for his part was uncharacteristically cooperative.

Langdon's eyes searched frantically for the origin of the noise. Three boys came around the corner of the motel clutching a paper bag. They were sixteen, maybe seventeen, typical burnouts. Of course they stopped a mere ten feet from Langdon, passing the paper bag between them. Langdon considered simply jumping down and going about his business as he'd been planning—but the last thing he needed was to draw attention to himself. The boys' conversation was typical teenage boy stuff, seasoned throughout with obscenities, F-this and F-that. The alcohol in their bag couldn't last forever, so Langdon simply waited. Slowly he drifted back into his own thoughts, trying to organize the past few days events. Where did Shakespeare enter into the whole picture? The Chief was being blackmailed, but by whom? Harold Dumphy was killed but for what? Abbigail Austin-Peters was covering something up, but was it what the Chief was being blackmailed for or what Harold Dumphy was killed for or something entirely different? It seemed to Langdon that there must be a connection.

As Langdon sat on the balcony waiting, a wave of terror suddenly washed over him for he began to understand the true scope of the mystery in which he'd enmeshed his brothers and so many of his friends. This wasn't taking pictures of Mr. Smith having an affair with Mrs. Jones, or catching Johnny dipping his fingers into the cash register at Cumberland Farms or even a simple murder investigation—this was a conspiracy possibly endangering the lives of thousands, with the evidence such as it was pointing at this moment to the governor. This was the big leagues.

To go back to the very beginning of the case, to Langdon's first suspicions—if there were problems at DownEast Power, then who was covering them up? Who would benefit the most from the plant's staying open? Casco Bay Power, of course. Langdon made a mental note to check and see what Danny T. had found out about the chief executive officer, Johnson Halperg.

Who else would benefit from keeping DownEast Power open? Or, to rephrase the question, who would be hurt most if the power plant closed? The people who lived in the town of Woolington, in which the plant was situated, would certainly be affected. For years, since the 1960's, they'd paid next to nothing taxes, the power plant taking up all the slack. Who owned the most land in town?

Several farmers would probably be put out of business if they suddenly had to start paying taxes on their huge tracts of land—but a farmer probably wouldn't be in a position to hire Shakespeare to commit murder. The one other possibility was the ski complex, Mount Chamberlin. The owner of Mount Chamberlin Ski Resort would be faced with millions of dollars in increased taxes if DownEast Power shut down. Ellsworth Limington, who'd eyed Langdon and Pepper so strangely the other night in Goldilock's bar, was the controlling owner.

One of the boys below suddenly flung the brown paper bag against a nearby rock, smashing the empty container within. The three boys moved on, laughing, and Langdon was free to go.

With aching muscles he dropped Coffee Dog down from the bottom landing of the fire escape, the dog's legs collapsing as he hit the ground, reminding Langdon that Coffee was not a cat. Coffee Dog looked up at him with forlorn eyes as if to ask, 'what did you go and do that for?' No doubt Coffee felt better when Langdon jumped the short distance to the ground below and also crumpled to the ground, the impact jolting his stiff bones.

The shadows of the December day jotted the parking lot provided enough cover for Langdon to slip quietly to room 13—where a young lady with a big crush on him waited, a young lady he'd perhaps led on.

Langdon took a deep breath and knocked on the door so as not to surprise Pepper, just a polite knock. And then he inserted the key to room 13 and swung the door open. Pepper lay on the bed. Naked. Dead.

Langdon let the Coffee Dog in behind him and pulled the door shut. Coffee immediately lay down on the floor, covering his muzzle with his paws and emitting a low-pitched whine.

Langdon found himself gasping for breath as if he were having a heart attack. The room tilted first one way and then another. And there was pain as if his body were being ripped apart. The floor came rushing up to meet his approach, and Langdon was lost in blackness.

Langdon fought the nausea and pushed back the darkness. With immense force of will he put the pain away, locking it tightly in a small compartment of his mind. This was no time to fall apart. He needed to know what had happened, and to find that out he had to remain professional, impartial, to examine the evidence of the room.

But first he approached the body on the bed. It lay flat on its back, legs twisted like a pretzel, ensuring that there would be no violation of the virgin from Texas. Her naked breasts were an angry red that would soon turn to the yellow and purple of bruises. There had been a struggle.

Her red hair billowed out behind her, dark and bright at the same time against the white sheets. A bit of dried blood dotted her chin from a cut lip and there was clotted blood in her nose. there was skin underneath her short nails. She had marked whoever had done this to her. The telephone cord was twisted around her neck, wrapped tight. Pepper lay with her eyes open, staring, burning a hole in Langdon's soul as she accuse him of the great wrong he had done here. It was his fault that this student from away had been murdered in what appeared also to have been an attempted rape, in a seedy motel room. Fall for what? Langdon pulled the sheet up to cover her body, and closed her eyes. He rested his hand on her forehead for a brief moment.

And then he made himself banish any thoughts of her as a living person. For the moment he had to see her as nothing more than a puzzle to be solved. He searched around the room. Everything was fairly orderly, showing no signs of the crime that had been committed here. There were papers scattered on the floor, papers Langdon picked up one by one, sliding them back into Pepper's briefcase. The table lamp lay broken on the floor. And a damp towel lay just inside the door. But that was all.

The body was still warm and there was a faint smell of pipe smoke—and Langdon suddenly realized that the murderers most probably had arrived while he had been distracting Lord from watching the room, a space of no more than twenty minutes.

But all Langdon could do right now was try to figure out what had happened, find out who had done this thing. He had always had a knack for looking at a room and being able to reconstruct what had happened there. In this particular instance he was helped by the tape recorder he found beneath a towel in the bathroom.

It was still recording. Purring gently like a cat happy to see him home.

Langdon hit the rewind button and glanced around the bathroom. The shower had been used, explaining the fact that Pepper's hair was damp against the pillow. There were various perfume bottles, eye liner and other make-up accessories scattered around the sink.

The tape clicked as it reached the beginning, and Langdon reached out and hit play. Whoever had done this had made a huge mistake in overlooking this tape recorder—but who would have expected a tape recorder to be plugged in behind the trash can underneath a towel?

Pepper's voice suddenly filled the room.

"Abbigail Austin-Peters, please? This is..."

Langdon hit the fast forward button, the recorder whirring in the stifling silence of the room, then pressed 'play' again.

"What I don't understand is how there hasn't been some sort of..."

Fast forward. Pepper had recorded her phone calls as Langdon had asked her to, and while the content was of great interest to him, it wasn't what he was looking for right now. Langdon had to stop - play - fast forward several more times before he got towards the end of the tape, Pepper's voice once again filled the room.

"What we have so far is one, Abigail Austin-Peters has agreed to meet with me privately tomorrow at noon in an off the record interview. Two, the press secretary for the governor said that he was out of town for a week but I could set up an appointment for early next week. And three—" Her voice broke off at the faint and unmistakable sound of a knock at the door.

*Su*ddenly it was as if Langdon were back in time, *watch*ing *the events issuing forth from the tape recorder, able to see everything but unable to participate, to help in any way.*

After Langdon was done vomiting in the toilet, he looked up and saw that the screen to the bathroom window was gone. The window was open, letting the cold December night air into the room.

He had been mere minutes from either saving Pepper's life or being killed himself, either way you cared to look at it. He leaned his back against the bathtub and bent his head down between his legs, trying to breathe slowly. He made himself review what he'd heard. On the tape there two men who'd called each other Elwood and Stanley. They were responsible for the attempted rape. They'd been sent to scare Pepper. But Shakespeare had done the killing.

Langdon's cellular phone suddenly rang.

Langdon stared at it as it continued to ring, finally making himself push the talk button. He rose and walked into the bedroom.

It was Lord, sounding anxious. "The police are out front with the night manager. They're coming your way. I don't know what's going on there, but you better get out!"

There was a sharp knock at Langdon's door. "Police. Can we come in for a moment."

Langdon grabbed Pepper's briefcase and the tape from the recorder, scooped Coffee Dog into his arms and was headed towards the bathroom when the door opened. Langdon didn't stop to look back as the night manager and two policeman watched him flee into the bathroom. Langdon promptly threw Coffee out the open window and dove out after.

Nobody made any attempt to follow him. It wasn't often that a Brunswick police officer arrived at the scene of a murder to find the suspect escaping out the bathroom window carrying a dog. Langdon would guess that he probably looked pretty guilty. He didn't know why he ran. But run he did.

Chapter sixteen

"I know this is difficult for you, Chabal," Gary Stout spoke quietly. "But we do need to bring Langdon in, if for nothing else than to help him."

"Looked to me like some kinky sex game gone awry," Patrolman Max sputtered. "Her all naked on the bed..."

Chabal stared blankly at the two men, still in shock. "How did she die?" She said. As if in a dream Chabal noted that another customer had come into the store and was browsing in the far corner.

"She was strangled with a telephone cord." Max answered.

"She was...naked?"

"At this time we can't be certain," Gary Stout broke in gently, "but it doesn't appear that she was sexually violated in any way."

"What was the manner of her relationship with Langdon?" Max asked in a sharp tone.

"Manner? of their relationship?" Chabal was confused and upset, tears beginning to form in the corners of her eyes.

"Ya know," Max said with a broad grin. "Were they doing the nasty?"

"Pepper was doing some research for Langdon on a case." Up to this point Chabal had been ready to be helpful, but this was just too much. If they wanted any more out of her they were going to have to arrest her.

"What case?"

"Langdon didn't discuss his cases with me."

"So you can't tell us anything about what they were doing in a motel on Pleasant Street?"

"No."

Max smirked.

"We need to have you come in some time and give an official statement," Gary, the good cop, said quietly.

"How about tomorrow evening at 6?" Chabal said. Gary nodded his assent just as the phone rang.

Chabal let the phone ring twice more until the two cops were safely out of the store. She croaked a greeting she was sure was incomprehensible into the receiver.

"Chabal, is that you?" It was a fairly drunk Jimmy 4 by Four.

"Pepper's dead," was all she could say.

Between the alcohol, the background noise of the highway and the static of his cellular phone, 4 by Four didn't think he had heard what he had heard. "Say that again."

"Pepper is dead."

"Shit."

Over the suddenly quiet line Chabal could hear the steady, rhythmic slap of the car wheels against the pavement.

"What happened?"

"She was strangled with a phone line out in the motel."

"Where was Langdon?"

"According to the police he was standing over her body when they arrived." Chabal leaned heavily against the counter. "Langdon is the prime suspect for the murder."

"Murder? She was killed?" 4 by Four was having a hard time taking all this in.

"Langdon is also wanted for questioning in the murder of Chief LeFebvre."

"Guyton? Murdered? What the hell has been going on in Brunswick while we've been out of town?"

"Where are you?" Chabal suddenly realized that she probably shouldn't be saying anything important over the phone. And the lady in the back of the store seemed to be working her way to the front.

Even in his drunken state, 4 by Four also grasped that it was time to get off the phone. The conversation was too sensitive for inquiring ears. "We're coming through Augusta on our way back to the 'safe' house."

"The 'safe' house has been moved," She said. "When you get off the highway in Topsham, call this number." She gave him the Fort Andross number. "I'll meet you there."

Jimmy's head was still spinning with this new information but he managed to say, "On the brighter side of things we're bringing back a witness."

"What?"

"Jonathan Starling. One of the original law partners of Harper Truman." 4 by Four failed to mention that the man was currently passed out on the back seat, and failed to mention also that this had happened just before they'd left the restaurant. They hadn't known what to do with the man—roll him into a gutter and just leave him? So they'd decided to put him in the car and bring him along for the ride. This was possibly kidnapping, but Jimmy felt as though he'd left the law far behind him.

"Forty-five minutes," he said.

"We'll see you soon."

Chabal hung up the phone to see the lady that had been browsing in the back now standing at the counter. She held the book 'Handling Sin' by Michael Malone in her hands, one of those odd exceptions to the mystery category that Langdon insisted on having in stock.

"Hello, Chabal."

The voice was familiar, but Chabal couldn't place it.

"It's Amanda," the woman said.

Langdon's ex-wife. But the woman who stood in front of Chabal was not the Amanda she remembered. In place of the shy, awkward, young girl from the South stood a cool, poised lady of the world. A beautiful silk scarf was wrapped over her head and tied below her chin—pastel colors, light purples and greens all held together by a silver clasp, a handcrafted dolphin. Amanda had neglected to remove the designer sun glasses, even though it had been dark for several hours now, giving her a cool, mysterious look. And her hair had changed from a sandy blonde to jet black, cut short with bangs falling over her face.

"Chabal, are you still with me?" Amanda asked with a friendly smile teasing the corners of her eyes.

"I've just had some bad news, that's all," Chabal replied with a shake of her head to clear the cobwebs. How have you been?"

"Things are starting to fall into place for me," Amanda said. "My painting is starting to take off, actually I'm having a show down in Boston. "I thought, heck, Brunswick is only two-and-a-half hours away, why don't I pop up and see my daughter. Do you know where she is?"

"Missouri?"

"Do I have another daughter?"

"She's..." Chabal was at a total loss over what and how much to tell Amanda, "She's with Richam and Jewell and their kids."

"I called their house but there was no answer. Do you know where Goff is?"

"Nooo, not really..." Chabal was surprised by Amanda's poise. The old Amanda would have been throwing a hissy fit by now, as she'd done in the past whenever she hadn't gotten her way. She was spoiled old Southern money, used to having things work out for her and if they didn't her daddy would take care of it.

"What's going on, Chabal?" Amanda asked pointedly, "Where is my daughter? Where's Goff?"

"Missouri's fine." Chabal made her mind up then and there to fill Amanda in on everything. After all, she was the mother and ex-wife. She deserved to know. Chabal sighed. "Langdon on the other hand is in a real bucket of trouble."

* * *

Both Chabal and Amanda were on their second glass of wine at The Wretched Lobster, sitting side by side on the plush couch in the lounge, having the place to themselves on this midweek night. Chabal was probably the closest thing to a friend Amanda had in Brunswick, but they'd always maintained a reserved coolness—perhaps because Chabal worked for Langdon, or perhaps because she was in love with him, or perhaps because Amanda had been incapable of friendship, so caught up was she in how much she'd hated Brunswick.

"So Langdon is wanted in connection with the murders of Chief LeFebvre and of this Bowdoin College student?"

"Right." A few tears still streaked Chabal's face, but the wine was helping, stiffening her back.

"And this is all connected to the suicide/murder of Harold Dumphy? Wasn't he married to that tramp?"

"Janice," Chabal said. "She's the one who hired Langdon in the first place, to investigate her husband's death."

"Where does she fit in to all this?"

"I'm not sure she does. But technically speaking Langdon is still her client."

"And you think think the governor is involved?"

Chabal nodded. "Yes."

"And who is this Shakespeare fellow?"

"He's a very gentle man," Shakespeare himself—sitting down on the armchair facing the two ladies, "A very nice fellow indeed."

Chabal gasped and her hand fluttered instinctively to her neck, where the point of this man's knife had pricked her skin that very morning. "What do you want?" she hissed.

Shakespeare's banana-shaped head seemed to glow a faint yellow in the gloom of the lounge. "I came to meet your lady friend, Chabal. Would you do me the pleasure of an introduction?"

"My name is Amanda." Amanda had not so much as changed expression in the presence of the new arrival.

"Mrs. Langdon herself? What an honor you bestow upon us. I thought I might have to go looking for you, but now here you are." Shakespeare spoke quietly, biting each word off as if he were having a very hard time controlling his temper. "Do you know where your husband is by any chance?"

"He's not my husband any longer, Mr..."

"Shakespeare. William Shakespeare."

"Do you mind if I call you Bill?" she said, smiling sweetly. "Or Willy?"

Chabal laughed a low mocking laugh.

"You can call me whatever you like, Mrs. Langdon." Shakespeare was still struggling with his temper. "Have the police spoken to you yet by any chance?"

Amanda's smile grew sweeter. "As a matter of fact my good friend Jackson Brooks of the state police is supposed to be meeting us here any minute for a drink. I'm sure he'd love to meet you."

Chabal eased back in the plush couch and watched the cat and mouse being played, not sure which was the cat and which the mouse.

"I have nothing to hide from the police, Mrs. Langdon," Shakespeare said with his hands held wide and a sallow grin. "Your husband on the other hand is wanted in connection with two murders. And the possible rape of one of the victims as well." "Is that all?" Amanda spoke in a tone that was tight but controlled and at ease all at once. "If you're done here, we were having a discussion."

"I was just wondering if you had paid a visit to your daughter since your arrival in town." Shakespeare was not going to be brushed off so easily, even though the possible arrival of a state cop made him uneasy. Who did this woman think she was? "Bill, let me tell you something," Amanda said in a confiding whisper. She leaned forward in the couch to get closer, "My husband is a cream puff next to me. Don't mess with my daughter. Don't mess with my family. Don't mess with my friends. Understand?"

There was something about Amanda's eyes that told Shakespeare this lady meant business.

Into the uneasy silence that followed, Chabal set forth her trump card. "And you don't think Jackson Brooks of the State Police will be interested to know about the connection between a punk like you with the governor?"

Punk? "I believe you have some wrong information, Miss Chabal, for I don't have the pleasure of knowing the 'Governor'." Shakespeare smiled inwardly, for the his late night discussion with the governor must have been observed. "Ladies, if you will excuse me..."

"No, why don't you stay for a minute?" Amanda asked, all politeness.

"Yes, please stay, we do so want you to meet Mr. Brooks."

"Remember who's in charge here." Shakespeare said. "You both should fear for the safety of your families." Shakespeare was now shaking, small shivers of anger rippling through his body. "Good evening." And he turned to go—running smack dab into an enormous man, a 6'4", 240 pound twenty-five year old ex-football player for the Brunswick High School Varsity team and then Bowdoin College out drinking with a couple of friends.

"Is there a problem here?"

"No, no problem." Shakespeare was now quivering from head to toe in frustration.

"Ladies, is this man bothering you?" The ex-football player was looking for an excuse to pulverize the little faggot and then bask in the good graces of the two very attractive females.

"No, Bobby, he was just leaving, but thank you." Chabal recognized Bobby Goodrich as everybody in Brunswick still did. He'd been the closest thing to a football star the town had ever had.

"Excuse me." Shakespeare stepped around the ex-football player.

"I'm not done with you yet, pimple face!" Bobby Goodrich said reaching out one huge hand and grabbing Shakespeare by the shoulder.

That was enough. Shakespeare drove the flat palm of his hand halfway to the back of Bobby Goodrich's neck, and followed with two cupped hands clapping his ears. The giant slumped to the ground without another word, his ear drums popped, a slight hiss the only indication that he was desperately trying to get some oxygen.

His two friends didn't move except to get out of Shakespeare's way as he walked out, the thin man a current of red-hot energy, wanting, begging—for more—a human bolt of destruction wanting to unleash and wreck everything in sight. Shakespeare paused at the door and looked back—and Amanda saw a hardness in his unguarded eyes that for the first time made her truly scared.

* * *

"Do you have a gun?" the shaken Amanda asked the equally shaken Chabal. Nobody in the bar had even noticed the altercation that had just taken place. Bobby Goodrich's being pummeled in less than one second could easily have been both Amanda and Chabal being murdered—and not a soul would have noticed.

"No."

Bobby's two drinking friends had half-carried him from the lounge, not realizing yet that their next stop would be the hospital.

"I do," Amanda said.

"I think I need one. Richam could probably get one for me."

"Speaking of Richam," Amanda said, rising, "maybe it's time for me to go see my daughter?"

Chabal rose with her on shaky legs. "You said you had to call your husband," Amanda reminded her suddenly. Chabal realized that it was about 7:30 at night, and her husband had expected her at 6:00. Chabal called her husband from the payphone near the front of the bar. He was unhappy with her, but she didn't have time at the moment for his feelings of neglect. "I'm going to stay with Richam and Jewell and help out with he kids tonight."

Her husband ventured a guess that hit closer to the truth than he knew. "Does this have anything to do with Langdon?"

"You mean am I sleeping with him?" Chabal shot back.

Amanda, standing next to Chabal, grinned at this exchange.

"Yes," he said.

"As a matter of fact," she said, "I'm standing here with his wife."

She wasn't exactly calming his anger. "You call to tell me you're not coming home and the only explanation you're going to give is your not sleeping with Langdon, which may or may not be true?"

"Right." Chabal really didn't have the time or patience for her husband's emotions, and she idly wondered if this meant the end of their marriage. Her husband was nice but her life with him lacked passion, and she'd been treading water for long enough. The adrenalin coursing through her veins terrified her—but at the same time she felt vibrantly alive for the first time in years.

Her husband hung up the phone, but she didn't care. Without another thought for him Chabal called the number at Fort Andross.

"Yes?" Jewell answered.

"Chabal. Let me in in about five minutes."

Chabal and Amanda left The Wretched Lobster, peering out the door before stepping onto the freezing sidewalk to make sure Shakespeare wasn't lurking in the shadows.

"We'd better take a roundabout route to make sure we're not followed," Amanda said, holding her purse tightly in one hand while the other hand grasped the gun that lay within, one finger curled around the trigger. Langdon had given her the pistol and told her a trick if she ever needed to use it: don't bother pulling it out but merely tilt the purse and pull the trigger. Much quicker, more efficient and more of a surprise.

"Follow me," Chabal said, taking the lead and heading immediately across Maine Street and into the video store. They took just one second to look out the plate glass doors to see if anybody was crossing the street in pursuit, and then hurried on through the store and to the parking lot out back. This is where Chabal parked her VW. In seconds the car was zooming away into the night.

"Other than this whole mess," Amanda began cautiously, "how has Goff been?"

"You mean since you left him?" Chabal wasn't one to mince words.

"Yes."

Chabal was once again surprised that Amanda hadn't tried to weasel out of responsibility for having left Langdon. She seemed to possess a calm assurance that hadn't been there before. "Not real good."

"Has he been drinking?"

"Like a college student."

"I think marriage and parenthood made both of us feel trapped in many ways." Amanda was reflective, trying to put her thumb on something elusive. "Not because we were, but because we looked at our friends out carousing, going away on trips. There are a lot of good things about being a parent, but it's a lot of hard work and freedom is one of the traits you have to check at the door."

"I can vouch for that," Chabal said quietly, thinking of her three children and her husband fuming at home, of the perfect life they'd carved out for themselves and the feeling of being a caged animal that went along with it.

Tonight was the first night Chabal had been out away from her family in years.

And suddenly Chabal realized that what Amanda had done, packing up and leaving without any prior notice, was what she herself was on the verge of doing. For what?

"I got a chance to think over a lot of things while I was gone," Amanda said.

"Like what?" Chabal now felt as if she were a disciple in the presence of a master, learning some great lesson.

"Marriage is sort of like a career."

"In what way?"

"95% of people go through life hating work, disliking their job, unhappy with the thing they spend seventy-five percent of their waking hours doing." Amanda was speaking slowly, picking her words with great care as she went. "Often as not working more hours than necessary so as to be able to buy a new fishing rod to be used on their one day off a week, or to save up for that one big week in Mexico they treat themselves to each year."

She's just described my husband, Chabal mused, with a wry smile perking the corners of her mouth.

"And then if they're single," Amanda went on, "they go home from work and go out in search of the man or woman they want to marry, who'll make their every wish come true..."

"And if they're married," Chabal continued the dialogue for Amanda, "they go home to their families and wish they were out at the bars, hanging out with their single friends who are trying to find a mate to spend the rest of their lives with and be married."

"My mother and father were never happy as homemaker and provider," Amanda stated with a sincerity realized some years earlier. "So when I found something in life I enjoyed—"

"Your painting," Chabal interrupted.

"My painting," Amanda agreed. "I decided that whether painting ever made me money or not, it was what I chose to do with my life. It's better to be happy in your work and broke for your free time than vice versa."

"And how are you relating all this to marriage?" Chabal had been following along, but had lost the gist of the conversation in the last turn.

"I always looked on my marriage with Goff as a lot of work."

"Marriage can be like work," Chabal agreed with years of knowledge.

"And I looked on being a parent as a lot of work," Amanda continued.

"That's for sure!"

"And the winters in Maine sure weren't easy."

"So—it was a lot of work to be married to Langdon, a lot of work to be a parent and a lot of work to live in Brunswick and it all got to be too much so you got out."

"Exactly," Amanda said. "But I never had a chance to stop and reflect that all of this hard work was something I enjoyed. Sure, Goff can be a pigheaded stubborn irresponsible fool. But he always treated me right and sure could make me laugh. And sure, changing diapers and fighting with a three-year-old over clothes and food and taking a bath can be darn tedious work. But we're talking one cute little girl. And sure the winters are hard here in Brunswick but that's a lot better than burning up in the summer. And the people are all so friendly..."

Chabal was silent for a long minute before replying. "So married life with a family in Maine was a life of work, but it was a life you enjoyed—and that's better than the occasional weekend of bliss with some Greek god on the beaches of Atlanta"

"Something like that."

They'd pulled into the back of the parking lot at Fort Andross. Chabal turned off the engine, and then turned to Amanda in the sudden silence of the car. "You're coming back?"

"If that pighead will have me."

Chapter seventeen

Chabal called Richam as they walked across the parking lot to let him know they'd arrived. Apparently he could see them, because the first thing she heard when the phone was answered was an obscenity on the other end. "I'm not sure she was on the invitation list for this party," Richam said.

Chabal hung up without bothering to answer. Amanda frowned across at her. "So he's not too happy to see me."

"He'll get over it." Chabal led the way, her legs skimming over the pavement, Amanda having to hustle to keep up, even with the advantage of longer legs.

"Tell me something, Chabal, and don't lie to me," she said. "Do all Langdon's friends hate me for what I did?"

"Hate you?" Chabal wouldn't look at Amanda, keeping safely a half a step ahead.

"The way I left him. Took Missouri. Left a note on the kitchen table." Amanda stared at the ground as she spoke. She hadn't made a single friend in her time in Maine. She'd known Goff's friends, had had them over and gone out with on occasion, but they'd never been her friends. When she'd left they'd found no reason to be sympathetic.

"You could have been gone weeks before he told me and I wouldn't have known, would I?" Chabal said. But she realized as she spoke that Amanda had never really been given a chance. She'd been treated as an outsider from the day Langdon had brought her home like some prize he'd won at the fair, a trophy to be shown off for a while and then put away.

Chabal stopped just behind the little shack in the parking lot that had been vacant for years, but still had the sign proclaiming fresh lobster and steamers for sale. Chabal remembered coming here on dates with her husband before they were married, picking up baskets of fried clams and onion rings and cokes and parking the car down by the river, eating, then making out energetically with all the wonder of new discoveries.

"People in Brunswick are plenty ready to be polite," Amanda said, hugging her arms for a moment in a defensive posture she quickly checked. "But when it comes to opening up to a stranger, especially some blonde from down South brought home from college, a stranger who likes to eat crawdads, has never shoveled snow and talks with an accent..."

"And wears a skimpy two piece bikini on an absolutely gorgeous body," Chabal continued for her with a rueful grin, "Okay, okay, so maybe you were different and maybe I was a little jealous as were some of the other women. And maybe we did look on you as more of a passing fad than somebody here to stay."

"I'm not here to cry on anybody's shoulder," Amanda said with conviction, "I just want to lay the cards on the table. Initially, I did come up here to Brunswick with a bit of a chip on my shoulder." She made herself smile, trying lighten the mood. "I mean, the culture consisted of going to Hog Heaven for dinner and then the movies, which, by the way, usually consisted of sequels to teenage flicks like the Mighty Ducks 2."

Chabal touched her arm gently for a moment and spoke softly. "Well, girl, I'm sorry I never gave you a chance." She grinned mischievously. "You come on back and I'll invite you over to the next tupperware party I have."

Amanda wasn't sure whether Chabal was kidding or not. "Thanks," she said in a dry whisper, just a little sarcastic but not too much, because maybe she would appreciate going to a tupperware party.

"We'd better get going," Chabal said with a friendly smile, "Or Richam is going to get worried and call the cops."

Richam was smoking a cigar, a thin, two dollar variety, sitting out on the steps partially shielded by the railing. He was enjoying the fresh air and happy to be away from the chaos and the suffocating feeling of being stuck inside with his wife, three kids, two drunks (Bart and 4 by Four), and a wino (Starling). "Halt, who goes there," he called jokingly as Chabal and Amanda approached. "What's the password?"

"I am Arthur, King of the Brits, and am traveling with a band of brave knights in quest of the holy grail!" Chabal replied.

"None shall pass!" Richam returned in similar jest.

Amanda smiled uncomfortably, not sure whether she should join in. "Hi Richam," she said. "How have you been?"

"Amanda." Richam nodded, his eyes piercing the night in search of something in her face, his lips compressed. "Your daughter will be happy to see you. She's talked about little else but her mommy all day."

"It doesn't seem like it's exactly been a sterling weekend with dad," Amanda said dryly.

"I'm not sure why Langdon brought her up to the middle of this mess," Richam replied with candor.

"Try going without your children for a few days, then imagine a few months and you'd probably know," Amanda said, defending Goff's actions.

Richam was surprised at this. Being a bartender he was used to the ex complaining about one thing or another and doing little else.

The hallway to the elevator was poorly lit. One dim bulb, hidden by a dusty glass cover, swayed in the rush of cold air from the open door, casting eerie shadows across the floor. At the end of the hallway were double cast iron doors, which Richam swung open on creaky hinges. These were the doors to the service elevator, the type utilized in warehouses before modern technology brought electronic doors. Richam slid up the gate that housed the elevator and they all stepped in, the silence of the huge building deafening. Amanda grabbed the gate and pulled it back down once they were all safely inside, clanging the metal and sending vibrations echoing throughout.

Richam operated their ascent with a lever—up fiver floors to the top of the building.

They emerged in a hallway that led between locked storage spaces, holding the possessions and secrets of various citizens. Chabal idly wondered what each of these dark boxes held that was so important to keep but not important enough to have.

Richam turned right at the end of the hallway and opened a set of huge double doors with a key—and Chabal suddenly felt as if she were Jack approaching the lair of the giant.

"MOMMY!" Missouri shrieked in a voice that could be used to cut diamonds, "Mommy, mommy, mommy." The tiny figure came racing across the wide expanse of floor, leaving a kickball game behind, a game that seemed to be pitting Bart, Jewell and Missouri against 4 by Four, Will and Tangerine with some stranger as the designated pitcher. "Mommy, do you like my new home," Chabal asked with excitement.

Quite a home it was. A huge, wide open expanse the size of a football field with ceilings that ran twenty feet high. A baseball diamond was laid out in the center, a diamond currently being used for the kickball game but usually used by the owner for whiffle ball games with his friends, a practice they especially enjoyed when really stoned. A basketball hoop and backboard adorned one massive pillar, in front of a basketball court painted in wild art deco colors. Gigantic canvas paintings hung from all the walls, wild colors strewn haphazardly, following a minute pattern only a trained eye could perceive. To Chabal they looked amazingly like her children's' works hanging from the refrigerator at home.

"I would love to live here with you," Amanda said, surprising even herself by not correcting her daughter and telling her that this was just a temporary arrangement.

"Do you want to play ball-kick?"

"Sure, honey, just give me a minute," Amanda said with a shortness of breath as she tried to keep up with the craziness.

The stranger who was pitching took the momentary break to lie down. Jewell talked to Will and Tangerine, choosing for the moment to ignore Amanda. And Bart glared over the distance between them. Only 4 by Four followed Missouri over, giving Amanda an exuberant kiss on the cheek that was just a tad too friendly. He was quite drunk. "Amanda, honey, great to see you. Chabal, don't let me leave you out." 4 by Four swept Chabal into a huge embrace and locked onto her cheek with his lips.

Richam pried him off Chabal with the practiced grace of a bartender and the disgust of a friend. "Jimmy, maybe you better stick to weed because this alcohol thing is just not you."

"Richam!" 4 by Four shrieked, "I almost got in a bar fight today, well I did, actually, technically speaking, but then Bart grabbed the guy and knocked him out, but I was playing pool..."

"If you tell me this story one more time I'm going to have Bart knock YOU out," Richam muttered, walking away.

4 by Four's expansiveness was undaunted. "Chabal, come meet Jonathan Starling. Former partner of one Harper Truman. And now a key witness for the case against the governor!"

"What case against the governor?" she said, wary of 4 by Four's state.

His tone was that of a genius making a bold pronouncement. "I think Harper Truman has been siphoning money from DownEast Power, money supposedly allotted for regular maintenance."

"Hold on just a minute," Richam interjected, "The only connection we have between the governor and anything is that Shakespeare was supposedly seen on his doorstep late at night!"

But Chabal was intrigued by Jimmy's fraud theory. "What does Bart think?" she said. The kickball players had all wandered over—all except for Jonathan Starling, that is, who had remained in a prone position on the pitcher's mound, probably waiting for play to resume the following day.

Bart shrugged. "I'm not so sure that Harper Truman is in this for the money. You know 4 by Four's thinking has always been a little obsessive where money's concerned."

"What else could it be other than money?" 4 by Four demanded belligerently.

"Power." Bart said with hushed voice. "Truman is stealing uranium or maybe nuclear waste to use as some kind of terrorist tool."

"That was Pepper's initial theory," Chabal commented tightly. They were all silent for a moment. The memory was painful for all of them.

4 by Four, not about to have his thunder stolen by Bart, finally broke in. "Power? If that's not the pot calling the kettle black. So I'm too concerned about money—but here we have Mr. Power himself. How do I get power? I think I'll be a policeman. You disagree with me? I think I'll beat you up. The one consuming passion of your life, Bart, is power. But that doesn't mean this is what drives everybody else. No, he's definitely in it for the money."

"You didn't mind me taking care of that punk who was about to rearrange your face earlier today?" Bart bellowed at his friend. "Maybe I should have let him do his thing instead of giving into my passion for 'power' and beating the crap out of him!"

"Would you children stop your bickering," Chabal spoke sharply as if to her own kids. "The problem I have with the governor is the fact that he was part of Flower First. And I really believe he has a genuine concern for the environment. I mean, sure, maybe he's been corrupted—but it's a little extreme to go from a tree hugger to spreading radioactive waste or causing a meltdown at DownEast Power..."

"It's sort of like tree spiking." They all froze in their heated discussion, surprised at the new voice. Jonathan Starling was speaking from his prone position.

"What do you mean?" 4 by Four demanded.

"You spike one tree, it doesn't actually hurt the tree." Starling said, propping himself up on an elbow. "Maybe somebody comes along and bangs their chainsaw off it and cuts their face off. But what's one casualty in a war to save millions of acres of forest?"

"Its still murder," Bart interjected.

"How does this relate to DownEast Power?" Chabal said.

"Perhaps a potentially disastrous situation occurs at DownEast Power. The theft of nuclear waste, a close call with a meltdown, a total breach of security, whatever the case—something happens of epic proportions. What do you think the public reaction will be?"

"People would be scared." Chabal said.

Richam nodded. "Five Mile Island all over again."

Starling lay back down and addressed the ceiling. "If the people were scared enough, it wouldn't take much to shut the entire plant down. I mean the cost would be exorbitant, but what politician could possibly go against the wishes of a bunch of terrified constituents?"

Bart finished his thought, suddenly seeing the whole plot unfolding in front of him. "It would be an easy step for the Governor to shut the plant down. Maybe there would be an investigation and some safety breaches would be discovered, maybe the plant really is a liability—whatever the case, it'd be a huge victory for Flower First. Hell, it would probably shut down other plants around the country if the scare were big enough." Even the drunk 4 by Four saw the truth in this theory. "If Harper Truman handled the situation properly, it could give him the national exposure to make a run for president in two years!"

"It's sort of like playing with fire, though, isn't it?" Amanda said in a small voice.

"Boooom!" Jonathan Starling yelled, then broke into a cackling laugh that gave them all a chill. "Either way, there's no more DownEast Power. Ha, ha, ha, ha." He stumbled to his feet and went off in search of his bottle.

Chabal wandered over to where Jewell was getting something to drink from a refrigerator in the portion of the room that passed as the kitchen. Against a huge column were placed the fridge, a range, a microwave and a bar set. There was also a counter with a wash basin, suggesting that while electricity was a viable option in the warehouse space, water was a little harder to come by.

"Things okay here?" Chabal asked gently.

"I look on it as an education for my children," Jewell said. There was a real anger behind her dry tone. "They get to play games with a wino, a drunk police officer and a drunk lawyer all at once. Not to mention that now we have a shirker in our midst!"

"Shirker?"

"You don't leave a four-year-old marriage behind with only a note to guide the way. And you don't take a three-year-old child from a daddy that loves her without at least letting them say goodbye."

"She had some issues to resolve..." Chabal defended Amanda's actions, though not five hours ago she herself would have been condemning them. Chabal realized she was also defending herself and some of the thoughts she'd had recently on leaving her own life and starting a new one.

"Issues? Marriage is a responsibility you enter into, knowing there are going to be some difficult situations. And doubly so for parenthood." Jewell shook her head, looking suddenly very tired. "But I don't want to talk about little miss muffet any more. Tell me what's new in the world of crime fiction."

Chabal shrugged, deciding that now wasn't the time or place to argue Amanda's cause. "I was thinking that after the kids go to bed we could get together and fill each other in on where we stand and what we know." Chabal had always been good at organization and practicalities.

Jewell glanced at the small bistro-style table where Tangerine sat with her head resting precariously close to the half-finished popsicle slowly melting into a pool of deep purple. Will was busy picking at his foot where a scab from some injury was in danger of being peeled away, his face pinched with responsibilities and concerns that shouldn't weigh on the mind of one so young. "I'd say they'll be off to bed soon."

As if reading his wife's mind, Richam ambled over, happy to leave behind 4 by Four and Bart's bickering. "Time to put these two monsters down?" he asked, mussing Will's hair with one hand while delicately removing the remnants of the popsicle from the vicinity of Tangerine's hair with the other. "What about Missouri?"

Missouri and Amanda were sitting by the windows that overlooked the town of Brunswick. They sat in an outdoor swing seat, rocking gently as they appreciated the lights, the view, and the intimacy in the midst of all the chaos. Missouri sat in her mother's lap, resting her head gently on Amanda's shoulder while she held on to her waist as if she were grasping everything she was missing.

"Is daddy going to be okay?"

"He'll be fine," Amanda reassured her.

"What does 'murder' mean?"

"Where did you hear that word?" Amanda bought herself time as she struggled with the appropriate reply.

"I heard 4 by Four tell Richam that the police want daddy for murdering somebody. But I don't know what that means. And Uncle Bart is a policeman, so does that mean he wants daddy for something?"

"Your daddy didn't 'murder' anybody, honey."

Missouri frowned bor a moment before asking. "Is murder when you hurt somebody?"

"Yes," Amanda said, keeping her voice steady. "But your daddy didn't hurt anybody, not even a little."

"I know." Missouri picked her head off Amanda's shoulder and implored with eyes that were wide and innocent. "But shouldn't somebody tell the policemen that? Then he can come back and see me."

"Tomorrow, honey," Amanda said. "We'll do that tomorrow."

Now that Missouri had been sufficiently reassured, her mind skipped ahead like a colt in a field. "I brought 'Goodnight Moon' with me, Jewell said I could and I did. I'll got get it and you can read it to me." And the excited little girl raced off across the room.

Bart was about fed up with 4 by Four, who'd been claiming all day that he'd been about to tear the kid in the bar apart when Bart had intervened. The truth was that 4 by Four had been standing there with his neck stuck out and eyes pressed tightly together, probably about to cry. And they hadn't brought Jonathan Starling back because he had any real use against Harper Truman, as Jimmy was claiming. He'd simply been passed out in the street and they hadn't known what to do with him. When Bart's beeper went off, he took the opportunity to break off his ongoing argument with 4 by Four. Bart had several messages to return. He checked the numbers, the first belonging to the station.

They wanted him to come in because of his known connection with Langdon. In their starched request Bart sensed the hand of an outside force, possibly even the FBI. He told them he'd be in to the station in an hour.

The third number was Langdon's—indirectly, of course. Danny T. answered the phone with a slight quaver to his voice. "Who is this?" Bart demanded.

"Aren't I supposed to ask you that," Danny T. muttered into the phone, terrified of the role he was suddenly playing in a high-stakes game.

"Danny T.? Is that you? How did you get my pager number?" Bart demanded, even though he had a fairly good idea. Danny T. didn't answer. Bart stomped his foot impatiently. "Just put Langdon on the damn phone, Danny T., and quit your whimpering."

It was a dark night. Langdon had borrowed a parka from Danny T., a parka that had once been red but had dulled to a dark brownish color guaranteed not to draw attention. It was hard to be inconspicuous in a town where you knew most of the people by their first names, including the police.

Pepper was dead, and it was Langdon's fault. He found himself unable to think of anything else. She was dead and her death could have been prevented in more than fifty ways, each and every way filtering its way through his brain time and again at a rate of about seventy-nine a minute.

He spoke more to keep himself sane than anything else. "Coffee Dog, what do you say we try to work this out? Make some sense of this whole mess?"

Coffee looked up at Langdon with his wise brown eyes in full agreement, and then continued trotting along at Langdon's side with his nose low to the ground—discovering a whole world of events that had transpired on that very sidewalk, events that came and went but lived on through the smells they left behind, smells as telling to a dog as memory was to a person.

Twenty-five minutes later, Langdon found himself in Fort Andross, presenting his thoughts to his friends. They sat around him on the floor, far enough from the sleeping children that they couldn't be heard. Amanda had watched as Langdon had gently kissed Missouri's forehead—but Langdon had hesitated to say hello to Amanda, and she'd seemed standoffish as well.

Langdon was now standing at an easel that had been dug out from a dusty corner, and making his presentation as if to a war council. He had formed the words he would use on the walk over the help of the Coffee Dog.

"(A)," he began. "We have the murder of an employee at a nuclear power plant.

"(B) We have a cover up which it turns out was ordered by the Chief of Police.

"(C) We have a man named Shakespeare, who has some connection with Governor Harper Truman, trying to scare us off of the case.

"(D) We have a very nervous Public Relations director, one Abigail Austin-Peters.

"(E) We find out the Chief of Police is being blackmailed and at about the same time he commits suicide,

"(F) I find a partially burned blackmail note threatening the Chief with exposure of some illicit affair with some mystery woman.

"And (G)." He cleared his throat for a moment, then made himself go on. "Pepper is tracked down and killed after having spent the day making phone calls."

"Do you have the blackmail note with you?" Bart was curious, though nervous about the note's content. He'd worked for several years with the Chief, and even though they hadn't always seen eye to eye, had a great respect for the man.

Langdon fished in his pocket and carefully took out the crumbling paper. Bart spent several minutes inspecting it before handing it to an eager 4 by Four.

"The letter claims they had photographs. Too bad you didn't salvage any of those," Bart noted with a look of deep concentration.

"Hold on." Langdon reached in his pockets, digging this way and that, finally managing to pull out the crumbling, partially burnt picture. "Unfortunately it's a little worse for the wear. But does anybody recognize this woman?"

The picture was passed from hand to hand to everyone but Jonathan Starling, who appeared to have passed out on the floor.

"I think it was a set up." Langdon had reached this conclusion on his walk and talk with the Coffee Dog, "I've done work like this before, taking pictures of illicit affairs for spouses needing proof. And I'll tell you, getting pictures is not easy. People involved in affairs don't go check into a motel and leave the curtains wide open, or have wild sex in the hot tub out on some deck like the movies would have you believe. Pictures aren't easy to get—"

"Unless one of the participants in the sex was willing to be photographed." Amanda spoke up for the first time, having meant to remain aloof but forgetting in her absorption in the matter at hand to stay quiet.

"Exactly," Langdon said with a grimness to his tone that could have been a result of his wondering who exactly Amanda had been having sex with since their separation—though he knew this wasn't fair on his part.

"It looks as if he were having the affair with a married woman," Chabal said as she read through the note. "The blackmail note refers to the woman as Mrs."

"The real question seems to be," Richam said, having quickly scanned the note, "why would these pictures be of interest to the police into a recent murder investigation'?"

"It has to be the Dumphy murder," Jewell decided. "It's not like we have numerous murder investigations going on."

"The woman must be Janice Dumphy." Chabal put into words what had crossed all of their minds but hadn't yet been spoken.

"Why is that?" Bart demanded to know.

"It would be 'of great interest' to the police if it was her, don't you think?" Chabal stuck grimly to her guns, not letting Bart bully her.

"The widow has slept with every other man in town, why not the Chief?" Amanda jumped in to Chabal's aid. Bart merely shook his head in exasperation.

"I'm going to go out on a limb here and say what everybody should have noticed," Langdon spoke in a slight lull in the fighting. "The woman in this picture is not—doesn't have-" Langdon stuttered, embarrassed in front of the assembled crowd.

"Hooters!" 4 by Four yelled triumphantly as the realization came to him, obviously having no reservations about body parts and dimensions. "The girl in the picture doesn't have the hooters Janice Dumphy has!"

Chabal looked like she wanted to scorn this remark—but the truth of it hit them all. It was obvious that Janice Dumphy wasn't the woman in the picture.

"Okay, okay," Langdon said jumping into the conversation. "The only suspect we have as the 'mystery' woman is Janice Dumphy, and we need to keep her in mind. But it's certainly not a foregone conclusion."

"What else do you have to go on?" Richam said with bitter sarcasm. He hadn't wanted anything to do with this case from the beginning.

"Give him a chance, Richam, would you?" Chabal hissed, tired of his complaining.

Jewell swung around with a vengeance, about to utter a retort. She was the only one in the room who had the right to criticize Richam.

But before she could enter the fray, Jimmy broke in, backing Chabal up against Richam. "Maybe you better back off tough guy!" 4 by Four was still stinging from his earlier conflict with Bart, and was till drunk and looking for a fight.

"MAYBE you better lay off the booze!" Jewell retorted, on her feet.

"SIT DOWN!" It had been a long day and Langdon just wasn't up for this eternal bickering of his friends—who he knew didn't mean a word of what they were spitting back and forth at each other, or they wouldn't be here in the first place.

Like a group of children chastised for disrupting the classroom, everybody settled back down into their seats on the floor. Langdon paused for a moment to make sure the room was in control before continuing. "Pepper recorded all her phone calls from today. Now I'm not going to play the entire recording over, but I'll sum up for you what I heard. Pepper talked to a number of people, mainly information gathering or trying to get through to others. The people she talked to with some relevance to the case as far as I can tell are.

"(1) the press secretary for the governor,

"(2) the press secretary for the actual Flower First Party, a different person than the first,

"(3) and Abigail Austin-Peters.

If anybody wants to listen to the tapes for anything I missed, please feel free to. There's about two hours of it and I've only had a chance to play it through once."

Langdon had played through the tapes at Danny T.'s house. They were mostly long, winding attempts at working through channels to get to the right person—busy lines, being put on hold, transferred, given new numbers. All the while Pepper delivered a monologue bitching about this person and that, about the government, red tape, bureaucracy and the whole nine yards.

There was nothing much useful there, but that Pepper had had a date with Abigail Austin-Peters for tomorrow at noon.

"4 by Four, do you think you can talk on the phone with a minimum of slurring," Langdon half-joked to ease the tension of the room. "I think you need to contact Ms. Peters as the legal counsel for the estate and investigation of Pepper's death."

"Gladly, I'll call right now," 4 by Four was eager for an excuse to go visit the ice queen of DownEast Power. "And I think that I will be able to speak plenty clear enough, thank you very much."

"Bart, when do you go back to work?"

"I was supposed to be at the station about an hour ago," Bart said with a start. "Anybody got a toothbrush I can borrow?"

Jewell wrinkled her nose. "Here, have a piece of gum," Richam said. "And try not to shoot anybody until you can at least see straight."

Bart took the gum with a light smile playing at the corners of his mouth. "Richam, one of these days I'm going head butt you so hard you'll need stitches from the crack of your ass to the crack in your nose!"

Langdon was exhausted and exasperated from the day, and from having to return and baby-sit a room of juvenile delinquents. He spoke in a loud, impatient tone to halt this exchange between Bart and Richam. "Bart—be careful. And don't jeopardize your job in any way."

Bart looked with beet-red eyes at Langdon's face in wonder. Bart's hair was askew, his clothes reeked of cigar smoke, his half-open mouth sent waves of alcohol tumbling across the gap between them. His shirt was half tucked-in, his pants were twisted around to the side with some sort of ketchup/mustard/relish stain all the way down. But Bart snorted at Langdon's admonition. He took the gum, pooped it into his mouth, went to the sink, rinsed his face, pulled a small black comb from his rear pocket and ran it through his hair, undid his pants, tucked in his shirt, and left without another word. Langdon realized he didn't need to worry about Bart. Bart knew how to take care of himself.

Langdon ran to catch up to him as he waited by the elevator. He wanted to impart one more piece of information about the case—though not in front of the others, because he feared it might prove to be yet another wild goose chase.

"I had an interesting conversation with Danny T.," Langdon began, ignoring Bart's snort of disgust at the mention of Danny T.'s name. "He found out for me that Johnson T. Halpberg, who is the CEO of Casco Bay Power, also happens to be an old school friend of Ellsworth T. Limington III."

Bart grunted in recognition. "The guy that's been slowly buying up the entire town of Woolington."

"Ellsworth is known to his friends as L.," Langdon said. "Which is how the blackmail note to the Chief was signed."

"Shit," Bart said, leaning back against the wall.

"Yeah. Shit." Langdon frowned, choosing his words carefully before continuing. "I think you need to go out of the department on this one." It went against political correctness to take a local issue outside of the department. But Bart merely nodded his head, aware of the implications. "I have a friend with the state police, Jackson Brooks, who's a good man," Langdon said. "I need you to get in touch with him and tell him everything. Don't hold anything back. The governor, Ellsworth, everything."

Bart nodded grimly and left with a look of deep concentration on his face.

When Langdon returned to the vast room, he found his friends still assembled and waiting. "I know the governor's wife fairly well," Chabal said right as he entered. "I could try to hunt her up for a lunch date tomorrow and see if I can pump her for information."

"If the governor is really involved in all of this, I'm sure they're well aware of your connection with me," Langdon reminded Chabal. "And Mrs. Truman isn't going to come within a hundred miles of you."

"You're assuming there's some sort of communication between the two of them," Chabal retorted, smiling with her superior knowledge. "As far as I can tell, the two of them haven't had a conversation in years."

"She's a fine looking woman," 4 by Four said with a sly look, "It's always nice to hear of a dissatisfied married woman living nearby."

Jewell smiled. She knew that the lawyer was trying to get her goat now—and with that one single sexist comment the entire group seemed to jell back together again. The one thing they all had in common was an ability to appreciate humor, no matter how twisted, perverted, or just plain sick.

"Richam, you working tomorrow?" Langdon said.

"I'm supposed to work the noon to six shift. But I was thinking I'd call in sick."

"No. Go to work. If there's any gossip to be heard, bartending at The Wretched Lobster is where you'll hear it," Langdon replied. "Now, what's the scoop on Lord?"

"They picked him up at the motel when Pepper was killed." Jewell said. "When the police showed up he came running down to see what the hell was going on, and they put him in custody just under general principles. And when he tried to say he was just passing by, the manager happened to point out that he had an upstairs room. And before you know it the police were in the room and discovering a rifle with a scope pointed at Pepper's room. And then somebody recognized him as your brother—and off to jail he went." Jewell had gotten this information over the phone from the motel manager's wife.

"What are they charging him with then?"

"Nothing," Richam said, looking pointedly at 4 by Four. "He should be out by morning with a good lawyer."

"If you have another drink, I'm going to beat you mercilessly Jimmy," Langdon said. Jimmy was the best lawyer he knew when sober. "I don't want my brother in jail a second longer than he needs to be."

But 4 by Four had fallen fast asleep in the past minute, passed out in the bean bag chair in which he sat. A thin line of saliva hung from his lip, and one hand was tucked into his pants with a faint smile clinging to his features.

Langdon sighed. "Any word on Nicky?" Not a word. But Nicky was out there doing his thing, and Langdon was sure that when they heard from him it would be with a bang.

Chapter eighteen

Bart had gone to the station, Chabal had gone home to her family, and Jonathan Starling was passed out. Jimmy 4 by Four was snoring in his bean chair. Jewell and Richam hastily said goodnight and retired to their corner. Langdon and Amanda were alone. Needless to say, it was a fairly awkward situation.

"So, did you come to pick up Missouri?" he said finally.

"Maybe," she said, curling her legs up beneath her in the chair.

"I guess you've got the gist of what's going on here?"

"Sort of."

Amanda's chair looked like a bad mushroom trip, as though it belonged at a beach for burnt out hippies. The lounge chair's fabric had been painted over in wild, haphazard colors. Langdon was reminded of an image from a Curious George book. George, working as a window washer, had happened to notice some painters going on break and had climbed into the apartment and painted a scene on the wall, of trees, vines, bushes and wild animals, complete with a little monkey. The image was too silly—and before Langdon knew what he was doing, a giggle had escaped him. Amanda looked at him crossly.

In an attempt to refrain from another inappropriate giggle, Langdon pressed his lips firmly together—but all that did was cause a squeak.

"What's your problem?" Amanda demanded hotly.

"I'm sorry, but—" And Langdon burst out laughing hilariously, huge convulsive gulps of pure hysteria wracking his body. "You remind me...of...Curious George," Langdon managed to leak out.

"Curious George?"

And then suddenly Langdon's body froze, and his laughter turned to tears of anguish. Men weren't supposed to cry, certainly not in Amanda's family. But he cried like a baby. The emotion of the past few days, discovering the chief's suicide and Pepper's dead body all came out. Langdon wasn't the hard boiled detective he strove to be. The death of a friend was too much for him.

Amanda left her lounge chair, and Langdon thought she was leaving in disgust—never having ever been one of those females who needed a sensitive man around. But she returned in a moment with a bottle of Jack Daniels and two glasses. She poured Langdon's glass full and then took just two fingers for herself before recapping the bottle.

"I'm not drinking." Langdon said, even though he desperately wanted the Jack.

"Drink." She handed Langdon a tissue, and then on second thought the whole pack she carried in her purse. "Even whiskey has its time and place," she said with a smile. "Just like anything else. It's only the abuse of alcohol that makes it bad."

Langdon tipped the glass up and took a shuddering gulp of the burning liquid. Another grin was teasing the corners of Amanda's mouth, a mouth Langdon loved for its full, pouty lips set delicately in the middle of narrow craggy cheekbones, like a fresh water basin in the depths of the canyon they'd hiked down together once in Arizona. It was strange how this image came to him all of a sudden—Amanda and he coming down a narrow trail between cliffs pressing them on either side, and then the narrow canyon suddenly opening into the small clearing, a small waterfall spattering down to a crystal clear pool surrounded by the only natural vegetation they'd seen in all of Arizona. They'd taken a siesta there, one of the most amazingly memorable afternoons they'd ever had, bubbling happiness. Langdon saw this in Amanda's face and it made his knees weak and his throat dry. "Too much of anything will suffocate you." Amanda continued. "Too little will tease you."

Langdon had always been a person who was all or nothing. He didn't eat a lot of meals, but when he did eat he consumed all he could. The only way he could exercise was to be obsessive about it; the occasional workout was not his style. he wasn't the sort of person who could go to work and put his eight hours in and leave it at the office; he tussled with improvements and problem solving around the clock. When he drank, Langdon didn't have one drink, but rather consumed to get drunk. Perhaps he could even be overbearing in a relationship.

Langdon tried a small nip of the Jack in the glass, taking just a snort to get the taste, and found it to be as satisfying as a gulp.

"Do you want to talk about it?" Amanda asked quietly, the smile gone from her mouth.

"There's a lot I want to talk about." Langdon said. He wasn't ready to talk about their relationship yet, not now when he was so tired—but she seemed to read this.

"Let's start with this girl...Pepper? Is that her name?" She spoke tentatively as if stepping barefoot across a gravel driveway.

"Peppermint Patti Smith," Langdon said with a ghost of a smile, thinking of the shy girl who had first approached him in the Bowdoin library just several days earlier.

"Were you...romantically involved with her?"

"No, not physically..." Langdon said as if in a trance. And he told his wife about Pepper, everything without any reservation—who she was and what she was to him. As Langdon talked he took random nips of Jack, and slowly the world righted itself and he knew that he could continue and that for the living, life went on.

* * *

Langdon woke several hours later with his head in Amanda's lap. She was sound asleep on the futon next to him, sitting slumped with her hand lying gently on his cheek. Her fingers were long and slender, those of a piano player.

Langdon's silent enjoyment of her sleeping caress was interrupted by a gentle sobbing in the overpowering silence of the cavernous space of the warehouse building. Cautiously he slipped from Amanda's touch and rose to his feet, unsteady and unbalanced from his crooked sleep. But his mind was clear with no cobwebs.

Langdon hurried over to where his daughter lay crying on a blanket on the floor next to Will and Tangerine. Fearful of waking the other two children, Langdon lifted Missouri, sleeping bag and all, from the floor and carried her over to the window. He sat down cradling her carefully but firmly to his chest, patting her back as she cried into his shoulder. "What's wrong, honey?"

"What does 'dead' mean, daddy?" she said.

Langdon knew this was going to be one of those life forming conversations, and hoped he was up to the task. It was as if the coach had suddenly thrust him into the game with four seconds left, his team down by five points—and now all of a sudden the quarterback had had the nerve to throw him the ball! But this was much more than a mere game.

"Dead is when somebody is gone for good," Langdon replied in direct fashion. He had always been of the belief that children were far more mature than most people gave them credit for.

"Is Pepper gone for good?" Missouri asked in a small voice, the tears gone for the moment as she gave her father the deep searching look only children can give, forcing candor.

"Yes, in some ways."

"I don't think I want to die."

"You don't have to worry about that for a long time, honey." Langdon hoped with all the power of his being that this was true.

"Where has she gone to?" Missouri squeaked.

"Different people think different things. Some people think that when you die you go to heaven which is where god is and everything is better, and some people think that when you die you disappear forever."

"I think I want to go to heaven. Do you want to go to heaven, daddy?"

"The way I see it," he said, struggling to find the right words for his thoughts, "is that there is no actual place called heaven, but that what people think of as heaven is the world all around us. I think that when a person dies they live on through everybody and everything they have touched. And whether their spirit is in a happy resting place depends on whether they've positively touched the surrounding circle of their lives." Langdon realized this was helping him as well, trying to put into words what he believed and did not believe. "Let's use

Pepper as an example, honey. I only knew her for a few days but in that time she made me smile, made me laugh, made me proud of myself. Although I'm very sad about what happened, I have a lot of good memories that make me smile. And through those good memories, Pepper's spirit lives on."

"What is spirit?" Missouri was intent and focused, not going to let Langdon off the hook easily.

"Spirit, to me, is who you are. It's what allows you to think and feel and to have emotions, happy, angry, sad..."

"Can I have a snack?" This question threw Langdon for a loop. "Can I?"

Langdon realized that the conversation was over for now. She was, after all, three years old.

He made them both peanut butter and jelly sandwiches and got them each a glass of milk, and they sat down to this feast at 3 A.M. in the silent warehouse building in Brunswick, Maine.

"I was having a bad dream, daddy." Missouri muttered through a mouthful of peanut butter.

"Monsters are scared of daddys, did you know that?" Langdon said.

"No," she shook her head earnestly. "These monsters eat daddys." So much for Langdon's ego. "But Gasoline saved me," she continued.

Langdon honestly had no insight into the creative, fertile place that was his daughter's mind. Missouri filled him in as she finished her sandwich, chattering on as he carried her back to her sleeping bag and tucked her in. Gasoline, it seemed, was the name of the winged dragon that protected her in her sleep. Langdon crouched next to her until her voice trailed off and her breathing slowed, and she'd fallen asleep again.

* * *

Langdon had never needed much sleep. Here it was, four in the morning, and he was wide awake. The bathroom had a shower, really just a modified bathtub—but even with the clinging curtain, the shower felt great, washing away the grit of real and imagined dirt he'd acquired over the past day. Langdon found shaving utensils, and there was a radio next to the sink which he turned on hoping to catch the news. It was an old fashioned shaving kit, a brush and a tub of stuff that looked like cool whip, a substance that proved somehow much more satisfying than the normal rubbing on of can-dispensed foam with his fingers.

The radio droned in the background.

Police are still searching for the man seen at the scene of the murder in a Brunswick motel of the woman now identified as Patricia Smith, a college student at Bowdoin. Patricia Smith is the daughter of Senator Harding Smith from Texas. Senator Smith could not be reached for comment but a spokesman for the Senator said that he was devastated and wanted a full scale investigation into the events surrounding her death.

Pepper was the daughter of a senator? Langdon struggled to process this fact as he foraged the closets for clothes. He found some that were tasteful, if rather short and tight. A short sleeve Polo shirt made his arms look huge, his back stretching the material tight over his entire frame. There were a pair of Brooks Brothers pants that were okay in the waist, but stopped a full four inches above his ankles. Even so, they smelled better than his clothes from the past day.

Langdon found the coffee. He was one of those people who couldn't find his way around most kitchens with a map, but never failed once in locating the coffee beans, grinder, pot and mugs. For the next few hours Langdon drank cup after cup coffee, writing down what he knew about the case.

The key to the whole puzzle seemed to be whatever the connection was between the governor and DownEast Power. The only evidence they had that there was any sort of connection at all was Shakespeares late night visit to the governor's house.

A voice suddenly startled him out of his musings. "You writing your memoirs?" Jonathan Starling had finally stirred from his position on the pitching rubber and shambled over. He plunked himself down, setting his nearly empty bottle of Jack Daniels down with a whack on the table.

"Just trying to figure out a problem that it seems you might be able to help me with," Langdon said.

"Okay with you if I have some coffee?" Starling surprised Langdon with the request, reaching for the pot which sat on a hot pad next to him. With shaking hands Jonathan Starling poured a half a cup, sloshing some on the table. But then, destroying Langdon's surprise, the alcoholic Starling tipped the bottle of JD and filled the remainder of the cub.

"And how can I help you?"

"It seems that an ex-law partner of yours might be mixed up in some sort of cover up at DownEast Power. And possibly involved in the death of several people." Langdon had laid all his cards on the table. He sat back to see what his opponent had to offer.

"She was always prone to being a little violent," Jonathan Starling said.

"She?"

"Jordan Fitzpatrick. That's who we're talking about, isn't it?"

"Jordan Fitzpatrick is a she?" Langdon had forgotten that there had been a third partner in the firm. And never once early on in the investigation had he considered the possibility that Jordan was a woman.

"That I know for a fact," Starling said with a leer that spoke of intimate knowledge of this fact. But she could be as mean and tough as any man. And the way she could put back Wild Turkey was a sight to see."

A thought tickled the edge of Langdon's mind but he couldn't grasp it. "So," he finally said, "Jordan Fitzpatrick is a she. And she was always prone to being a little violent?"

"Took most of the skin right off my back one time," Starling cackled with delight in the memory. "Ripped the shirt right off me she did, first time we met it was, some sort of fund-raiser for the spotted loon or some garbage like that."

"I wasn't talking about her bedroom antics..." Langdon began to interrupt. But Starling would have none of it.

"Sex was the perfect example of her tendency to violence. Not only did she like it a little bit rough, she used sex to get what she wanted and then moved on. She sucked the very life out of me." Starling swished down the remainder of his coffee and Jack, and poured himself another. "And to tell you the truth, if I had it to do all over again I wouldn't change a thing. There was something about that woman. No, I don't know if I would change a thing..."

the reality of this man, old before his time, broken, drunk, and willing to accept this fate if given a second chance for the experience of Jordan Fitzpatrick was gritty and not all that glamorous. Langdon tried to move the conversation on. "What did she want from you?"

Jonathan Starling looked surprised. "Power. Legitimacy. She needed a foot soldier for her army. She had fantastic recruiting skills."

"Her army?"

"I'm speaking figuratively of course. But I do think Jordan wanted to conquer the world."

"Wanted to?"

"Wants to, I suppose, if she's still out there. Maine was much too small for that woman." He took another stir of his drink before continuing. "Flower First and then Terror were organizations that had aspirations on a national scope. And I'm fairly certain that Harper Truman isn't being groomed just to be the reigning Governor."

"So it's all about power?" Langdon asked the old drunk, hanging on his words, as if her were Moses come down from the mountain with the ten commandments.

"Don't get me wrong. Harper Truman, even in the very depths of his corrupted soul, would do anything for the environment. Power for his is only a means to achieving more green reforms. Both Harper Truman and Jordan Fitzpatrick would do anything to preserve mother nature just as she is. That's the scary part. They will do ANYTHING."

Langdon desperately wanted a slug off the JD, a shot in his coffee—but he was restrained by the image of Amanda saying there was a time and place for everything. Somehow he didn't think that included whiskey for breakfast. "Were Jordan Fitzpatrick and Harper Truman romantically involved."

"Jordan Fitzpatrick slept with anybody and everybody." Starling said. "Sex was a weapon used to gain her power. But I don't think there was ever any romance involved."

"The three of you had a law practice together?"

"Harper Truman and me were room-mates at Maine law school down in Portland, room-mates and best friends. We both had the same ideals. We were going to save the environment from civilization. And what better battleground to face creeping civilization than right here in Maine, where there's something still left to be saved. And where the enemy is right there to be seen in the form of the paper companies.

When we graduated we moved up to Madison because there we could stare the paper companies right in the eye and force them to blink, but at the same time be close enough to Augusta to go lobby against the destruction of the Maine woods and the Maine way of life.

Langdon could see the energy and passion that was once Jonathan Starling, but remained quiet, not wanting to interrupt the monologue. From the raspiness of his voice, Langdon was betting it was the most the man had spoken in quite some time.

"So Harper and I moved to Madison and rented a small house together, right downtown, and in the front of the house we made our office and hung out our sign and we went to work. We worked all day and night. We took on any case opposing the paper companies. We fought and struggled and starved and loved life. We weren't in it for the money. We weren't in it for the power. We had a cause and that was enough."

The cold December sun had now risen in Brunswick and the light came flooding through the windows of Fort Andross, illuminating Jonathan Starling's face, stripping away the wrinkles and the mucus in his eyes, glinting off his brown, cracked teeth and Langdon almost cried as he imagined the man that had been. Jonathan Starling had set out to stop the paper companies, some of the richest and most powereful people in the world, with nothing but his strength of will and a law book.

"We had just won an important battle," Starling continued, "I don't remember exactly what it was, we blocked a vote that would have opened up even more land for clear cutting. So we decided to go out and celebrate. We went out to hear some environmental group give a lecture, but the banquet that followed was really why we went. Me and Harper were really tying one on—and then there were three of us, drinking, laughing, high fiving each other over our victory. Somehow Jordan Fitzpatrick became part of our victory. She was just there. Celebrating with us. We had never seen the woman before, but she fit in with us as if she'd always been there. I already told you how I ended up in an empty conference room with her, madly ripping clothes off. What I didn't tell you is that months later I discovered that Harper Truman had had the exact same experience. She seduced both of us that night and we both fell in love. And from there it was only a matter of weeks before she was an acting partner in our small law practice. And Jordan Fitzpatrick now stood between us and things were never the same again."

"Woman will do that to best friends," Langdon commented dryly.

"We both vied for her attention, almost coming to blows on several occasions. For a while I thought I was the victor. I'll telly you I the best sex of my life. I was willing to keep our relationship secret for awhile so as to not rub Harper's nose in it. But then one night when Jordan was away on business me and Harper had it out. We'd both been drinking and got to arguing. And we discovered both of us had been sleeping with the woman!"

"So how is it that Harper Truman ended up governor of our state and you ended up a broken drunk in Madison?" Langdon sincerely wanted to know this, and realized that Jonathan Starling had no illusions and no pride. Calling him a drunk wasn't an insult but merely the truth, and Starling well knew this.

"I can only guess at what decisions Harper Truman made, but I can tell you exactly what happened to me."

"Let's start with your...decline," Langdon said carefully, knowing that he was on the verge of unravelling the entire puzzle.

"There was no official policy change, no change in the mission statement of the law firm. But at some point I realized we'd become more aggressive in furthering our objective of saving the environment. Instead of using the law to protect the forests and streams, we began to bend the law. Skirting the edges of what was legal and what was not. This happened so gradually, I wasn't even aware of it at the time. It wasn't until much later that I realized I was no longer proud of what I was doing or who I was."

"That happens to everybody in this life, at one time or another," Langdon broke in gently, trying to give just a little comfort to this man who had obviously been torturing himself for so long over this. "We start out thinking we're going to change the world, that we're going to make a difference, the dreams of children and the innocence of babies—and then at some point we realize that we're just pawns in the larger game of life, and it's hard enough just to make ends meet. And then before we know it we're middle-aged and jaded."

"I think I'm a little past the jaded stage," Starling said dryly with a faint sparkle in the recesses of his dark, unforgiving eyes. "There's more to the story." He spoke with the patience of one who had waited years to unload his story and now had a willing audience. "Our law office became the meeting place for radical hippies. One by one they crept up on us until one day I realized there were a total of seven extra people sleeping in our house. The house reeked of marijuana and at any given time of the day I could find two of the hippies having sex in my bed. Sometimes more than two. They were into free speech, free love, freedom from government interference and against corporations. I didn't know it at the time, but they were Jordan Fitzpatrick's strike force. I came home at the end of one long day to find them in the middle of a meeting. Jordan was presiding. The objective was to block a particular stretch of woods from being cut, a stretch of woods that I do have to admit was one of the most beautiful areas I've ever seen in my entire life." Starling suddenly buried his head in his hands for a moment and then looked up. "I've thought about what happened that night every waking hour since. It was a Friday night. They were going to start cutting Monday morning. And I'd used every legal means I could think of to block it, but nothing worked." He took a deep breath. "And then Jordan said something about, what if the skidders didn't work. And someone else suggesting putting sand in the gas tanks. I fought them for hours. I said we couldn't defeat the beast by becoming the beast. Pain gripping Starling's words even now, ten years later, "We finally called an impasse sometime in the early morning hours. They hadn't been able to budge me. I'd even gone so far as to threaten to turn them all in. And then Jordan Fitzpatrick came to my bed for the last time and gave me a slice of heaven. When I woke in the morning the planning was already in the active stage. And I realized I'd cast my vote of consent the night before." Starling looked at Langdon with the pain of memory and whispered, "And to this day I'm sure I'd do the same thing again. I was no match for Jordan and I'm still not."

"What happened?"

"They vandalized the skidders—but that was only a temporary delay. The paper companies brought in new skidders with security guards and dogs. So, we spiked the trees."

"What happened then?"

"A man I knew from Madison was in the woods with his chainsaw and found the first spike. His chainsaw kicked back and imbedded itself in his forehead."

"Dead?"

"Dead."

"And then you fell apart?"

"I started drinking, and Jordan discarded me." He pushed his empty cup across the table, away from him. "The day the man from Madison stuck the chainsaw in his head was the day I became what you see in front of you now. Nothing."

Chapter nineteen

The warehouse, now fully lit with bright December sunshine, was silent for just a moment. "You can always start again, Jonathan." Langdon said with feeling.

"I don't need your pity, Langdon, I just need you to be truthful with me."

Langdon considered for a moment what Starling was asking—realizing that some part of Starling did want to move on. "You're not likely to be some hotshot lawyer again. But we can probably come up with some menial job for you down here. It would be a start."

"Like what?"

"If nothing else you could work in the bookstore for me," Langdon said on the spur of the moment. He meant it.

Starling shook his head. "Where would I live?"

Langdon smiled. "If this whole mess gets cleared up and I don't go to jail, then there will be an unoccupied house in town we could rent for you. Front you the money off of future wages to get you started."

"Empty house?"

Langdon's smile broadened. "Mr. Harper Truman should be going off for an extended vacation. We could see about getting his house for you to live in." For this, Langdon was rewarded with a large smile from Jonathan Starling.

The smile slowly faded. "You didn't tell me why you needed all this information on Harper and Jordan. But I guess I knew they were up to no good.

A sudden pounding at the door interrupted their conversation. Richam appeared at Langdon's side in an instant. "Langdon, get out the back window onto the fire escape."

It seemed to Langdon that he'd been spending much to much of his time on fire escapes lately, but he supposed that couldn't be helped. Langdon nearly stepped on 4 by Four as the lawyer crawled out from the table he'd been sleeping under. "What is that infernal banging noise?" 4 by Four muttered, bleary-eyed.

"Open the damn door!" Bart's muffled voice boomed through the door's heavy metal, stopping Langdon in his tracks on the edge of the windowsill.

"Better keep going." 4 by Four shouted at Langdon. "The police are here!" And then 4 by Four giggled—suddenly stopping with a strange green look to his face. He rushed off to the bathroom. 4 by Four wasn't much of a drinker these days.

Chabal was with Bart at the door. The war conference convened. Tangerine and Will came running over yelling hello to the both of them. Langdon looked around for Missouri and found her curled up with Amanda, both of them fast asleep. Neither of the girls in Langdon's life were morning people, and they'd be able to sleep through a nuclear explosion if it happened in the A.M. hours.

Chabal was carrying donuts, muffins and coffee. Bart carried a beer. The man was just amazing.

Jewell took a coffee from Chabal and settled heavily into a chair at the table. Her hair was all crazy in the morning and her eyes full of bleariness.

Bart sat down across from her for his breakfast of beer and donuts. He took a look around the room. "What a sorry ass sight you all are," he said, before proceeding to stuff donuts into his face. He took a swig of beer.

"Unlike the poster child for health and happiness you are," Jewell retorted crossly.

Amanda came wandering over and went about searching for a tea bag—until Chabal handed her the tea she'd gotten specifically for her from Dunkin Donuts. It wasn't often that somebody remembered a tea drinker when getting coffee. A surprised but gratefully Amanda accepted the cup. "Thank you, Chabal."

When 4 by Four emerged from the bathroom, the first thing he saw was Bart shoveling donuts into his face and noisily slurping beer. This sent him stumbling back to the porcelain god for round two.

"Bart, what news do we have of my brother?" Langdon had been patient but couldn't wait any longer. Lord was in jail because of him.

"You mean Lord?"

"Yes." Langdon wasn't in the mood for playing Bart's game of cat and mouse. Bart's eyes twinkled with the look of a man who held all the cards.

"Cranky bunch this morning," he said, disappointed that he wasn't going to be able to take his time parcelling out his information. He sighed. "They had Lord up all night for questioning, but it doesn't look like they're going to charge him with anything yet. They don't have a whole lot on him. Other than that he was in a motel room facing the murder scene with a high-powered rifle."

Jewell smiled. "Yeah, not much."

"They don't think he murdered Pepper, do they?" Chabal wanted to know.

"No, they're pretty sure it was Goff. As a result, they're keeping their options open so they can try to hook Lord up with an accomplice to murder charge. But they're not quite ready to do that yet."

Jewell was concerned. "We need to turn over that tape to the police to clear Langdon's name and let the police get after the right people."

Langdon shook his head. "Let's not tip our hand yet, or the real bad guys will run for the hills and we'll be left with just the patsies like Shakespeare."

"Okay. Let's not get away from the subject," Richam interjected with the facilitator skills of a practiced bartender. "Are they going to let Lord go or does he need to be bailed out?"

"They were in the process of filling out the appropriate paper work to get him out of there on his own," Bart said. "Brunswick P.D. will not be pressing any charges at this time is the official word."

"Do you have to be back at work, or are you done for awhile?" Langdon desperately hoped that Bart had some time off to help them.

"Funny you should ask," Bart smiled. "The new acting Chief, Commander Bickford, suggested that I should take some paid vacation time until this whole thing blows over. It seems he knows of my friendship with the main suspect."

Langdon was all innocence. "I don't see how that would affect your sworn duty."

"Well, he thought I might pass along privileged information to the suspect." Bart shook his head in mock consternation.

"No! They didn't suggest that!" Langdon was grinning.

"And furthermore, Commander Bickford seemed to think that I might have a problem arresting my friend Goff Langdon if I happened to come in contact with him."

"The gall of some people!" Langdon snorted in mock disgust. "If they want me to vouch for the fact that you would never be compromised—well then, I'll come down and give a statement to that effect."

"Would you guys stop being men for just a minute and get back to the problem at hand," Jewell snapped. Her patience was apparently at a low ebb this morning.

"Okay, okay," Langdon said with a grin. He knew that everything would be okay one way or another, as long as he retained this group of friends. "Game plan! We need to talk to Abigail Austin-Peters and see how she fits into this mess. Anybody want the honors—seeing as Don Quixote is in the bathroom throwing up his internal organs..."

4 by Four of course took this moment to return from the bathroom, wiping his hand across his mouth. "I get Ms. Austin-Peters all to myself," he said.

"Just try not to bark on her," Chabal said with a mischievous glint in her eyes. "Some girls might take offense at that."

"Make fun all you want," he retorted. "But I will obtain the key information that will bust this case wide open. And then we'll see who has the last laugh." 4 by Four was regaining some of his trademark flair.

"Greasy onions," Bart said.

"What?" 4 by Four was confused.

"Greasy onions mixed with floor lint." Richam chimed in.

"Greasy onions with floor lint and squirming leaches," Jewell added.

"Imagine you were at a restaurant and they served you that as the main course by mistake," Langdon spoke up, giving in to the cruelties that made them friends. "And you took a bite before you realized it."

4 by Four once again stumbled off to the bathroom. It was good to be friends.

"So, it looks like Romeo will work the DownEast Power angle." Langdon said with a suppressed smile, "Any takers on paying the governor a visit?"

"I got that one," Bart said with satisfaction.

A suspended cop hanging around the governor's mansion would bring too much attention. "I have a better idea for you," Langdon said. "Why don't you go pay a call on the Widow Dumphy?" Langdon had always had a suspicion that Bart might have a thing for the widow.

"Sure." For the first time in his life, Bart agreed to something without argument. Langdon smiled. He must really like the widow.

"Why don't I go poke around the Blaine House and see what I can find?" Amanda suggested with interest.

"They would probably connect you to me," Langdon said weakly, not wanting her involved in any of this, not after Pepper.

"I'm the perfect person," she said. "Nobody knows me. I only lived here for a few years so I'm not liable to run into somebody from high school like Chabal would. And what's more, I've been out of town..."

What could Langdon do? She was right. Langdon shook his head. He was convinced that Truman himself wouldn't do anything violent. He hoped that Nicky was hot on the trail of Shakespeare and his henchmen.

* * *

Jimmy 4 by Four made a phone call, and found himself connected fairly easily to Abigail Austin-Peters. Probably too easily, as if she'd been waiting for him to call. She agreed to a lunch date at The Wretched Lobster. Even a queasy 4 by Four recognized the danger signals, and was on his guard. Langdon had further warned him about the Wild Turkey which in his own wretched state, Jimmy knew he could easily refuse. He was remembering why he had for the most part given up drinking. He went home to shower, shave and change, tying his hair back into a tight ponytail and spraying a fine mist of scent over his body, just enough to tease the sensation but not enough to overwhelm. He dressed in black jeans, pressed at the dry cleaners, a white shirt from Brooks Brothers, a thin leather tie and a tweed jacket that hugged his hips and squared his shoulders. He surveyed himself in the mirror. His stomach had recovered, but his face was still a pasty white—nothing that wouldn't be repaired by a little food and maybe, just maybe, a drink if he could stomach it.

Two hours later, 4 by Four stood in front of The Admiral Perry Inn, room 17, fumbling with a key as Abigail Austin-Peters pressed herself tightly up to his back, rubbing, breathing and caressing.

* * *

Bart grabbed a twelve pack from the fridge for the road, stuffed one last donut into his mouth and headed for the door. It would be good to see Janice Dumphy again. She was obviously a woman who did what she wanted and to hell with the consequences or the public opinion. Bart had a lot of respect for that approach to life. The widow might be a woman he should get to know better. And what better opportunity than now?

Langdon walked to the door with Bart, needing to ask him some questions in private. "Did you get in touch with Jackson Brooks?"

Bart nodded. "He told me he has a friend in the FBI. This friend told him several months ago that Ellsworth Limington III was being investigated. It turns out the man was involved in some pretty shady dealings in New York City. He moved to Maine one step ahead of a jail sentence. They weren't able to prove anything at the time. But it seems that Ellsworth wasn't above hiring thugs to rough up anybody who got in his way.

"Ellsworth has a history of getting his way through violence." Langdon repeated.

Bart shrugged. "They could never prove anything against him. But they did convict a man for beating up one of Ellsworth's competitors. And though the man never admitted any connection to Ellsworth, the Feds were pretty sure there was one.

"What happened to the man they convicted?"

Bart looked Langdon straight in the face. "The man's name was Lawrence William Shakespeare."

The hallway was silent as Bart moved past the storage spaces. Bart locked himself behind the metal bars of the elevator with a finality that was like jail. Although he wore a badge, he was committing a crime in not arresting his friend. He'd become a police officer because there had always been a straight line drawn in his mind between right and wrong. But that line seemed at the very best hazy in this case. Sometimes a stand had to be taken between what was legally right and what one's own morals demanded.

But onto more immediate concerns—home for a quick shower, a shave, a quick change into civilian clothes...

Janice Dumphy answered the door immediately as if she'd been waiting for just this intrusion into her life.

"Hello, ma'am. My name is Detective Jeriamiah Bartholomew. I'm with the Brunswick Police Department. I was wondering if I could ask you a few questions in regards to the death of your husband." Bart flashed his badge at her. He was shaved, showered and flushed with excitement as if he were picking up his prom date. His hair was combed neatly, still wet and freezing slightly in the chill air. He wore his black overcoat over his tweed jacket and dress pants, to look every part the detective he was not.

"Yes. Please come in." The widow was dressed in a pink halter top that must have made it difficult for her to breathe, with a man's white shirt unbuttoned over it. Her pants were a shiny material, vinyl or something similar—Bart wasn't quite sure what, and didn't rally care.

"I understand you've retained Goff Langdon to do some investigative work into the nature of your husband's death?" Bart asked this as he settled his frame into the doll-like house, resting his bulk in a delicate arm chair.

"I did initially. But I had to fire him because he couldn't be trusted," Janice said with large eyes that were ringed with a faint green. "Isn't it awful what he's done now?"

"We're not sure Mr. Langdon is guilty of the two recent murders in town. One of the reasons I'm here is to find out anything you might know about his connection to them. But more importantly—we're going to reopen your husband's case. It seemed to be the starting point for more murders than Brunswick has seen in fifty years' time."

"Would you like something to drink, Mr..."

"Bart, call me Bart, Ma'am. And yes, I would love something to drink." Bart could barely speak with his eyes having so much trouble staying on Janice's face and away from her inviting body.

"I was going to have a glass of wine for myself, but I have juice, coffee, water..."

Bart looked at his watch. Eleven in the morning. "A glass of wine would be just fine with me."

Janice Dumphy cast a surprised look at Bart and murmured, "Of course." A tinge of excitement sent a pink flush to the back of her neck, a color not unnoticed by Bart.

Half-way through the second bottle of wine, Bart finally managed to glean some information. "I don't know if this is important or not," Janice said as she leaned forward in the chair she'd already pulled to within a foot of Bart. As she leaned forward, Bart was rewarded with a generous view down the front of her halter top. His shyness at showing his full appreciation for the woman in front of him had disappeared when he'd realized that Janice Dumphy like to be looked at and admired. With her lips no more than four inches from Bart's, her eyes glassy from the morning's wine, Janice Dumphy continued. "Harold did say something to me a couple of days before he died, something I forgot. By the time I remembered, Langdon was already under suspicion—and there was nobody left to tell."

"What is it?" Bart murmured, not sure if he'd replied or not, so caught up was he in getting a full view down the halter top.

"He said something about them vandalizing the reactor," Janice put her arms lightly on Bart's shoulders and pulled his head forward and down towards her bosom as if to whisper in his ear. "He said he thought the inspectors were actually vandalizing the fuel rods."

Bart's head snapped up. "Vandalizing the reactor? Christ! The inspectors are in on it?"

"He was tipped off by Clayton Jones, Harper Truman's stooge at DownEast Power."

"And you forgot to tell Langdon this?" Bart was incredulous.

Janice swayed the last inch forward and kissed Bart lightly on the lips. She then put her forefinger lightly against his lips and said, "Hush. That's all I know."

Bart shook his head lightly to remove her feel from his lips—but not so much that he couldn't get it back. "Let me get this exactly. Harold told you the reactor was being vandalized. And told you he thought the Inspectors from the Nuclear Regulatory Commission were part of it? And that he was tipped off by Harper Truman's man?"

Janice nodded her head up and down twice in agreement, her eyes wide, her lips parted just slightly. She slowly licked her lips with her tongue, gently. "Is that important?"

* * *

She was a wild woman, there was no doubt about that. 4 by Four lay back in the bed and surveyed the damage. Scratches, bruises, and an all-pervasive body ache that went right along with a feeling of deep contentment. Abby was in the bathroom, taking a shower by the sounds of it. 4 by Four stretched his arms high over his head and wriggled his back to get more comfortable—realizing suddenly that there was a strange object digging into his back. Reaching around, he pulled out the remote control to the television set. He tried to remember how it might have gotten there—but then again, anything was possible in the chaos that had just passed. It was a scant twenty-five minutes since they'd first entered the room.

Idly, he flicked on the power.

Bob Walters and Kate Conley flashed onto the screen, the channel 6 news team 4 by Four always watched, not that he watched the news all that much. They were talking about what Kate had done with her family over her recent vacation.

"And this just in on a late breaking story," Bob Walters began as Kate shuffled her papers and looked serious. "It appears DownEast Power may be closing its doors for a while at least. A series of cracks have been discovered in some of the cylinders used for containing radioactive material. In a standard, annual test, Nuclear Regulatory agents discovered a number of potentially

hazardous cracks in some of the equipment at DownEast Power. This is all the information we have at this point. We do not know exactly the extent of the damage, but we will keep you posted.

"Jimmy?"

"Huh?" 4 by Four tore his attention from the television set to view the nude body of DownEast Power's public relations director.

"Do you think you may be able to set up a meeting with Goff Langdon?" Abigail pulled on her underwear with a fluid, graceful movement.

"Did you know about this?" 4 by Four motioned to the television where Bob and Kate droned on about the potential for disaster at DownEast Power.

Ms. Austin-Peters stood mostly naked, applying a thin line of lipstick to her ample lips. "Of course I knew about this," she said with candor.

"Were you going to tell me?"

"I need to get together with Mr. Langdon, all of you involved for that matter. To see what you have for information about any possible wrongdoing." Ms. Austin-Peters spoke with an icy edge to her voice. "That's what this is all about, isn't it—your Mr. Langdon has stumbled upon some sort of cover up at DownEast Power?"

"Yes, it appears that way," 4 by Four said weakly. "But I don't know if I can track down Langdon." 4 by Four wasn't so sure he should be bringing the public relations director of DownEast Power to see his friend. But after all, how could it hurt?

"Some of the big wigs at DownEast Power have contacted me, asking whether I could find Mr. Langdon and retain him to do some investigative work for us. Actually, CBP would be footing the bill, but Mr. Langdon would be well paid. Something has gone wrong at DownEast Power and we just want to find out what. We're talking about a potential disaster that could make Chernobyl look like the circus. Help me, would you?"

"You have to remember Langdon is currently wanted by the police."

Abigail Austin-Peters turned from the mirror, pursing her lips ever so gently to let the lipstick dry. "I'm sure you could probably help me out, Jimmy, don't you think," she said. Her smile lit up her face like a bonfire on an autumn night.

* * *

Amanda had to walk the few blocks back to where she'd left her car the night before. The air was stiff with the kind of cold that hurt your face when you breathed. Amanda had a light scarf wrapped around her face, leaving her black hair uncovered, gleaming richly in the sharp air. Things were going well, as far as she was concerned. Langdon had seemed receptive to some sort of reconciliation, and the others had stopped one step short of being rude. She couldn't expect much more than that. Of course, Langdon was wanted for murder and Lord was in jail...

Her car sat where she'd left it, a Volvo station wagon she'd bought in preparation for coming back to Maine, trading in the almost-new Mustang convertible she'd been driving around for the past few months. She was glad she had the Volvo; it would prove much more efficient in the snow.

Instead of heading for the highway and going up to the Blaine house in Augusta as she'd planned, Amanda decided she might just swing by the house here in Brunswick to see if the governor's wife, Karol Truman, was in. Amanda had kept this notion to herself, her ace in the hole. She figured she was much more liable to pry something from Karol Truman than from some stuffy secretary who would claim to know nothing and would probably be telling the truth.

The Trumans lived up behind Bowdoin College in an area known as Meadowbrook, up-scale but just short of real money. Their house was a big, old but well-kept white Colonial, on about an acre of land with a three-car garage that had been added at some time. The perfect picture of contentment. Amanda decided to brazen out the situation and go ahead and just knock on the door. If the governor himself were to answer, she wasn't quite sure what she would do.

But Karol Truman answered, letting out the noise of bedlam from somewhere behind her that bespoke four children between the ages of two and eleven and possibly a few friends as well. "Hello Karol, how are you?"

"Amanda Langdon?" Karol Truman was cool, surprised to see her but reserved, her interest reined back in check. This was after all, the wife of a murder suspect, and she was the wife of the governor.

"Can I come in?" Amanda had no real plan of action other than to feel the situation out, definitely a page straight out of Goff's handbook for living life.

Karol Truman swung the door open hesitantly, but was too polite to refuse.

Amanda eased by the stiff figure of the first lady of the state, and into the bedlam beyond. Randi Petersen sat on the floor with one of the children, reading a board book that was probably from The Coffee Dog Bookstore. Randi was the nanny, about twenty years old, someone Amanda knew vaguely but not too well. For her part, Randi Petersen barely looked up from the book.

"Come on up to the study," Karol Truman said from behind Amanda, having closed the door and shut out the chill air. "I didn't think you were in Brunswick these days," she continued as they headed up the stairs, leaving the rowdy noise of the unseen kids below.

"I just came back to town yesterday." Amanda wasn't going to give out any more information than she had to—though she knew she'd have to open up to Karol Truman somewhat if she wanted to get anything from her.

"I'm sorry to hear about Langdon. Is that why you came back?"

"Missouri was up here with him."

Karol frowned with sympathy. "During this whole mess?"

"He called me, told me to come get her. I knew if the trouble was bad enough to be sending his daughter away again, it must be serious indeed."

Karol Truman was troubled as only a mother can be, imagining the pain of having one's children being placed in danger. "Is she okay?"

"She seems fine. But she sure is going to miss her daddy."

"Have you seen him?"

Amanda measured the question carefully, realizing this was the time to give out a little information. "Yes."

"What's going on, Amanda? I find it hard to believe that Langdon would shoot the Chief or some college student or anybody else for that matter."

"You want the truth."

Karol Truman seemed genuinely surprised at the question. "Yes. I do."

"Langdon is being framed because of a case he's working on."

"Framed?" The disbelief in Karol Truman's face was clear, though she vaguely tried to hide it. "This isn't some Hollywood movie, Amanda."

"I'll pass along a little bit of information from Langdon. He's fairly sure there's a real danger at DownEast Power and..." Amanda stopped in mid-sentence at this point, because Karol's face had frozen. "Karol?"

"DownEast Power?" Karol Truman managed to ask.

"Langdon was hired by Janice Dumphy to look into her husband's death—which she felt to be related to his job as head of security there.

"The Harold Dumphy case? But the man committed suicide!"

"That was the police verdict. But it turns out Chief LeFebvre ordered the case dropped. And Langdon discovered that someone had forced the cover-up. The Chief was being blackmailed for some illicit affair he was having." At this point, Karol Truman's face went from white to almost transparent.

"Blackmailed?" The words came as if dredged from the very bottom of the ocean.

"Langdon found some charred photos and a blackmail note to the Chief burning in he wastebasket, right after he shot himself." Amanda was going with the flow, but was not quite sure where the flow was taking them—only that there was something on Karol Truman's mind.

"He shot himself?"

"Goff said it sure looked that way."

"Because he was being blackmailed?"

"It would appear so."

"There were pictures?" Karol still spoke as if from a great depth, the words cracking and stretching to reach the surface.

"They were burnt. You can just make out the Chief in a couple of them but you don't get a good look at the woman's face, just body parts that tell more than enough." Amanda wondered if this were going anywhere. It was about time for Karol to come out with some return information.

As if Karol had looked into Amanda's mind, she now spoke. "I'm the woman in those pictures."

"You?"

Karol Truman sank visibly in the chair in which she sat, reduced to a woman confused and hurt and nothing more. "I found out Harper has been having an affair for several years now. I wanted to get even."

Amanda nodded, a slight buzzing in her head. This couldn't be real. It was as if a disease had spread throughout her entire town, touching everyone.

"I just wanted him to appreciate me. To tell me to stop. I made it obvious to him—and he ignored me! This isn't a marriage but a business," Karol was sobbing now, her face sticky with cascading tears. "I don't think he ever cared for me. For all I know he's been screwing that slut from the power plant since we've been married!"

"Who?" Amanda asked in a tiny voice. But she already knew.

"Abigail Austin-Peters." Karol Truman hissed.

"How did you make your affair 'obvious'? Amanda asked with cool reserve.

Karol Truman's voice now had an edge bordering on hysteria. "One night when I'd a few drinks I told a friend, and he suggested a way to bring the affair to my husband's attention. I'm sorry, I know this all sounds pretty cheap, but I let him take pictures of me with Guyton. That particular time—I wanted to get my husband's attention. I did things..."

"Who was your friend?" Amanda asked, not wanting to hear any of the more explicit details.

"Ellsworth. Ellsworth Limington III. One of my oldest and best friends. He sent the pictures to my husband anonymously."

"I think your husband may be involved in more than just an affair," Amanda spoke with complete calm, almost as if she were not connected to her own voice. "I think that vandalism on a grand scale is occurring at DownEast Power. I think your husband might be playing with more fire than he's capable of controlling."

"What do you want from me?"

Amanda paused to collect her thoughts for a moment. "Ellsworth didn't send the pictures to your husband. He used the pictures to blackmail Guyton into covering up Harold Dumphy's murder."

Karol merely looked at Amanda, not disputing what she'd said.

Amanda continued. "I think your husband may have the best interests of the environment at heart..."

"I have no doubt of that," Karol interrupted. "Harper would do anything to protect the environment. He hates the nuclear power plant. It's a symbol for him of everything that's wrong with technology. He'd do anything to shut it down."

"I need you to tell the authorities everything. I need you to give a statement about Ellsworth Limington. Your husband is guilty of sabotage, but that's all. If you don't help me he's going to be implicated in several murders. We have to stop this whole thing right now, before anybody else gets hurt." Amanda spoke with precision, but inside she was all keyed up. Everything had come down to this. Would Karol Truman help her find evidence that would incriminate her husband?

* * *

It was late afternoon when Abigail Austin-Peters and Jimmy 4 by Four pulled into the parking lot at Fort Andross. There was just a flake or two of snow spitting out of the darkening sky. It was cold, the temperature hovering somewhere in the zero degree Fahrenheit range and falling by the moment.

Unseen by them, another car pulled into a dark corner of the lot right behind them. Shakespeare had been tailing Abigail Austin-Peters, knowing this tremendously resourceful woman would find a way to locate Langdon.

Unknown to Shakespeare, a third car also pulled into the lot. A third party had been following him.

"Langdon is in Fort Andross?" Abigail Austin-Peters was amazed at the man's audacity. Didn't he know what he was dealing with? "Sleeping right under the nose of the police? I have to give him credit, he has balls."

They walked through the mostly empty lot along the shadows, keeping a low profile, to the door Jimmy 4 by Four opened with his key. "We'll take the elevator," he said, letting her get on first. 4 by Four slid the metal grate down, closing them in. He squeezed her hand gently, but she pulled it roughly away. She was the ice queen again.

"Who is here with him?"

In answer 4 by Four simply opened the elevator and walked off down the hallway, his footsteps echoing against the surrounding storage units. He swung open the door and waved her in with a grand sweeping gesture.

Abigail Austin-Peters stepped tentatively into the room. There were a group of people eating at a table in the center of the vast hall. Langdon sat with Amanda on one side and Missouri on the other. Tangerine was next to Missouri and then Will, with Jewell and Richam across from them. Bart was at the fridge getting a beer, while Jonathan Starling sat on the floor with his back against a pole drinking straight from a bottle. Chabal was at the sink rinsing out some dishes. But Abigail had eyes for nobody but Jonathan Starling, and he for nobody but her.

"Hello Jordan," Starling said quietly, his voice quavering slightly.

"Hello Jonathan," she replied with an easy smile gracing her face, taking none of the hardness away from her eyes. "Long time no see."

"Jordan Fitzpatrick? We've heard much about you," Langdon picked up immediately on the connection he hadn't quite been able to make before. Of course Abigail Austin-Peters was Jordan Fitzpatrick, director of the militant arm of the Flower First Party. "I do hope you've been showing Jimmy a good time?"

4 by Four found his face turning tomato red from embarrassment, shame, you name it—but he still couldn't quite grasp the reality, "This is Abigail Austin-Peters," he said in a halting voice.

"I don't know what her name is now," Starling said with rancor, swigging off the bottle. "But she used to be Jordan Fitzpatrick and my law partner before she kicked me out on my ass."

"Damn!" 4 by Four had really screwed up. He walked jerkily over to Starling and took the bottle from him, pouring a huge amount down the back of his throat.

"Ms. Fitzpatrick, what can we do for you this evening?" Langdon asked politely. There was nothing to do but go with the flow at this point.

"You couldn't let well enough alone, could you?" Jordan said with pain.

"I was hired to resolve a murder being passed off as a suicide."

"The Widow Dumphy doesn't want you on the case any longer."

"Yes she does." Bart chimed in from the fridge.

"You shouldn't have threatened me," Langdon said candidly.

"I never threatened you. I tried to avoid you, but you kept popping up in my life, trying to ruin everything I'd worked for."

"What about your man Shakespeare?"

Jordan shook her head in denial. "I don't know what you're talking about. All we wanted to do was to get the nuclear power plant shut down. And we did. It's too late now to stop it. The NRC is swarming the place, finding numerous safety violations. DownEast Power will never open its doors again."

"Why?" Langdon didn't bother to ask who the 'we' was, for he knew the second party was Harper Truman.

"For the environment. Nuclear waste isn't a disposable item. And there's no reason to have it. There are much safer, less environmentally damaging alternatives. It's not even cheaper. What is nuclear power except a big scam to make the rich richer?"

"There are other routes to be taken," Langdon replied with concern. "Your man Harper Truman is the governor after all."

"We tried that. But there's just too much money behind nuclear energy. Believe me, it's not the governor who really controls this state or any other state. It's money and nothing else. Money controls everything." Jordan Fitzpatrick spoke out bitterly, letting down her ice queen facade just a little, letting them see the fragile girl inside, a view none of them, including Starling and 4 by Four, had seen before.

"You can't go around killing innocent people to attain your goals," Langdon continued to argue. "What chance did Harold Dumphy have in all this?"

"Harold Dumphy committed suicide. Which was too bad as it set our plans back. He was going to blow the whistle months ago but then the pressure got to be too much and he killed himself." Jordan replied sincerely.

"He was killed." Langdon spoke flatly. "And Chief LeFebvre was blackmailed into covering it up. And then to avoid the scandal, Guyton LeFebvre killed himself."

Jordan Fitzpatrick seemed genuinely shocked. "But you killed the Chief."

"You're being used, Jordan. By forces bigger than you. You're in over your head."

"I know nothing about any of this. All I know is that DownEast Power will be shut down for good. And if I have to disappear again to avoid prosecution, it will have been worth it."

Inside Langdon was burning. With effort, he controlled the anger in his voice. "Stir up the hornet's nest and then run and hide, is that the game you play?"

"If you're going to play with fire, Langdon, you have to be prepared to get burnt." Jordan Fitzpatrick had faced her own demons and come to grips with what she was doing.

"What do we do now?" It was as if there were nobody else in the room but Langdon and Jordan Fitzpatrick. Langdon wondered at her audacity in coming to face them—and then realized she must not be alone.

"Let me answer that," came Shakespeare's nasal voice from the doorway. "We're going to have to kill all of you and see if we can't straighten this whole mess out. It might be too late to save DownEast Power. But we can't have a whole roomful of potential witnesses running around pointing fingers." He entered the room with three of his thugs behind him, all with guns. There was a short, chunky man who appeared to be arriving at a party, so big was the grin on his face. There was a woman who had a shiny look to her eyes that suggested she wasn't all there. The third, a tall, thin man, had scratches on his face. Scratches of the kind somebody's fingernails might make when she was fighting for her very life.

Chapter twenty

"Hello Mr. Shakespeare, would you care to come in?" Langdon said to the man that resembled a banana, "Did you bring some playmates with you today?"

Shakespeare smiled tightly. "We've come to kill you Langdon!"

"I kind of figured you weren't here to play pattycakes." Langdon replied with warmth, all the while racking his mind for a way out, a way of survival. Things indeed looked grim. His daughter couldn't grow up without a dad. Bart was sliding away from the fridge on Langdon's left, not moving as far as the eye could see, but now he was three full feet further away. Missouri ran over to Langdon and hugged him with a worried look on her face.

Everything slowed.

Almost to a standstill.

And suddenly as if a light had been turned on in his mind Langdon realized they weren't just planning on knocking him off, but on killing the entire room of people. Everybody who knew anything was in that room.

Except for Nick, Lord and Larry. But there wasn't a credible one among the three—nobody would pay any attention when they claimed the whole group had been murdered to cover up nuclear sabotage. For all Langdon knew, they'd be set up as the prime suspects.

"Are these the bad men, daddy?" Missouri looked very troubled for a three year old, but Langdon guessed some ugly guy with a gun would be enough to upset even the most naive three year old girl.

"You don't need to hurt the kids," Langdon said, his voice quavering, almost sobbing.

Shakespeare shrugged and smiled in mock apology. "No witnesses."

Langdon began to get angry. He had been truly angry only one other time in his life, and that time hadn't ended happily. There was no stopping or slowing the emotions until they'd run their course. "What I don't understand," Langdon said, while the control of his speech was still within his power, trying to buy time. "Is how you fit into this whole scheme, Shakespeare." He chided the foppish thug gently. "Do you really think Jordan's going to keep you around after the rough stuff is over?" Langdon was hoping if nothing else, to force Shakespeare into making an error in judgement. All Langdon needed at this point was one crack in the facade. Bart was now twenty feet to his left and Langdon knew he carried a pistol, and wouldn't hesitate to use it.

"Fat boy!" The female assassin shouted. "You move another inch and you'll be the first to die."

Bart raised his massive arms in his best helpless fat boy pose.

Jordan Fitzpatrick or was it Abigail Austin-Peters stood in between the two groups with a look of confusion. "What exactly is going on here? Who are you?" She directed the last question at Shakespeare.

"You know damn well who he is," Jewell spat out. "He's your hired gun."

"I've never seen this man before in my life." Jordan stated with an honesty that was disarming.

Shakespeare stood shivering with anticipation.

Langdon tried again to slow him down. "Perhaps we should lay all our cards on the table. Let everybody know what's going on."

"You tell us, Mr. Smart Guy!" Shakespeare snarled.

"Okay," Langdon replied, still intent on buying time. "Jordan Fitzpatrick and Harper Truman have been trying to shut down DownEast Power for years. Ever since they first began the environmental group known as 'Flower First'. Stop me if I'm wrong, Jordan?" Jordan merely stared woodenly at him. "They decided the only way to attain their goals was from a position of political power. So they built their environmental group into a political force that eventually gained Harper Truman the nomination, and then his election as governor. What they didn't realize is that he wasn't any more capable of shutting down DownEast Power as governor than he had been as an activist. There was just too much money behind it."

"When they realized this was the case, they hatched a plan to close DownEast Power by sabotaging the plant. I'm not sure exactly how they managed to breach security. But after the sabotage, they made Johnson T. Halpberg, the CEO of Casco Bay Power, aware of the situation. It didn't take much prodding for him to cover the problem. Halpberg had to bribe members of the NRC for this to happen—but that worked well within the plan. A cover up of faulty equipment would be more effective in promoting public outrage than just the faulty equipment itself."

"When the time was right, Jordan tipped off Harold Dumphy to the fact that there were problems at DownEast Power, using her position as Public Relations director. Then Harper and Jordan sat back and waited for Dumphy to uncover the whole plot and alert the media, covering their backsides so it couldn't be connected to them in any way. Am I right, Jordan?"

Jordan nodded.

"What Jordan and Harper didn't realize is that the man they were using for their scapegoat, Johnson T. Halperg, had certain friends who weren't willing to let DownEast Power be closed. It was Halperg who was supposed to take the fall for the cover up, because he'd been responsible for hiding the problems. After all, his job as CEO of Casco Bay Power was at stake, he couldn't afford for DownEast Power to be closed down. What Jordan didn't realize was that there were other players. When Johnson T. Halpberg told his old school chum, Ellsworth Limington III, about the problems at the plant, the game took on a new dimension Jordan and Harper weren't aware of. Ellsworth Limington couldn't afford for DownEast Power to be closed. It would have been financially disastrous to him. As the sole owner of the Mount Chamberlin Ski Resort and owner of several related businesses in town, his taxes would have gone up millions of dollars a year. The town of Woolington has about a third of the tax base other towns of the same size have, making it a very inviting place to own real estate. But if DownEast Power were shut down permanently...It would have ruined him. And to a man like Ellsworth Limington, this was unthinkable. Any means of preventing this closing were worthwhile. Even murder. Am I right so far, Lawrence?"

Shakespeare grinned insolently, "You're right on target so far, Mr. Big-Shot. Why don't you continue, since it doesn't matter any more. Seeing as you're not going to be alive in ten minutes."

"Ellsworth called in his hired gun, Lawrence Shakespeare," Langdon continued, "who was just recently out of prison for doing similar work for him in New York City. Shakespeare arrived just in the nick of time to murder Harold Dumphy before Dumphy could expose the leaks and cover up to the authorities. Shakespeare didn't have much time to make the death appear 'accidental', so he did his best to make it look like a suicide. And then they bribed the Chief of Police with some illicit photographs featuring none other than the governor's wife. Ellsworth and Halpberg were hoping this would buy them time to correct the problems at DownEast Power. But then the Widow Dumphy decided to hire me, a fact she let slip to her friend Ellsworth, one of her many suitors. Before she even had a chance to officially hire me on the case, Ellsworth had his man Shakespeare threatening me."

Shakespeare nodded his head in consternation, impressed in spite of himself. "You don't scare easily, Langdon. But I'm afraid this will prove to be your great downfall. Because now you, your family and your friends are all going to die."

Langdon continued with a calm expression. "There's no reason to go any further with this, Shakespeare. It is too late. Jackson Brooks of the State Police has been made aware of the entire situation, and he's contacted the FBI. Ellsworth and Halperg are going to jail. If you kill us, you'll only add to the charges against yourself. Do you think your friend Ellsworth is going to go to bat for you? Just like he did in New York City where he let you go to prison while he escaped to a new life in Maine. You are once again the scapegoat, Shakespeare. If you surrender now, I'm sure you can work a deal with the state, maybe even immunity. They don't want you. They want Ellsworth Limington III."

"Either way, DownEast Power will be closed and I'll have won," Jordan Fitzpatrick said defiantly. "I may go to prison but it will have been worth it."

"Langdon, I'm going to kill you, but not before I kill that little girl of yours." Shakespeare was now visibly frothing at the mouth, somewhere beyond the point of reason. He wasn't a man to take defeat easily. He shifted the pistol and a blackness began to descend upon Langdon. He knew Shakespeare was going to do it.

"What you are going to do is lay that gun down at your feet and take three steps back with your hands over your head," came the voice of Lord Langdon, who had suddenly appeared in the back door—quickly stepping aside to let Nicky and Crazy Larry in.

The three of them held high-powered rifles that would do quite a job on a person at close range. Goff still hadn't taken his eyes off of Shakespeare.

The female assassin swung her gun from covering Richam and pointed it directly at Nick, who shuffled to the side to take the rest of them out of the line of fire. "Stop! Don't take another step." She spoke in chopped tones, a dangerous light rising up in her eyes.

"Hello, honey, what are you doing when this is all over?" Nick asked her, flashing a smile.

"Cooking marshmallows over your burning carcass," the woman hissed.

Larry had sidled the opposite way from Nick, moving towards the two hit men. It was now a real Mexican stand-off. Shakespeare was still pointing his pistol at Langdon, Bart was pointing his now-drawn pistol at Shakespeare, Elwood was pointing his gun at Bart, Crazy Larry had his rifle directed at Elwood, Stanley was pointing his gun at Larry, the woman still had her gun on Nick and he had his rifle trained on her.

"Looks like you better lay down your guns and throw yourselves on the mercy of the court," Langdon said with a smile towards Shakespeare. "Better yet, why don't you three thugs walk out of here?" But Langdon knew he couldn't let that happen. He had seen the scratches on Elwood's face, and knew what they meant. Langdon couldn't let Pepper's killers walk away.

"Daddy, I'm scared." His three year old girl. The thing he loved most in life.

Langdon put one protective arm around her and raised his eyes to Shakespeare and all of his weakness must have been in that gaze.

"I'm going to kill you, Langdon, but first I'm going to shoot your little girl right in front of you." Shakespeare chuckled, sounding possibly even a tad more unhinged than before.

Langdon knew he meant it.

The room around Langdon slowed down. Missouri clutched his shirt front with frail fingers and the strength of trust. The ugly black anger that had been brewing in the base of Langdon's spine, boiling in the pit of his stomach, tingling in his arms and clutching at his neck came together in a solid ball in the base of his skull, tightening, condensing.

Shakespeare brought the pistol to bear on Missouri. Langdon's Viking heritage replaced his rational being.

Langdon leaned forward and whispered to Missouri, "When I stand up honey, you run like the wind, you run faster than you've ever run and in a minute I'll come catch you and everything will be okay."

Langdon knew Shakespeare was going to shoot about one tenth of a second before he knew it himself. Langdon saw the increasing tension, the flutter of his hand. He set Missouri gently on the ground and hissed, "RUN!" He came out of his chair with one quick movement and stepped in front of her, blocking his daughter, his flesh and blood, with his own expendable body.

The first bullet took Langdon in the shoulder, spinning him sideways. And then gunfire erupted from everywhere.

Langdon let out a guttural bellow that drowned out the snapping sounds of guns being fired and charged towards Shakespeare.

Once again time stood still and sound disappeared.

The room went dark as if night had suddenly fallen as Langdon's anger overflowed.

Epilogue

Langdon opened his eyes to a white room with a solitary vase of purple flowers resting on a small table. He knew he wasn't in heaven, for he'd never in his entire life done anything to merit his admittance into that institution.

There was a dull ache that was his body, and a pounding that was his head. Langdon shifted his neck and was rewarded with a shooting pain—erased by the sight of Amanda slumped asleep on a small couch. She was dressed in black jeans with a baggy white t-shirt. She was beautiful.

He lay for what must have been a full minute watching her with wonder and longing before the events of the (previous day?) came back to him in bits and pieces. He cleared his throat to get her attention.

She was awake instantly. "Goff?" Her black was tousled, her eyes wide and hopeful and Langdon noticed for the first time the black smudges beneath them, and the puffiness to her face. She had not gotten much sleep, and she'd been crying.

"Is Missouri...okay?" Langdon croaked through the passage of barbed wire that was his throat.

"She's fine." Amanda eased his mind with those words as she rose to her feet and came to the side of the bed.

"How about everybody else?"

"Everybody's fine. Bart had a bullet take a little bit of extra skin from his side, but he was drinking a beer while the doctor stitched him up. Jimmy 4 by Four had his jaw broken—but we all pretty much determined that he deserved that after bringing them all right to us." Amanda shook her head with a smile.

"How long have I been here," Langdon interrupted with another croak.

"About three weeks."

"Three weeks!"

"You've been in a coma, Goff. But I knew you were too darn pigheaded to lay here without moving for the rest of your life."

Langdon could remember nothing but the first shot hitting him high in the shoulder. Apparently events had continued to unfold around him.

"Let me get a doctor to check you out before I go on. And then I'll fill you in."

"Get me a beer while you're at it," Langdon said with sincerity, for the thought of a cold beer filtering down his throat was as close to heaven as he was likely ever to get.

* * *

Langdon had apparently wrapped his hands around Shakespeare's neck, killing him almost instantly. In the process Langdon had gotten another bullet in the thigh and one in the forehead. When the ambulance arrived, the paramedics had had to pry Langdon's fingers from Shakespeare's neck one by one. Bart had only gotten off one shot, a clean miss, before Elwood had dropped him with a flesh wound. Crazy Larry had shot Elwood in the leg with the large hunting rifle he carried. Amanda?! had winged one of the men with a bullet but the man had managed to escape out through the door. The hired thug had been picked up in the parking lot by the police, who were responding rather quickly to the report of shots fired in Fort Andross.

Nicky had blown most of the hit woman's head off before she could get a shot off in his direction. When the shooting had started, Jimmy 4 by Four had lunged toward Jordan Fitzpatrick, more recently known as Abbigail Austin-Peters. She had knocked him to the ground and broke his jaw with a karate kick. She had then disappeared—and while there was a huge man-hunt out for her, not a trace had been found. It seemed that Jordan Fitzpatrick had disappeared back into the obscurity she'd emerged from fifteen years earlier when she'd first met Jonathan Starling and Harper Truman.

The three kids had had several visits with a therapist, who seemed to think there would be no lasting mental scars. But Jewell was pretty pissed off at Langdon. Langdon didn't blame her.

Langdon was now in a hospital in Boston, having been airlifted there by helicopter. Langdon hoped his insurance would cover the bill. Just his luck to miss out on his first helicopter ride.

"So, am I still wanted in connection with the murders of Pepper and the Chief?"

This had been a close call, because there was just the word of Langdon's friends against that of the governor, the CEO of Casco Bay Power and the financial mogul Ellsworth Limington. Senator Harding Smith had arrived at the scene to run the investigation into the death of his daughter personally. And with the aid of Jackson Brooks of the State Police and the FBI's case file on Ellsworth Limington, justice had prevailed.

Harper Truman had been arrested for his part in the sabotage, but was currently out on bail. Amanda had heard that he and his wife were in couples therapy. Johnson T. Halpberg had been arrested for his part in covering up the sabotage, and had been put on a leave of absence from Casco Bay Power. Ellsworth Limington III had not had any charges brought against him yet as the FBI hadn't been able to come up with any evidence that would stand up in court.

DownEast Power was shut down, and the process of dismantling the nuclear power plant was being discussed—with estimated costs in the hundreds of millions of dollars. Jordan Fitzpatrick had accomplished her immediate goal.

While she may have lost the war, she had definitely won the battle over DownEast Power.

"Senator Smith gave me this letter to give to you when you woke up," Amanda said, pulling a crumpled letter from her purse and handing it to Langdon. The envelope was sealed.

Dear Goff Langdon;

While I cannot say that I absolve you of my daughter's death, I would like to tell you that the first time I had heard her happy in several years was right after she met you. There was no denying the lightness of her spirit when she told me of the case you were working on and the strange ensemble of people she'd met through you. You treated her as a person, and for that, I thank you. I do feel that it was wrong for you to involve a child of twenty in a murder case. I cannot tell you that I forgive you. But you should know that you were a bright spot in what was otherwise a troubled life.

Sincerely,

Senator Paddington Smith

Langdon folded the letter gingerly and then handed it to Amanda to read.

"The bookstore," he asked, trying to tie up loose ends.

"Chabal and Jonathan Starling have been running the store in your absence," Amanda replied. "He claims you spoke to him about that the morning of the shootout."

"Yes. He's not living at the governor's house, is he?"

"What?" Amanda asked, confused with his jibbering.

"Nothing," Langdon said with a faint smile.

Richam and Jewell had gone home with the kids and were not seeing any of the group for the moment, needing some time to themselves. 4 by Four, embarrassed about being seduced by Jordan Fitzpatrick and unable to argue with Bart in his own defense due to his broken jaw, had taken an extended vacation and gone ice fishing at Moosehead. Bart was back to work.

"What about us?" Langdon asked his wife. There was the sudden pitter patter of little feet running down the hallway—and the door burst open and Missouri came rushing in and jumped on Langdon, and it didn't hurt in the slightest.

"Daddy, you've been a sleepyhead!"

Amanda came over to the bed and rested her hand of Missouri's head. "We'll have to see," she said.

"If Chabal and Jonathan Starling are running the bookstore, I might need to become a full time private detective, you know," Langdon said with a smile as he hugged his daughter and clutched his wife's hand.

"Maybe you could write that mystery novel you keep talking about."

Maybe.